BOOKS

PROUDLY PRESENTS

The Lock Box Murders

Copyright TX 599-474

Library of Congress Catalog Number 94-60771

ISBN 0-9635404-0-8

PUBLISHED BY 24U BOOKS (9635404)

1994

A

Novel

by

DICK BEYER

The
Lock Box
Murders

OUR APOLOGY

In characterization we find it necessary to
use language that is essentially appropriate for the
person being portrayed.

You may find "gutter language" in the text
objectionable. Unfortunately, it is
widespread in our sociaty.

****

On June 10, 1978,
an attractive real estate agent
was found in a bloody heap
in a field
behind a gas station
in Scottsdale, Arizona.
Attacks on real estate agents
form the basis
of this story,

Introduction_____

INTRODUCTION

Not a blade of dry grass quivered.

The air was so still.

It was as if the very earth had been smothered.

A new moon was pasted on the pale blue-green sky as filaments of dark gray clouds floated beneath it. Beyond the horizon the sun began to butter the sky a creamy yellow, but then as the glowing yellow ball appeared over a distant mesa, it portended another day of record temperatures.

It was 5:12 a.m.

The sun awoke the red-tipped ocotillo that were scattered across the vista. The ocotillo had spent the night sweeping up the blossoms with witch-like broomsticks.

Magestic saguaros, lined up like chess pieces, stood silhouetted against the sky as colors and textures sprang to life across this panorama of Arizona desert. Crimson, ochre, shades of green accented by slashes of purple and dusty shades of violet-red, added to the drama that unfolded.

With the sun rising ominously into the heaven, a hawk circled over the dense thickets of ironwood and palo verde that grew along a wash. Then it swung in a

1

wide arc towards the blue Ford pickup that marred the landscape.

Near the driver's door, light reflected from an empty bottle of Southern Comfort lying on the sand. Ants swarmed through the neck and clambered over it in an endless ribbon. Aside from an occasional shrill cry from the hawk, the desert stillness remained unbroken.

The man sprawling on the front seat stirred. His face was caked with sweat and grime where it had pressed against the vinyl seat. As his hand reached out it came in contact with the unfamiliar surroundings. He raised his head awkwardly, squinted into the sun and cupped a hand over his eyes to stop the throbbing pain that the brightness had triggered. Pulling himself up on the seat he brushed against the horn. The blast defiled the solitude and startled the hawk which flew off into the distance. The sound also jarred the man. He breathed deeply, mouth open, then licked his dry lips. His breath still stank from all the liquor he had consumed. Angling the rear-view mirror towards himself, he saw the shrunken, light brown pupils. Threads of red spiderwebbed the whites, mute testimony to his drunken spree.

This wasn't the first time he had awakened in some desolate spot. Whenever the world seemed to close in on him he sought escape from the pressures that boxed him in. A recent head injury triggered this feeling more frequently, clouding his judgement, prompting violence on his part.

His hand struck out at the door latch and simultaneously pushed the door open. He lurched out painfully and stiff, muscles cramped from spending hours twisted on the seat. He leaned against the truck and urinated.

Seeing the ants crawling over the bottle, he shuddered involuntarily. His inards were crawling, too. He zippered up his trousers and tried to focus on his wristwatch. 5:30. Stretching skyward he tried to get some of the kinks out of his body before climbing into the truck. His body straightened to its 6'3" height. Despite his disheveled appearance, Ed Kimball was a handsome man. Muscular, without any sign of fat. His cheekbones were high and pronounced, his piercing eyes framed by thick, bushy eyebrows. His hands were covered with dark, masculine hair. They seemed unusually large and strong, the type that made a formidable weapon when used aggressively. His hair was matted at the moment, usually brushed back without a part.

The nighttime temperatures had hovered in the upper 80s. In this short period since the sun had burst out over the mesa, the temperature had already climbed 10 degrees. Beads of perspiration formed on his head. He glanced towards the gravel road nearby, then at the rock-strewn vista and the ridges of mountains. He recognized where he had spent the night, near the Ft. McDowell Indian reservation.

Climbing back into the truck he started the engine. Somewhat uncoordinated, he backed onto the road in a series of lurches. Driving cautiously, he managed to reach the Beeline Highway and continued to drive south, unsure of his vision and reflexes. Suddenly he pulled over to the gravel shoulder and braked hard. A cloud of sand and dust swirled up around him. He wiped the dust from his eyes, cleared his throat and spat out through the window. Finally the dust settled. He glanced down at his shirt and noticed bloodstains. His hands also had dried blood on them. It seemed to confirm the question in his mind that had caused him to stop. His eyes now focused on the closed glove compartment.

His heart started beating faster. His unclear mind was still trying to sort out reason. He rubbed his eyes and the back of his neck to relieve the dull ache. The glove compartment continued to stare back at him, and with a feeling of guilt and dread, he pressed away from it wedging his body into the corner of the cab.

The sun constantly beat in on him. His body was drenched with sweat. In the distance he heard an approaching car. It interfered with his thoughts. Glancing in the rear view mirror he realized it was almost abreast of him and involutarily lowered his body and shielded his face from view as it sped past.

The grim silence closed in on him again. When another car went by in the opposite direction, his hand shot out to open the glove compartment. "Christ!" he rasped. Where was it? His hunting knife was missing. His mind was still muddled. Had he gone to the desert to blot out what had happened the night before? He looked down at his shirt, clawing at it with his strong fingers. He yanked it off and threw it on the floor.

He pulled out onto the road and subconsciously headed home. At the junction of Shea Boulevard he put the sun behind him. The McDowell Mountains loomed on the right till he reached north Scottsdale. Ahead lay the Phoenix Mountains which embraced luxury homes on their lower slopes. Sun-brushed streaks of gold fell across the rocky slope as he approached.

Traffic picked up as he reached the shopping area around 32nd Street and fast food chains beckoned him to have black coffee. It was urgent that he reach home before being ticketed for DWI. He watched his speedometer constantly. The left turn lane led through

Dreamy Draw and moments later he passed the Pointe Resort. It brought back memories as he stood under the shower when he reached home. His clothes lay in a heap on the bathroom floor.

The hot spray beat against his upturned face and closed eyelids. Through the stupor of alcohol, he reflected on the day of his arrival in the Valley of the Sun nine years earlier.

PART I

The overhead sign came on. Flight 579, originating in New York, would soon be landing. Ed Kimball put down the paperback that had helped pass the time, fastened his seat belt and peered out the window. He could barely make out the mountains silhouetted against a moonless sky. In the distance he spotted lights scattered in clusters on the ground and as they flew lower and came closer to the city, the network of lights seemed to spread out in all directions.

The stewardess gave him a fleeting smile as she checked their seat belts and took down a coat from the overhead compartment for the older lady on the aisle seat. The seat between them had been unoccupied during the flight. While the in-flight dinner had been served, she engaged him in conversation.

"No, ma'am," he answered if Phoenix was his home.

"Getting away from the cold?"

"That's for sure, but I may stay on if I find the right job."

"You'll like it here. I've lived here most of my life. Kansas originally. You're young. You'll be all right."

Yes, thought Ed. He'd do fine. At age 24 he'd been around enough. Knew what he wanted to do, and more important, what he didn't want to do. The sales job with a major building supply company had been OK. It was a living, not too bad a one, and it could have been lots better if he had been willing to give it his all.

In college he had majored in English literature with an eye towards classical drama and the theatre. Empty promises of work opportunities quickly pointed up the real drama in life. Survival needs replaced ambitious dreams, and when a student friend of his steered him to the building supply job opening, he grasped at it.

Ed Kimball was the ascending star at first. The shining new light.

"Look at Ed's sales," his boss proudly told the others.

"Brand new at the job and breaking records."

The trouble with being a star was the built-in pressure to compete against yourself constantly, to surpass what you did the previous month, ad infinitum.

Pushed more and more by the sales manager, Ed rebelled inwardly. He resented the constant pressure. His sales remained good for a time, leveled off, then declined drastically. Under more prodding they gained impetus. Ed felt he was being boxed in, fought it and would have quit anyway, when one of his customers

6

approached him.

"Construction's going to hit a slump, Ed. This subdivision of mine, you know building materials. You can point out the quality material we use, quality workmanship to go with it. Help sell off the remaining units."

It took eight months to get rid of the half dozen unsold homes. The last house sold on November 6th. Having lived frugally during this period, he managed to save $4,000 and ten days after he got his final check was on the TWA flight to Phoenix.

His only regret in leaving New York was his friendship with Susan, who lived across the hall in their walk-up in the Bronx. He found her available, asking no questions, no commitment. Rather comely, her hazel colored eyes sparkled the first time Ed removed his shirt, that she had playfully unbuttoned. His body was surprisingly muscular, unnoticeable when clothed. She reached up and pulled his face down to hers and kissed him warmly. His broad, powerful hands picked her off the floor and he carried her into the bedroom.

Susan found him all animal. She cried out in pain at first, but then as her pleasure increased she gasped and groaned with delight as she climaxed again and again. "My God, what the hell are you?" she asked almost fearfully as he finally released her and lit a cigarette.

Flight 579 from LaGuardia taxied over to the terminal while passengers, ignoring instructions to remain seated, scrambled to be first in line to leave the aircraft. Kimball stayed in his seat. There was nobody to welcome him. It was still weeks before the Christmas holidays would swell hotel accomodations with sun-hungry visitors eager to escape the wintry blast else-where.

The stainless steel baggage systems were dis-gorging luggage like a mechanical monster regurgi-tating what a like machine had devoured elsewhere. He edged his way between two impatient travelers, stepped back as one grabbed a heavy carton by the rope tied around it, and unceremoniously swung it around. Moments later the Sampsonite suitcase with the big K that Susan had painted with nail polish moved up to where he stood. He grinned thinking of their amorous 'goodbye' this morning.

"I'll miss you, lover. Take good care of these," she said squeezing his groin.

With a snake-like strike his hand shot out to grab the handle. He picked it up effortlessly and stepped towards the transportation exit. Reaching the side-walk, he spotted a passenger van marked 'The Pointe Resort' loading up.

The driver approached him.

"The Pointe, sir?" he asked reaching for his bag.

"Why not."

He handed the suitcase to him and smiled in-wardly as the man strained under the unexpected weight.

The van pulled out into airport traffic, circled the short term parking area and moments later joined the flow of cars moving north on 24th Street. The area was nondescript until they reached Camelback Road. Old Ironwood trees landscaped the parking area of the Biltmore Fashion Park Shopping Center. Even though Christmas was almost six weeks away, small white lights glistened like stars in all the branches lend-ing an air of enchantment. Continuing north to Lincoln Drive skirting the base of the Phoenix Mountains, the driver turned west to 16th Street, then a quarter of a mile north to their destination. Nestled against rugged hills, the Spanish architecture was appropriate to this area proclaiming that the land had once belonged to Spain.

From his room he could see the lights of the high-rise buildings along the central corridor. So this was Phoenix. He wasn't one to form opinions based on first impressions. One thing he decided on, however, upon registering for a room. In the morning he would find an inexpensive room elsewhere.

In the lounge of the Pointe of View, where one saw the valley of lights spread out in the distance, he unwound with a couple of Coors while making small talk with several pretties at the next table. So this was the Valley of the Sun. From the looks of the girls, not a bad place to be.

The Pointe faded from his thoughts. The hot shower was bringing the blood vessels to the surface, opening the pores to act like little exhaust vents to release the alcohol in his system. His body came in contact with the handle as he turned around and searing hot water struck his back.

"Shit!" he shouted jumping back. He adjusted the temperature and stood under icy water that cascaded down his body. Drying himself off he realized that the throbbing in his head was gone. He had a tremendous tolerance to alcohol and recovered quickly. After he had finished shaving, he put his clothing away. The shirt he threw into the garbage bag.

Coffee was now in his mind. Good strong coffee.

As the water heated, he poured himself a shot of vodka. The 'hair of the dog' had worked many times before. "Won't you ever learn?" he asked out loud as he sat down with the mug in hand. "'You dumb bastard!"

His face was solemn as he looked around the room. He'd been alone in this apartment for a year. His marriage had been touch and go and ended the previous July. Julia had warned him if he ever manhandled her or young Jeff again, she would leave him. She kept her word. He asked around. None of his friends knew where she was. At least that's what they told him. He felt they were lying from their expressions. Evenings became drinking bouts in his attempt to counter the rejection and the resulting anger. He loved Julia who unfortunately was too much alike. Confrontations became brush fires that often went out of control.

Finally Julia started back fires and Ed Kimball would be full of regrets when his anger finally burned out.

Ed placed the blame for what he was on his childhood. His father was of Irish/Welsh stock, born in Boston and later raised in New York. Hot headed, tough fisted. He recalled how his father would strike his mother from time to time, taking out his frustrations. She was submissive, took the blows and retired into the bedroom to give vent to her humiliation and physical pain by weeping quietly. Ed accepted what he witnesses, never realizing that bullying was not the way. He grew to manhood feeling that a woman had to be submissive. Fortunately for his mother, she died at the age of 42 when he was 20.

His first sexual encounter at age fifteen helped to further the image instilled by his father. The girl he was with resisted his attempt. But Ed had heard from his friends that girls always would say no at first, but that it was their way of playing hard to get. Only a game. The way the girl bled when he forcibly entered her frightened him momentarily, but his desire for self gratification overcame her cries of pain. When he was through he threatened her with bodily harm should she tell anyone. Machismo became second nature to him as the years went by.

When his own son, Jeff, was going on five he struck him. It happened to be a rainy Saturday afternoon. One of those rainy days that infrequently washed down the dust. A good time for lovemaking. In the background Ed heard the TV cartoon program which Jeff was watching. Julia's eyes were closed as he was thrusting more rapidly. Neither of them heard Jeff enter the bedroom. Suddenly the five-year old started pounding his father with his small fists. He cried out tearfully, "Stop hurting mommie! Stop hurting mommie!"

Automatically, without thinking, Ed's big fist lashed back and sent him sprawling. Blood trickled from his lip. Julia sprang from the bed and cradled him against her.

"You lousy bastard!" she snarled. "He's only a child. How's he supposed to know?"

Ashamed of what he had done, Ed Kimball dressed and drove out into the desert. It was late Sunday evening when he returned, reeking of liquor but apparently sober. Julia didn't bother to look up.

"How's Jeff?" he asked in a low voice.

"Asleep."

"Say anything?"

"He wonders why you struck him."

"I didn't mean to. He snuck up on us."

"You can't understand, can you?"

"Understand what?"

"How could he know what it was all about? All he saw was you banging at me. Christ! He's an innocent child. And you? Booze it up as usual. You stink!"

"Shut up. I'm warning you."

"You going to hit me? Is it my turn now?"

He sank back in a chair and glared at her.

"I'm warning you, Ed. If you ever raise your hand to either of us again, I'm through."

"Sure," he said sarcastically.

Kimball heated more water and washed down a stale donut with freeze dried coffee. His eyes strayed to the wall clock. Not quite 7:30. The hell with being at work on time. Let Mel blow his stack. Right now he had to unscramble what had happened the previous night. The blood spattered on his shirt? What had happened? It wasn't his own blood. His shoulder was bruised but uncut. Cut? His hunting knife? Had he used it on somebody in a bar brawl without realizing it? He certainly couldn't remember at the moment. The hot shower, vodka, the three mugs of coffee were taking effect slowly. The pieces were coming together. He pushed the empty mug aside, spread out his elbows on the table and rested his face on his cupped hands. He closed his eyes and thought back hard.

Yesterday had been a bitch. Blistering heat sizzled up from the pavement, turning the vinyl seat in his pickup into a waffle iron even in the shade. It was on days like this that he hated his job, but the money was pretty good. As long as construction held up, it was OK. This was his third job in 9 years. He'd been fired from the last one when he failed to show up at work for three weeks.

Julia had left and taken his son, just as she had threatened to do. The drunken spree this time lasted 11 days, finally ending when a blow from a section of steel pipe caved in his skull. Just off Van Buren and 16th Street he was spotted lying in the gutter. The emergency room took a quick look and he was immediately prepared for surgery. The doctors at Good Samaritan removed slivers of bone that had penetrated the cranial area involved in thought and memory. The concussion in the temporal lobe area caused occasional blanks in his memory, even after he recovered. Drinking hampered his recall even more. Slowly the picture of the previous day now began to form in his mind.

It was mid afternoon when he had spotted Julia in the Sun City area driving along with her mother, Betty Hochstetter. He made a U-turn on Grande Avenue and followed them into the parking area at Boswell Memorial. Julia didn't notice him until he called out her name.

"Julia!"

Her expression was one of disbelief.

"Ed?" she whispered stopping in her tracks.

"Come along, Julia," said her mother tugging at her

"How've you been?" asked Ed.

"OK"

"And Jeff?"

"He's all right."

"Julia, come!" urged her mother. "You know I can't stand out here in this sun."

"Coming."

"I'd like a minute," he said reaching out this hand to stop her.

"You heard from my lawyer."

"So?"

"There's really nothing more to say, Ed."

She moved off. Ed trailed behind. Julia snapped at him. "Dad's ill. Go away! We've got enough trouble."

The way she said it there was no room for maneuvering. He sauntered back to the pickup and drove off. He was trying to control his anger. It was good to see Julia. Beautiful as ever. Never lost her figure except when carrying Jeff.

So the old boy was ill? He never got along with his father-in-law. Roger always bragged about how successful he was. Had tried to talk Ed into moving to San Diego and joining him in the Chevrolet dealership. About the time Ed had decided to make this move, good old Roger sold his business and took Ed's wife and son along on a trip around the world on the QE2. That was two months before Julia left him. Damn Roger! Maybe if he hadn't sold out things would be different. He shrugged it off. Now the old boy was in the hospital. That meant the Hochstetters were probably living in Sun City. Betty had often said that she liked the orderliness of the community and wouldn't mind moving there when Roger retired.

His anger began to mount as he drove from the hospital. He hadn't seen Jeff in almost a year. Would things ever be good again with Jeff? Or would Jeff be afraid of him? The papers from the lawyer said that visiting rights would be spelled out in the final decree. It was suggested that the boy could spend two weeks during his summer vacation with his father every second year. Why not start with this year? He had two

14

weeks coming at the end of the month. He'd ask Julia.

Ed Kimball raised his head. The formica table at which he was sitting was out of focus. Rubbing his eyes he glanced around. He hated this furnished apartment. When Julia moved out on him, he sold off everything that was left behind. He didn't want any memories of her. Not even a chipped plate was left when he got through. His eyes moved to the pile of unread Sunday papers stacked in the corner. The vinyl-covered couch had a burn mark where it melted the dark-green seat. Behind it on the wall hung a gilt framed pastel painting of a charging bull done on a black velvet background. A bloated Mexican pottery lamp boasting a soiled white fabric shade stood on a marred end table over in the corner between the couch and an old wooden armchair. The small bedroom was crowded by a double bed, an overstuffed chair with worn tufted brown fabric, and an eight-drawer double chest.

The wall clock showed that only a few moments had passed since he rested his face in his hands. Time! His mind again drifted back to his encounter with Julia. Where had everything gone wrong finally? He dismissed the marriage and recalled driving from Boswell to Farrington Construction's trailer at a new shopping center that was being built. He found young Farrington scheduling the next day's requirements. He looked up from his desk.

"You OK, Ed?"

"Goddamned heat," he said standing in front of the window air conditioner that was going full blast.

Tom Farrington laughed.

"We're not even into the hottest time of the year."

"I know. Luckily I'll miss some."

"Vacation time?"

"Couple of weeks."

"Where're you heading"

"Thought I'd take my kid to New York."

"Your divorce come through?"

"Not yet."

"Will she let you take the kid?"

"Sure! I'm entitled to two weeks with him every second summer."

"You'd better not count on it, old buddy. I went through the same business and until the court spells out exactly what your rights are, you don't have any unless she agrees."

"The hell you say."

"I'm dead serious."

"I'll be a son of a bitch," said Ed pounding his fist into the palm of his hand. "I bumped into her not twenty minutes ago."

"You'd better check with her."

Ed's anger mounted. The air conditioning was doing nothing to cool him off. Damn Julia! Suppose she didn't agree? He made for the door.

"What's your hurry?"

"I've got to talk to her. Goddamn her. I hope she's still there."

Tom Farrington shook his head as he listened to the tires of Ed's pickup squealing.

The flow of traffic was heavy in both directions at this hour. Facing the sun added to his misery as he drove. He didn't bother turning on the air conditioning. Instead he cranked down the window and felt the hot air blow in his face. Perspiration began to roll down his chest.

"Bitch! Goddamn bitch!" he kept repeating aloud.

16

He resented having to chase all the way back just to find out where she was living. Jeff was his kid, too. It was her responsibility to let him know where he could pick up his kid. Wasn't that how it should be? These fuckin' lawyers. Bet they told her not to contact him till they settled. Settled, shit. There was nothing to settle. She wasn't asking for anything, not even child support. That was a break. But, Christ, what if she changed her mind about visiting rights? What if she told the court about his drinking? What if she told about him having struck Jeff? Could they deny him his visitation rights? He had nothing to trade off, no concessions to make on his part.

His doubts were mounting as he hurried into the lobby of the hospital. Off to one side he spotted the receptionist.

"Hochstetter?"

"First name?" asked the bespectacled lady.

"Roger. Yeh! Roger Hochstetter."

"He's in intensive care. Are you a family member?"

"Son-in-law."

"That's all right then. Second floor. He's in room 218. Check with the floor nurse."

Kimball rushed off in the middle of her sentence. On the second floor he noticed Julia sitting in the waiting area. She looked up from the magazine she was reading.

"I have to talk to you," he said.

"Shush!" she said in a hushed voice raising her fingers to her lips.

He glanced around and noticed the people looking in his direction. "I didn't even know how to get a hold of you," he said in a low voice. "Where do you live?"

"You have my lawyer's number."

"Fuck him!" he barked.

"Ed! Please!"

"OK! OK! I've got vacation coming the first. I want to take Jeff to New York."

Fright showed in Julia's face for a fleeting moment. Gaining her composure, she asked, "Why there?"

"He's heard me talking about the big buildings. The ferry ride, Coney Island, Bronx Zoo. All that stuff."

"He's too young"

"Bullshit!"

"Ed, keep your voice down!"

He glanced at a woman staring at him with disapproval. He felt like telling her to fuck off. That would teach her to eavesdrop. Instead he reached over and grabbed Julie's wrist.

"You're hurting me," she said trying to free her arm.

"I want to take Jeff with me."

"Ed! Let go!"

"Not till you say it's all right."

"Up to your old tricks? Beating it out of me?" Her voice was no longer calm. The others were looking at them. The appearance of Julia's mother saved the situation.

"You!" she said seeing Ed.

He released his grip.

"He was just leaving, mother," said Julia stepping over to her mother.

"You can go in now, Julia. Only for a minute though, the nurse thinks daddy should rest."

Julia turned and hurried away down the corridor. He now stood face-to-face with Betty Hochstetter. She held her ground and stared him down. Taken aback by this sixty-year-old woman, he shifted

18

his weight awkwardly. He was beginning to feel foolish.

"How long will Roger be here?" he asked.

"Several more days, maybe longer."

"OK, then."

"I'm sure whatever it is you've come for isn't worth a ruckus."

"Yeh! It'll hold. I'll be back."

"I'm sure you will," she observed haughtily. She sat down and picked up a copy of Sunset Magazine. Without a good-bye, Ed turned and went towards the elevator.

He drove straight to the bar on 7th Street that had long-stemmed girls shaking their teats on the small stage from 11:00 a.m. on. His reputation as a 'swordsman' had been snickered around by two of the girls he persuaded to succumb to his amorous ways. The girls had a way of glancing down at his crotch whenever he appeared.

"Holly around?"

"She's off today," said the bartender. "Whatcha drinking?"

"Beer," he answered aimlessly.

The more beer he guzzled the angrier he became thinking about Julia. Who the hell did she think she was telling him to go away. Keep quiet and not make a scene. If he wanted all hell to break loose, they couldn't stop him if they tried. Goddamn her and her mother. After finishing off the eighth beer, he decided to head further downtown.

Parking his truck on a side street, he thought of the time when his skull had been caved in. By Christ! He wished he'd run into that big buck nigger again. He'd slice off his balls, trim him down to size.

Those lined up at the sleazy bar were a mixture of sweaty humanity. Some perched on bar stools like wary vultures ready to pounce on anybody who might be good for a drink. Among them a couple of starch-fed Indians with puffy round faces and T-shirted bellies hanging over their belts. One was arguing with a middle-aged Negress. The other was patting the back of a young, wiry Mexican American laborer who sported a coiled snake tattoo on his left forearm and another snake's head peering over the grimy jersey he was wearing. At the far end of the dimly-lit bar a white-haired older man with a bushy white mustache was apparently negotiating with a young whore. Good luck, old-timer, thought Ed. He looked around for possible action. Still too early.

The bartender, out to fill the till, poured a cheap shot of whiskey to go along with Ed's beer. "On the house."

Ed knew the game, but went along. He was bent on tying one on. "Thanks!" He emptied the shot glass and sipped the foam on his beer, nursing the glass before setting it down. The juke box was blasting out some rock. That was one of the things he and Julia agreed on. They liked the beat, especially to hump along with the rhythm. There was one word Julia wouldn't say. He'd often tried to get her to say 'fuck', but she wouldn't. Each time she wouldn't, he didn't bother to satisfy her.

Around eleven the bar became crowded. Two guys in leather vests squeezed in on either side of him. How could they wear leather on a stinking hot night? Macho cyclists, he guessed. Tattoos and all. He sized them up. One all muscle, the other weighing in at around two hundred. 5' 7", soft gutted, but built like a barrel.

"Easy!" rasped Kimball when the guy tried to push him over to give himself more room.

"Whatcha got there?" the beefy one asked his buddy as he glanced up at Kimball.

"Looks like we've got a midnight special." He glared at Kimball. "Got a problem?"

"Yeh! I don't like your stinking sweat all over me."

"Listen to him, Hank."

Hank stepped back from the bar and moved around Kimball to stand next to his buddy.

"No sweat to shut your fuckin' mouth," he said brushing Kimball as he walked by

Kimball pushed the fat one aside and with his right hand smashed the bottle the bartender had left in front of him. The remaining cheap whiskey spilled over the bar and onto the floor. He faced his opponents with the jagged glass edges directed at them.

"Outside you bums!" shouted the bartender brandishing a baseball bat.

On the sidewalk it was a standoff. Patrons moved to the entry expecting to witness a fight. They placed their odds on that jagged bottle.

"Come on!" ordered Hank leading his partner away. "Got an idea."

Kimball walked a little unsteadily to his truck. He started up the engine, glad in a way that it had ended like this. He would have gotten his ass kicked in for sure. Driving along Van Buren he wondered about the stuff he had been drinking He was seeing things. The headlights of the car following him were moving in and out like an accordion. The next moment one of the cyclists came roaring up alongside and swung a heavy chain against the door panel.

21

"You bastard!" shouted Kimball veering sharply towards him. The cyclist braked and dropped behind while the fat one pulled into a side street only to reappear moments later. This time both men swung chains. Kimball knew he couldn't outrun them. He still had the broken bottle on the front seat. Maybe. He turned into the parking area of the Caravan Inn, pulled to one side, turned off his headlights and shifted into reverse. As the first cyclist drove in, he accelerated smashing into the cycle sending both man and cycle skidding across the lot. Leaving the motor running, he jumped from the truck bottle in hand. The second cyclist came at him swinging his chain. It grazed his shoulder hard enough to make him wince. On the next pass he ducked and thrust out the bottle. It gashed the outstretched arm as the man rode up. The jagged bottle was knocked out of Ed's hand and shattered on the paving as the cyclist lost control.

The fight had ended, but the closed-in feeling he again experienced caused him to head for the nearest drive-in. It had added to his anger, the day having gone badly. With bottle in hand he drove north where he knew he could breath.

Ed Kimball put the mug into the sink. He now remembered meeting Julia, getting drunk, the swinging chains hitting the truck, but it all didn't go together for the moment. The clock showed 7:45. Like an automaton he got dressed. He sat down on the edge of the bed, cupped his face in his hands. He had to think. He tried to blank out the dull ache of his hangover that seemed to be like a spiderweb ready to capture his every thought before it could fly to him. His mind remained a jumble of disorganized scenes.

22

When he closed the apartment door and climbed back into the truck, he was already beginning to throw off the effects of the liquor. His capacity for getting drunk was equaled by his quick way of recovering. By the time he got to work he was feeling pretty good again.

In the front office the secretary was busy on the phone and nodded to him. She simply pointed to the boss' door. He knew what that meant. Mel was sure to give him hell for being so late. Mel raised his eyes and puffed heavily before grinding out his cigarette in the abused ashtray in front of him.

"Am I working for you, or the other way around?"

Kimball laughed. "I wish I were signing the checks."

"Since we both know where we stand I suggest you get your ass out there. Aztec's raising hell about the wrong windows that were delivered."

Without a word Kimball walked out past the secretary, giving her a knowing smile. He was about to drive off when the passenger door opened.

"What the hell are you doing?"

"Hi, Ed. Wanted to return something I borrowed the other day. Knew you wouldn't mind."

He reached for the glove compartment and pushed the latch and proceeded to replace the missing hunting knife.

Once again Ed was out on the Beeline highway wondering about the knife, the bloody shirt he wore at the time. His doubts.

"You bastard, Mark," he said grabbing his wrist. "Don't ever take anything without asking."

"OK! Sorry!" He backed away when Ed released his grip and slammed the door. Now the pieces fell into

23

place. The blood. It was the cyclist's blood. Good Christ! He hadn't stabbed anybody with the knife in a drunken rage. Leaning back he burst into laughter. Good old Mark, the dumb bastard.

It took several hours to straighten out the window foul-up for Aztec. By this time it was after twelve. From the development site it was only a 20-minute drive to Boswell Memorial. He had to get an answer on this vacation bit from Julia. There was no doubt in his mind that he had come on too strong the previous afternoon.

In the hospital lobby he bought a small bunch of pink tea roses in the gift shop. He protested the $7.50 price, but flowers always had a positive effect with Julia. At the moment he had to put his best foot forward. Her face lit up when she saw the flowers.

"How's your dad?"

"Mothers in with him. Seems better."

"Sorry about yesterday, heat and all."

He passed the flowers to her.

"They're lovely. Thank you."

"Where're you staying? With them?"

"I have been."

"Sounds like you're moving into an apartment again."

"House this time. I take possession at the end of the month."

"A house? That's great. They buying it?"

"My parents? No. I've gone back into selling real estate."

"I forgot you were doing that when we met."

"Never should have dropped my license. Anyway, what's on your mind, Ed?"

"The way we left things yesterday about Jeff and

my vacation. I think it'd be good for us to be together so he doesn't forget all about me."

"He hasn't. I told him I saw you."

"What'd he say?"

"Oh, he asked how you were? He wondered if you were still mad at us?"

"Why would he ask that?"

"He remembers. Don't you?"

Ed thought back to that 4th of July weekend.

PART II

Spring never really had a chance. Summer temperatures moved in early and by the time the 4th of July weekend came along pavements were sizzling and tempers were frayed. Air conditioning units everywhere were overworked and Ed Kimball's broke down Saturday morning. He slammed down the receiver.

"The bastard!"

"What did he say?" asked Julia.

"Not till Tuesday. Nobody's available. Only one guy working and he's got more than he can handle."

"Can't the manager call somebody else?"

"They're on a service contract. He said I can call anybody I want, but I'll have to pay for it myself."

"Well?"

"The hell I will," he said raising his voice. "I'll be damned if I'll pay overtime. Fuck 'em!"

"Please, Ed. Jeff will pick up that kind of talk."

"Good! Then he'll be ready for this stinking world."

"You hate holidays, don't you. Why do you ever bother to take time off? You never seem to enjoy your family."

"Sure I do."

"Well, for Pete's sake let's not sit around. Let's plan to do something."

"Such as?"

"Why do you always leave the plans to me? All right. How about Encanto Park? There're lots of trees for shade, picnic tables. Jeff likes the rides."

Julia expected some reaction.

"Well?"

"Sure. That sounds OK. I'll pack some beer."

"Just like you to think only of yourself. Beer? Do you expect Jeff to drink that too?"

She walked into Jeff's bedroom. "Jeff, honey, the apartment is going to get terribly hot. How about a picnic in the park?"

"Can I go on the rides?"

"I'm sure your daddy will take you over."

The day passed as expected. Julia wound up with all the work. She even had to stand by as Jeff went on all the rides. Ed had gone off to the men's room and became sidetracked by a baseball game. Angry at first when he didn't return to take Jeff over to the rides, she picked up all the things and put them in the car. Taking Jeff's hand she started walking towards the amusement area.

"Aren't we going to wait for daddy?"

"He can find us if he wants to."

26

Ed was sitting in the car with the doors open to let the breeze blow through.

" 'bout time!" he said.

"You didn't even bother," said Julia.

"Bother?"

"To look for us."

"I figured where you'd gone."

"What happened to you? Get stuck in the seat in the men's room?"

"Funny!" he said starting the car. "I was watching a ballgame."

"That proves what I said this morning. You don't know how to enjoy your family."

"Bug off!" he snapped.

A slight breeze was blowing through the apartment that night. The lights had been turned off, but a street light was casting a shadow across the bed. Julia and Ed were lying naked on top of the sheet. They had watched television for a time and Jeff had gone to sleep exhausted from all the running he had done. Julia could see that Ed's eyes were open. He had made no advances despite his organ standing erect like a maypole. Its shadow fell across her stomach.

"You going to let that go to waste?" she asked.

"Hadn't given it any thought."

She sat up in bed, leaned over playfully and bit it in the midsection. My God, she thought, he's really something.

"Want to play games, I see."

She went over and closed the door and locked it.

"Why'd you do that?"

"Remember when Jeff walked in on us?"

"There's no breeze," he complained as she climbed back in bed.

"Shut up and kiss me."

On Sunday they drove over to the zoo, rode the bus and looked at the animals. Ate hotdogs and popcorn and chocolate covered stick ice cream. That night they watched the display of fireworks at the ball park in Scottsdale. When a loud barrage of explosive firecrackers let loose, Jeff got frightened and wanted to go home, but his father insisted they stay. The program was about to end momentarily.

Jeff didn't want to sleep by himself as firecrackers sounded in the neighborhood. Julia finally gave in and lay down next to him on his bed and fell asleep there.

On Monday Julia again packed a lunch to take to Encanto Park. She didn't want to drive far from the apartment. There had been too many holiday accidents reported already. Jeff sat wide-eyed through lunch. Somewhere in the park he kept hearing explosions go off. Firecrackers. That's what his father said were making the noise. Ed crumbled the empty beer can and got up from the picnic table.

"Where're you going, daddy?" asked Jeff.

"Be right back."

"Another ballgame?" asked Julia.

"Ha! Ha!" he said in an irritated tone. "I said I'll be right back."

He headed in the direction of the sounds. He had spotted several teenagers over by some trees. As he approached them they started to move off.

"I'm not a cop," he shouted. "Want to talk to you."

"So start talking," said the apparent leader.

"Want to buy a couple."

"Sure. So would a lot of people."

"I want to show my son there's nothing to be afraid of. Sell me two?"

They glanced at one another. "OK. Buck apiece."

He wasn't about to argue the price. This was too important.

"OK!" He handed them the money and received two 3 inch firecrackers.

"What was all that about?" asked Julia who had watched him meet with the boys.

Thought I'd show' Jeff there's nothing to be afraid of. He pulled one of the firecrackers from his pocket.

"Get rid of that!" ordered Julia.

"Sure."

"What's that, daddy?"

"Firecracker."

Jeff immediately hid behind his mother.

"Get out from behind your mother," he ordered in an irritated voice. Jeff started to cry.

"What's the matter with you, Ed? Stop being a bully!"

Taking out his lighter he lit the first firecracker and dropped it off to one side. It exploded with a loud bang, showering them with pieces of powder-smelling cardboard.

"Damn you, Ed!" shouted Julia.

He lit the second one. It was short fused and went off before he could throw it. He brought his hurt fingers to his mouth.

"Shit!" he cried out.

"Serves you right," said Julia.

He shoved her. Forced backwards she tripped over Jeff who was clinging to her. Both fell onto the grass.

"That does it, Ed Kimball," said Julia helping Jeff

to his feet. She brushed dry grass clippings from her skirt. "You've really done it this time."

From the way Ed handled the wheel as they drove home, she knew that his fingers were aching. She felt no sympathy whatsoever. It was his own stupidity and served him right. Furthermore, she smarted from having been pushed down. Not so much physically as mentally. She had been embarrassed in front of her son as well as those nearby who had witnessed the episode. There were no reservations in her mind. This was it.

That evening Julia fed Jeff and herself. "Fix your own!" she told Ed who sat in front of the TV with a bag of chips and beer. When Jeff fell asleep she locked herself in the room with him.

Around eleven she heard the doorknob being twisted. She went over to the door and in a soft voice said, "Go away!"

In answer, he started pounding on the door waking Jeff. She sat on the edge of the bed with her arms around him. As Ed shouted for her to open up Jeff started to cry.

"Stop it!" shouted Julia above the racket as she heard him pushing at the door. "Stop or I'll call the police."

The molding around the door splintered as his foot kicked it in. He stood in the open doorway rubbing his ankle.

"You madman!" shouted Julia.

Ed advanced towards her.

"Don't hurt me again, daddy," Jeff cried out in his tearful high-pitched voice.

Julia could feel his body trembling. His father stopped, opened his mouth as if about to say something.

30

He pounded his hand with his fist, wincing as he struck with his hurt hand. Without a word he turned and left the apartment. Julia closed the bedroom door and propped a chair against the doorknob.

In the early morning hours she heard him return and with daylight listened to him showering. She knew his routine. Next, he'd shave. Jeff was sleeping soundly. She prayed Ed wouldn't create another scene. He didn't. After hearing the apartment door close, she sighed with relief. She didn't quite trust him and after removing the chair, opened the door and peered around the corner.

Jean and Harold Simpson quickly responded to her urgent call.

"You're walking out on him. Good! It's about time," said Jean when she telephoned the Simpsons.

"Not now, please, Jean" said Julia.

"We'll be right over. How many cartons do you think you'll need?"

"Three should do it for now. Can you spare them?"

"Sure, honey. We're not moving for several weeks. We can replace them if needed."

Harold brought tape along. He filled two cartons, cushioning fragile things in among clothing. Jeff's toys took the third carton. "Anything else? I can get a few more items in."

"Thanks, Harold. That's all I'm taking other than the suitcases."

He taped the cartons and marked the shipping destination in bold letters. "I'll drop them off at Greyhound. You should have them in the morning."

Julia watched as he carried the cartons out to his van. He gave her a hug and kiss on the cheek.

"Got to run. Jean will drive you to the airport."

He turned to Jeff who was watching television. "You take good care of your mother, Jeff."

He gave the boy his hand and Jeff pumped it up and down. "I will." He let go and turned around to watch cartoons.

On the way to the airport, Jean asked, "What did your folks say?"

"They've seen how Ed treats me. They weren't surprised. You won't say anything?"

"To Ed? Certainly not. I won't tell anyone else where you've gone, either."

At the airport, the sky cap lifted the heavy suitcases and carried them into the terminal where Julia needed to pick up her ticket.

"Write?" said Jean.

"I promise."

"Take care. We'll miss you."

"Me, too. Say goodbye to the others."

"I will."

Julia followed the sky cap to the ticket counter. At 11:42 a.m. she and Jeff held hands as their plane took off for San Diego. His hand squeezed hard as the acceleration affected his stomach. He was wide-eyed when he looked down towards the ground.

"Will daddy stay mad?"

"Let's not think about daddy right now, Jeff. Grandma and grandpa will be so happy to see you. I know you'll be glad to see them, too."

"Sure, mom."

All Julia could think about was the shattered door frame. How furious he'd be to find she had left him for good. Let him get good and stinking drunk. She no longer cared what he thought or did.

Ed Kimball looked uncomfortable as he recalled that weekend.

"I don't know what gets into me," he said as they sat in the waiting room.

'Too bad they don't have something like alcoholics anonymous for your problem."

"Hotheads anonymous?"

She laughed. "Why don't you start one?"

"About Jeff? Our going off together."

"New York?"

"We'll only be gone two weeks."

"I know." She kept looking at the flowers. Maybe it would be all right. Jeff would be leaving so soon, though. This was Thursday, the 15th. That meant Ed's vacation would start on Friday the 30th after work. Just 15 days from now. She started thinking out loud, mumbling to herself.

"What did you say?"

"Let me think about it over the weekend. I'll let you know on Monday night. All right?"

Ed hesitated. Think about it? At least she hadn't given him a flat no. This was a hopeful sign.

"For sure? You'll let me know?"

"Yes, Ed."

He took out one of the company cards on which he usually filled in his name. He wrote on the back. "My home number."

She took it from him. "Thanks for the flowers."

"Thought you'd like them."

He was a different man when he drove back towards Phoenix. Not the angry, frustrated Ed Kimball who only yesterday could have willingly killed off the Hochstetters. By contrast he found himself whistling.

33

On his way he stopped at a Burger King and ate unhurriedly as he glanced through the morning paper, he found on the next seat. He felt good about things. His constitution was rugged, no lingering effects from the hangover he had experienced this morning. Aside from that, the fact that Julia hadn't told him to go straight to hell had come as a pleasant surprise. If it hadn't been for the roses, he knew she would have. He knew her weak spots. He had explored them during seven years of marriage. Seven years. Christ! How the time had passed. Julia was a knockout the day he first laid eyes on her.

Ed had been working for Danny Williams, developer of a town house complex covering five acres. He had answered an ad in the classified after arriving in Phoenix. The fact that he had sold houses in a similar property back east appealed to Williams, and Ed got the job. Knowing that people wanted to escape from the snow and ice back home, he figured that it would be a snap to sell off the homes. Williams had also probed into his background before making his decision. He liked the idea that Ed had worked in building supply. That was a plus. Asked about his academic background, Ed mentioned his love for English literature, his early interest in classical drama.

"Did you do any acting"

"Only in college. Played the lead in Hamlet and Macbeth."

"Think you can do a good acting job for me? Convince people that my development is the soundest investment they could make. The best town houses this side of the Garden of Eden?"

"Just raise the curtain," laughed Ed. "I'll put on the best show you've ever seen."

One day heading for the studio apartment he had rented on the second day after his arrival, he spotted Julia. Didn't see her face, but rather her backside as she leaned over to pick up a sign from the grass. He pulled over to the curb in this residential section, backed up to take a closer look. He watched as she hammered a metal post into the lawn and fastened a real estate sign on it. Turning around, she noticed him watching her and smiled. He liked what he saw and climbed out of the car. Hammer in hand she edged over in his direction.

"I've just put it on the market. Interested?"

He smiled. Interested? Sure, but not in the house. There was no sense telling her that right off.

"Is it vacant?"

"They both work. I put it on lock box. Would you like to take a look inside?"

"Sure."

"I'm Julia Hochstetter."

"Hochstetter?"

"Let me give you my card. And you're?"

"Ed Kimball."

"Nice meeting you, Mr. Kimball."

The house was ordinary. A builder's tract home with average kitchen cabinets and bathroom fixtures. The floor plan was stereotype, 3 bedrooms, 1-3/4 baths. The carpeting was the exception. Ed made a mental note. From his selling experience, you accent the positive features.

"I like the carpeting."

"They replaced the carpeting last week. You can still smell the newness, can't you?"

"That's what I thought."

They walked out into the back yard.

"There's an alley behind these houses. If you wanted to have a pool installed it would be an easy job. Do you have children, Mr. Kimball?"

"I'm not married."

"You're really not looking for a 3 bedroom then, are you?"

"To be truthful, I only arrived here four months ago. I'm still getting my feet wet."

"I'm sure you did the last three days."

He laughed. It had been pouring on and off.

"Disappointed?" he asked.

"Not really. You have my card. When you're in the market for a house, I'd be glad to help you."

"Speaking of marriage, how about you?"

"Considering it. I'm going with someone."

"Sounds serious."

"We're making plans."

There was no sense coming on heavy. He had her card. Julia. He pictured her parents. Probably hard to swallow like their name. Hochstetter? He laughed at the thought. He saw her questioning look.

"I wasn't laughing at your plans. Happened to think of something else." He reached out his hand to her. "Thanks for your time. I'll get in touch."

Her hand was warm. He was partial to her blonde looks, pale dreamy blue eyes that had the effect of a Shakespeare sonnet.

"I'll look forward to that," she said.

His car wouldn't start. Ed had paid $1200 for this Chevette which he purchased directly from the owner. He now had 48,000 miles on it having added almost 2000 during the past three months. In the rear view mirror he noticed her watching She seemed undecided

36

as to offering him a ride in her car. Just as she stepped in his direction the engine started and he drove off, waving out the window.

Working for Danny Williams proved to be a good thing after all. He didn't care for the job once he got into it. He was just an order taker like the other salesmen working on the project. The contract work went through Williams' attorney who helped arrange the financing packages. It took a year to sell off most of the units. When they came down the home stretch, Ed asked Williams if he had another project in the works.

"I've had my eye on trying something else. You've met my brother, Joe, haven't you?"

"Once."

"Joe's syndicating a shopping center and wants me in with him. Too big for me to handle the construction. Frankly, I don't want the headaches. But there's room for you. Thought you might want to come along."

"I can't handle that. Too rich for me."

"Not as one of the syndicators, Ed. I know it's out of your ball park unless you've hidden an eccentric old aunt with lots of money. I'm thinking in terms of liason between the major contractor and our investment group. Someone to ride herd, keep a checklist on what's being done and keep us informed. It's too early to finalize, but keep it in mind, Ed. When the rest of these units sell, you can step right into another better paying job. Unless, of course, we can't come to terms."

It sounded good to Ed, but he didn't want to sound too anxious. "Let me think it over, Danny."

It didn't take long for him to come to a decision. First of all, he hated the idea of having to scout around

for a new job, answering ads, interviews, and all that garbage. The better paying aspect also sounded good. He was sure they could come to agreement on that score. Something also had been sparked by his meeting Julia that day. It was about time he settled down. These one night stands were getting him nowhere. A job with more money offered some semblance of security, the possibility to take a step in that direction. The way Julia had bent over that day had attracted him to her. Suddenly he desired to grab those rounded cheeks and pull her close while he made love to her.

The following day he singled out Danny.

"I'd like to go along with your proposition if it gets off the ground."

"Thought you would. I'll let you know next week whether or not it's going to fly. My bet right now is that it will. Keep your fingers crossed. I told Joe last night that he can count me in. If they can wrap up the permanent financing commitment, we'll get the architects started."

Timing was perfect. The last of the town houses sold, wrapping up that development. Meanwhile all the pieces fell into place in the new venture and Ed went on the new payroll. His earnings progressed as the months went by, commensurate with his responsibilities and an ever increasing work load. More than a year passed. The job tied him down and whatever free time he managed, he'd hop over to Vegas and try his luck. The big kill was always out of reach. Craps was his Nemesis. He had a bad habit of letting his winnings ride. Invariably they were wiped out. Instead of investing his earnings in real estate, seeing how much profitibility there was in the right investment, he maintained a level of dependence on the next payday.

Danny cornered him one day.

"You're playing penny, Ed. It's not as if you were in a tax bracket where losing constantly wouldn't phase you a bit. Give it up."

"You're right. Unfortunately I'm one of those hard headed people where good advice doesn't penetrate."

He should have taken Danny's advice. Instead he was always blowing his money on something. Ed Kimball and being a spendthrift went together like ham and eggs.

One evening soon after Danny had talked to him, he was standing in line at the Cine Capri. Critics had given rave reviews to this latest version of Hamlet. Reading about it reminded him of his college days when his first love would have been the theater. After he bought his ticket he spotted his favorite real estate lady inside the lobby. He walked over with a big grin.

"How's Julia Hochstetter?"

She looked at him quisically. Then her expression changed and she smiled. "Oh, yes. The Madison house. I was fussing with the sign."

"Did you sell it?"

"Someone liked the carpeting the way you did."

"You remembered? How about that?"

He noticed her glancing around.

"Expecting your husband?"

"We never got that far," she laughed. "At the time I thought we were all set, but you know how those things go."

"No. I've never gotten that serious." He reached into his pocket.

"Mind if I smoke?"

"It's all right, but I don't use them."

They sat together during the movie and remained

39

in their seats during the 15-minute intermission. They compared notes. Ed told her how he had aspired to be a Shakespearean actor when in college. A promising thespian was forever lost because of the more immediate roll that sustenance played.

Julia laughed as she recounted her roll in the 'The Cactus Flower' in high school back in San Diego.

Ed asked her out for a drink after the show.

"Some other time I'd love to. Call me!"

He wasted no time getting back to her and soon be came a fixture around her apartment. The second time they went out, he spent the night. He was adept in his lovemaking, forceful and possessive, taking complete control of her body.

There was a moment soon afterwards when Ed frightened her. Her parents paid a surprise visit, flying in from San Diego. They hadn't expected to find anyone in the apartment with her. Julia sensed immediately that the men didn't take to one another. Her father was an opinionated man who met his equal in Ed.

"Guess I blew it," said Ed after the Hochstetters left in sort of a huff.

"What do you mean?"

"Guess your folks didn't think too much of me."

"Don't mind dad. He's ornery at times, but you met him head on."

"What did you expect me to do? Kowtow to him? I'd just as soon kick his head in."

"Do you realize what you're saying? I love my dad."

"Figure of speech. Because he's your dad, I wouldn't hurt him."

Fortunately her menses gave her an excuse to send him home that night. She needed time to think. There were other moments when she glimpsed an underlying anger in his personality. An uncontrollable aspect of an otherwise wonderful relationship. She tried to analyze his character, weighing the pros and cons on a mental balance on which she closed her eyes by not weighing his deep-seated shortcomings. Ed's possessiveness in his lovemaking overwhelmed her and at times she found herself to be as insatiable as he. She was hooked.

When Julia found herself pregnant after they had been married for more than a year, she learned his true character and never forgot it.

One of the things he had done when she had accepted his marriage proposal, was to talk her into eloping and getting married in Vegas. He disliked Roger Hochstetter and thought it was one way of getting at him. He was right in his assessment. Hochstetter was hopping mad learning that they had eloped.

"You should have told us you were getting married."

"Bullshit!" said Ed. "Since when do you have the right to tell us what we can do or can't do. We're of age."

"She's my daughter. I have all the right."

"Please you two. Stop this!" said Julia.

"You should be ashamed of yourselves. Of course we're disappointed, but if you can make Julia happy, that's all we care about. Isn't that right, Roger?" asked Betty Hochstetter.

He grumbled something that was a half-hearted confirmation, but Ed knew he had made an enemy. It was only when they learned the following year that they were going to be grandparents, that Roger suddenly mellowed. He accepted the fact that Kimball had fathered his grandson. He knew that it would be a boy, and having raised a girl looked forward to the new addition to the family. He made peace. Sort of a truce, actually. A white flag flying over the trenches.

PART III

Ed Kimball awoke feeling good. After his seeing Julia the previous afternoon he spent a quiet evening in the apartment. He was so relaxed that he actually fell asleep in front of the television. After the drunken spree of the previous evening, his waking in the desert, and the hunting knife episode, an evening at home was in order.

As the day progressed, however, he became impatient to hear what Julia would decide. Monday seemed weeks away. What if she said no? Then what? He'd fix her somehow, maybe slap her around a little. That lawyer of hers would probably charge him with assault and battery. That wouldn't be good, wouldn't solve anything. In some ways he still loved Julia, loved her body, anyway. She seemed to know what to do and how best to please him.

Friday night was always a heavy scene at his favorite hangout on 7th Street. He got there around nine. At home he had changed into a lightweight pair of washed-out jeans and a sleeveless jersey. His belt had a heavy brass buckle with a large turquoise set in it. For a long while he stood along the bar, but later squeezed behind one of the small tables along the wall. From here he had an unobstructed view of the girls as each one came out to gyrate before the patrons. Holly was supposed to be on next and he didn't want to miss any of her act. He had watched her numerous times before and had her sit with him at the table, but she wouldn't go out with him. She'd drink with him, get him to spend his dough, but that's where it ended. Getting Holly into bed became an obsession.

During Holly's act a slightly-drunk twosome started making lewd remarks. One of the men reached out to grab at her G-string.

"Sit down!" shouted Ed. "And shut up!"

The men turned around angrily. "Fuck you, buster!" growled one of them.

"Outside, you bums!" said Ed getting up from behind the table.

"OK, fucker. Come on!" snarled the other man heading for the door.

Ed turned to Holly who was still on stage dancing but watching the confrontation. "Be right back!"

The men were waiting for him. As Ed went outside into the parking area, one of them had moved aside in the other direction and was eager to fight. A kick caught Ed in the small of the back and sent him reeling to his knees. Instinctively he rolled to one side as the other man aimed a kick at his head. He was more sober than they and scrambling to his feet, slipped off his belt. The first swing caught one of them on the side of the head. The sound of the buckle meeting bone told the story. The man crumbled, clutching the side of his head.

"OK, you're next!" said Ed moving aggressively

towards the other one.

Instead of standing his ground, the man ran between the parked cars towards the rear of the lot and disappeared in the dark. Seeing him run off, Ed turned his attention to the one on the ground. There was no fight left in him. He cringed and tried to roll his body under a parked car. Blood was flowing from the gash made by the belt buckle.

Holly was still dancing when he entered. He gave her a sign that all had been taken care of. A short time later, she came out of the dressing area and slid onto the seat beside him.

"Thanks, Ed!"

"No problem, Holly."

"You're really a nice guy, Ed. Do you come to a girl's rescue all the time?"

"Only if they're special."

"Does that make me one of them?"

"I've been telling you that all along, but you just drink this slop that they pass off as champagne. Where's the happy ending?"

"A girl can change her mind, can't she?"

"I'd like that. What time are you through?"

"I'm on once more. I'll be free around one."

"I'll stick around. Sit with me?"

"You know the rules, Ed. I've got to mingle." She squeezed his wrist and got up. Her smile said it all. He had waited a long time for this.

Ed nursed his beers over the next two hours until Holly had danced again and was now approaching his table. He settled up, took her by the arm and moved towards the door.

"Mind riding in a pickup?"

"I've got my own car. Why not follow me?"

"What if I miss a light?"

"1915 E. Osborn. Apartment F-205."

Ed walked with her to the car. "Be right behind."

Holly started up the engine and switched on her headlights. She screamed as she saw a flash and heard the shot that was fired at Ed's back. Holly screamed again as she saw Ed stagger and fall. Several patrons came running over as she was getting out of her car.

"My God, Ed's been shot!" she cried out as she saw the blood on the back of his shirt. He was on his knees, trying to get up. He seemed wobbly and leaned sideways supporting himself against his truck.

"Bastards!" he coughed. Blood oozed from his mouth.

"Don't talk!" said Holly."

"Call the police! Ambulance!" one of the men ordered.

More patrons had spilled out of the club as they heard of the shooting. They stood around gaping as the first squad car pulled up with lights flashing. Sirens were screaming from all directions as a paramedic truck and squad cars converged on the area.

"Where's the victim?"asked a stocky police officer with a large mustache.

"There by the truck."

He hurried over to where Ed was surrounded by onlookers.

"OK. Stand back!"

Glancing towards the arriving paramedics he shouted, "Here!"

Holly stepped back away from Ed as the medic knelt down to examine him.

"Anybody see this happen?" asked the police officer.

"I was here," said Holly. "I saw the flash."

"See who did it?"

"It was dark. Ed! Poor Ed."

The eirie light flashing around made it a stage setting. Blue-green emergency beams intermingled with red as the lights rotated. As the colors bounced off the people, it looked like an old Kinescope being played to a juvenile audience on a Saturday afternoon. Any moment the Keystone cops would chase the villain across the set. When the light struck Holly, her face showed a frightened expression.

"Would you have any reason to know why someone would shoot your fellow?" continued the officer.

One of the patrons answered for her. "There were a couple of guys giving Holly, here" he pointed to her "a hard time earlier. Guess Ed took them out. Maybe it's one of them."

"Can you give us a description?"

"Sure."

A quick check of the area by the other officers proved futile. They gathered back in the parking lot. Only a couple of minutes had passed since the first officers arrived. Holly walked along with the medics who helped the ambulance crew put Ed in the back.

"Where're you taking him?" asked Holly.

"Good Sam."

The small-caliber bullet entered his back between the 6th and 7th ribs and lodged in the inferior lobe of the lung. Deflected by bone on impact, the distorted bullet tore into soft tissue.

Outside in the pastel-green waiting room, Holly, who felt indirectly responsible, sat slumped in an uncomfortable chair while the operation was taking place. She shifted as the doctor approached.

"Are you Mrs. Kimball?"

"Only a friend."

So that's what his last name is, she thought. He'd never mentioned it. Ed Kimball. Nice ring to that.

"He's in recovery now. We're putting him on the critical list but there's nothing to really worry about. I'd suggest you run along and get some sleep yourself."

"Guess you're right. Would you give him a message when he wakes?"

"Sure, miss."

"Tell him Holly will be looking in on him. Would you, doc?"

"I'll tell him."

Because of the amount of blood seepage, the doctors thought he would run into pneumonia. Ed rallied quickly without complications and was released six days later. Holly picked him up.

"We'd better go by my truck," Ed suggested.

"Already taken care of. I had Pete drive it over."

"Pete?"

"Our bartender."

"Oh, that Pete. You take care of everything, don't you, doll?"

She smiled as she turned to glance at him. "Too bad you're not in shape at the moment. I want to express my thanks for what you did. I feel responsible for your getting shot, you know."

"Forget it, Holly. Is there any word on those crappy punks?"

"They've been identified from the police sketches, but they must have high tailed it out of town."

"Speaking of high tailing it, I'll take you up on that 'thank you' that you owe me. Just give me a couple of days."

"Sure, lover."

There was a letter from Julia in the mail. Ed sat down on the couch and ripped open the envelope. "Fix yourself a drink, doll."

"Fuckin' broad!" he snapped as he finished reading her note.

"Who, me?" asked Holly indignantly.

"My wife."

"Thought you were single."

"She's filed for divorce."

"That why you're angry?"

"Christ, no! It's my kid. She learned about me getting shot. She's decided not to let me take Jeff along on vacation. Goddamn bitch!"

"Maybe she'll change her mind."

"Not Julia. Once she's got something in her bugger, that's it."

"That's not fair. Getting shot wasn't your fault."

"It's where it happened. Had my skull caved in after Julia walked out on me. Drunk? Christ! Eleven days of boozing it up till that fuckin' nigger hit me with a pipe. I still feel the effects sometimes."

"Were you helping another girl?"

"Not that time."

She walked over, drink in hand, and kissed his cheek. Her breast brushed his shoulder. It roused him.

When he was discharged the doc had told him, "Take it easy for a week or so. Nothing to tax your breathing. "

He tried not to think about Holly, but he knew from seeing her on stage that she had the kind of breasts that swept upwards, with dark nipples pointing skyward.

Seeing his expression, Holly laughed.

"Down, boy! Let's keep your mind on something else. How about a drink?"

"Will you get me a beer?"

Holly took a can out of the refrigerator and pushed in the metal tab.

"Your frig is kind of empty. Want me to run over to that Circle K?"

"There's enough stuff around. I'll manage for a couple of days."

"OK, then, lover. I'll shove off. See you tomorrow, if you don't mind."

"Anytime."

She kissed him on the head and left.

Ed Kimball sat back in the couch slowly finishing his beer. He stared at the letter on the coffee table. The empty can crumbled in his hand and he flung it across the room into the kitchen. Julia's words had gotten to him. They had probed into his innards as easily as the doctor's scalpel had cut through tissue to get at the spent bullet in his lung. This pain he was undergoing was without the use of anesthesia, that could deaden it. Why should she punish him for something that wasn't his fault? Especially after all he had gone through this past week. He needed to talk with Julia, get her to change her mind. But how to reach her? He had no number. He tried information, but they had no listing for Roger Hochstetter. He felt certain that she was staying with her parents till the end of the month. Calling Boswell Memorial, he learned that the old man had been discharged on Monday.

"Shit!" he exclaimed.

In the middle of the night he woke up restless, uncomfortable. He flicked on the light switch and went into the bathroom for one of the pain killing capsules the doc had given him. When he lay down again he shut Julia out of his thoughts and dwelt on Holly. She had proven to be a real friend. With visions of her upswept breasts, he drifted off.

He felt cold in the morning and wished he had turned the air conditioning down when he had taken the pill in the middle of the night. Before putting on his bathrobe he looked at his back. Tomorrow they were going to remove the bandage. No shower till then, he had been cautioned. Remembering that Holly had said she would be over, why not ask her to give him a sponge bath? Would she?

Over coffee he found himself listening to the morning news on TV. Usually he was already on the way to work. The words real estate agent caught his attention as well as foul play. He put the mug down on the table and walked closer to the set. A real estate agent's car had been found in the long-term parking lot at the airport. He had been reported missing by members of his family for the past three days. Upon querying his movements the last day any of his associates had seen him, it seemed that he had had an appointment to meet a prospective client in the area around Pinnacle Peak. The man had told the agent, who was reported missing, that he had inherited a home in that area and wanted to put it up for sale. When a bulletin was sent out by the local board about the agent's disappearance, another broker came forward reporting on a similar situation. In fact he had met with the man who claimed he had inherited a house, but because of a previous commitment, wasn't able to go off with the client to view the house. When this prospective client wouldn't provide a phone number at which he could be reached, he wrote the man off as a flake. Not hearing from the man again, he dismissed the incident from his mind till now. From the description given, the police artist made a sketch of the suspect. The suspect, calling himself David Spencer, was wanted for questioning and anyone knowing his whereabouts was asked to contact Detective De Morro of the Scottsdale Police Department.

Ed's mind was spinning. How easy it was to deceive. If you waved dollar bills in front of somebody, how quickly they responded. This real estate episode made him think of Julia. At the moment, like the incident he had just heard about, he had to track her down. The news item had offered a way to reach her. The problem was that he'd have to wait till 9 o'clock. Promptly at nine he dialed the State Real Estate Department.

"I'd like to get the phone number of someone licensed with your department."

"Salesperson or broker?"

"Salesperson."

"Name?"

"Kimball."

"First name?"

"Julia."

"I'll put you on hold, sir." He listened to the music piped over the phone in the meantime.

"I'm sorry, sir. We don't have a Julia Kimball licensed with this department."

"That's impossible. I talked to her the other day. She may be using her maiden name again."

"What would that be?"

"Hochstetter." He spelled it out for her. He was again put on hold.

"We do have a Julia Hochstetter. She's licensed

with Scott Harrison & Associates, 2410 Northern Avenue, here in Phoenix."

"Could I trouble you for the number?"

"264-3205."

"Thank you for your help." He dialed the number he had been given.

"Good morning. Scott Harrison & Associates."

"Julia Hochstetter, please."

"She's not expected today. May I take a message?"

"Let me have her home number. I'll reach her there."

"I'm sorry, sir. There's been illness in the family. She's not to be disturbed. May I have her call you when she checks in?"

Reluctantly he left his number. Would she avoid calling back knowing that he'd be furious with her decision? He next called his boss. Mel Greer had phoned him at the hospital several times to check on his progress, and now he figured Mel would know that he'd been released.

"Peggi, Ed Kimball."

"Sorry about what happened to you. Feeling better?"

"Coming along. Mel there?"

"I'll ring."

"I heard they let you out. Called this morning and they said you had been released yesterday. How's it going?"

"OK. Seeing the doc tomorrow. Guess he'll say it's OK to get back to work."

"Let me know what he says so I can fit you into the schedule. The guys have been going bongo picking up your load. When you come back to work, for Christ's sake manage to stay out of trouble."

"Hey, Mel! That wasn't my fault."

"Never mind. But people don't get shot up for no reason, as a rule. Sure! If some crazy with an automatic rifle stands in the middle of an intersection and fires at the crowd, you may put your life on the line. But knowing you, Ed, you must have rubbed some guy the wrong way. You're a big guy. I'd hate to tangle with you on a one-to-one basis. But if I've got the only gun, I can cut you down to size pretty damn fast, and you can't do much about it unless I blow my advantage. Keep that in mind. If you want to come out on top, you better cover all the bases before you wind up on a cold gurney down at the morgue."

"I'll keep your advice in mind."

Keep the upper hand, cover the bases. Sound advice, all of what Mel said made sense.

"OK. Remember! Keep your nose clean."

As the day moved along, he became more and more impatient at not hearing from Julia. No longer using the Kimball name meant that she was really severing all ties with him. The only link that would remain would be Jeff. When the phone did ring, he expected it to be Julia.

"Julia?"

"Ed. This is Holly."

"Oh!" he said disappointed.

"Well, aren't you the cheery one."

"Sorry. I've been expecting the old lady to call. What's up? Coming over?"

"Wanted to know if you like pizza."

"Sure."

"Good. I'll pick one up on the way. See you in an hour, lover."

Shortly after six he opened for Holly. She kissed

53

him on the cheek and walked directly to the kitchen.

"Hope you like pepperoni and all the trimmings. Like mushrooms?"

"Sounds real good."

"Mind if we eat right away? I go on at 7:30 tonight."

"Too bad we have to eat first."

"Down, lover. Beer?"

"I'll get them," said Ed.

"Sit still," she said.

"Want one?" He was already up.

"Please."

Holly sliced the pizza and the aroma of hot cheese, tomato sauce, and all the trimmings quickly filled the air. "Smells good, doesn't it, Ed."

"Sure does. You bought one of the real large ones."

"You're no 90 pound weakling. You have two to feed."

"Two?"

Holly laughed mischievously. "That's what the girls at the club say. You've got quite a friend there," she said pointing with her knife.

Ed joined in her laughter. "You'll have to judge for yourself."

"Got any candles?"

"What for?"

"To put on the table, jerk."

"In the drawer. Think there's a small one."

Holly found it and remembering where she had spotted an empty liquor bottle, retrieved it from alongside the trash basket under the sink. She fitted the candle into the neck.

"How's that?"

"Just like old times."

"Your wife?"

"Candle nut. Always had one lit at dinner."

"I like that myself. What's the matter with romance?"

"Nothing, I guess."

"Just sex, Ed? Wim wham, thank you ma'am? Don't you remember how we ladies like to be treated? Slow and easy. Candlelight, violins, slow and gentle until we want it otherwise."

Ed laughed. He bit into the pizza slice. "I've had no complaints," he bragged with his mouth full.

"That's good pizza," he continued.

"It is, isn't it. By the way, did your wife call?"

"Don't remind me of her."

"She didn't then."

"No."

"I'm sure you can work something out. Maybe you can postpone your vacation. Give her time to cool off. Give her a breather, and you, too."

"Guess you're right, Holly. She never stays uptight long. I'll set it back a month. You're a smart cookie."

Ed liked Holly's idea the more he thought about it as they ate. Before long he accepted the idea and dismissed Julia from his thoughts. Holly filled his plate and watched as he ate in silence. She wondered about his being so pensive.

"Hey, tiger. You're really the big silent type. What gives?"

"Wondering what I'd do with Jeff if I had custody."

"That's not likely, is it?"

"No. I'm not contesting the divorce."

"When's it final?"

"Anytime now."

"Then there's nothing to think about then, is there?"

"If something happened to her, then what?"

"Ed, things can happen to anyone. Look at you. You might have been killed."

"But, what if?"

"The court would decide."

"That would rule me out."

"The way you take chances, you're probably right. Unless you changed your ways."

Ed laughed.

"I've always accepted a brawl, Holly. Where I lived in New York, you didn't stand a chance if you were a milksop. My old man would have kicked the shit out of me if I'd come home crying. I can't change my ways, Holly."

She passed him another piece.

"Who'd wind up with the kid?" Ed asked.

"Probably the grandparents. Your's living here?"

"My old man's still alive back east. I guess he's alive. I've never looked into it since I've been here."

"Your in-laws, then. What are they like?"

"Respectable. Dull. Hochstetter. Get a load of that name. But they've got money. That's what it takes. Money."

"Like another beer?" she asked getting up.

"Thanks."

"That's the last one. I'll go across the street and get some later."

He reached into his pocket and gave her a fiver.

"You didn't have to do that now."

"So I don't forget later."

"Big deal!" She offered him the last slice. He lifted his hand to refuse it.

"You need it. I'll take a bite."

The ringing phone caught them off guard. With the pizza bite in her mouth she asked, "Shall I?"

"Why not?"

She put the slice on Ed's plate and wiped her fingers off before picking up the phone on its fifth ring.

"Hello."

Holly put her hand over the receiver. "For you. Probably your wife."

"Hello!" said Ed.

"You left a message."

"That letter of yours. I want to talk about it."

"Sorry about your getting shot, Ed. You all right now?"

"I'm doing OK. About this vacation bit. I'm going to postpone it for a month. Jeff can go with me then."

Julia didn't answer.

"Did you hear me, Julia?"

"I heard. What makes you think I'll change my mind?"

Ed tried using charm. He knew how anger backfired.

"To tell the truth it was Holly's idea Not mine."

"Holly?"

"The girl who answered the phone. She's been looking in on me since I got shot."

"Oh?"

"Think about it, OK? There's time."

"I'll see."

"Jeff OK?"

"He's fine."

"Tell him I love him."

He put the phone down and stood there for a moment. His last words were still reverberating.

Strange. He couldn't remember the last time that he openly admitted loving Jeff. He did, even though he hardly ever expressed it. Love? Was he capable of it? Or had he cunningly tried to soften Julia's attitude by stating that he loved Jeff?

"You all right?" asked Holly.

"Yeh!" he said gruffly. He picked up the slice of pizza.

"What'd she say?"

"She'll see."

"At least she didn't say no. Give her time."

Holly glanced at him from the kitchen where she was getting rid of the pizza carton. The way he had said 'Yeh!' showed he was ready for another brawl with his wife. Some rough cookie she was mixed up with. But she owed him one. She decided to unruffle his feathers.

"I still have a little time, lover. Like me to get the beer first?"

"Wouldn't mind that."

"Be right back."

He walked to the window and watched her crossing the street. The loose fitting white dress swished sideways with her hip movements. Christ! She had a good ass. It reminded him of what first had attracted him to Julia as she bent over her real estate sign. For the moment he didn't know what to make of Julia. She had him by the balls and he didn't like that. Being a man, he had to be in control at all times. But she, goddamn her, was pulling the strings, making him dance to her tune, sit up and beg like a dog. Shit! He should beat some sense into Julia once and for all. Let her know who was master.

His emotions flooded over him like water from a

broken dam. He found himself submerged in self pity momentarily, feeling a sense of weakness from his recent hospitalization. His macho stance was on wobbly legs. The undercurrent anger was also dragging him along. Deeper and deeper where the blue-green water changed to murky dark blue ink. A change in the current of his mind swept him upwards towards the surface and pushed him like driftwood onto the shore. As the surf pounded this human relationship between him and Julia, it was made up of love-hate. Their love-hate, in the past, had brought special emotional fulfillment to their combined sensuality, adding just the right amount of spice to their lovemaking, after hanging up their war bonnets. There were still moments when he conjured up tender thoughts towards Julia, but more often these were outweighed by resentment. It was only a matter of a short period before their connecting lifeline would be severed by the divorce decree. It would end. Or would it?

Monsoon rains battered the city. In the pre-dawn hours Ed was awakened by dust infiltrating around the window in the bedroom as gale-like wind rolled a dense cloud of sand before it. Thunder reverberated through the South Mountains, coming ever nearer. As he lay there watching the sky light up from streaks of lightning, he anticipated the large drops of rain that would accompany the thunder. He got up out of bed, lit a cigarette and stood naked by the window and pondered over the torrential rain that suddenly was overflowing in the street and cascading down from the roof of the apartment.

It reminded him of the rainy day when Jeff had surprised him and Julia as they were both about to climax. He had often regretted having struck out at Jeff. Standing by the window also reminded him of watching Holly the previous day. He had tried to convince her to stay over.

"Lover, I'd like nothing better, but I want to buy more pizzas for some helpless slob some day. If I don't show, there'll be somebody to move into my job."

"They couldn't replace what you've got, no matter how they tried."

"Why, Ed. You'll have me blushing."

"Come back later?"

"Ed Kimball! You just got out of the hospital. Remember?"

The rain made him thirsty. Beer at 4 in the morning? So what? Beer was beer, anytime. Twenty minutes later he was sound asleep, oblivious to the continuing storm.

The weather eased up a little in the morning. He had an appointment to see the doctor and fortunately telephoned to confirm it. Because of heavy flooding on some streets, and long delays at river crossings, all appointments were cancelled. The answering service suggested phoning Monday to arrange for another appointment. That bothered him. He wanted to get the visit over with and put this latest episode behind him, like a bad review after opening night. As the day progressed he felt like a virtual prisoner.

The storm shuttled back and forth between the ridges of mountains dropping rain varying in intensity between torrential and heavy. Four inches had fallen within a 12 hour period and constant bulletins were ribboned over the televised picture of the ball game being played in Philadelphia. Ed wasn't surprised to learn about major river crossings being shut down. This hard baked desert saucer on which the city had risen and spread out, was easily filled with rising water. He had witnessed four occasions over the past nine years when traffic was possible at only three crossings over the Salt. On one occasion southbound traffic on Interstate 10 was routed to the northbound lane because of a sagging roadway.

Around eight the doorbell surprised him. Holly was outside his door grinning. Her dark hair hung in strands from which water dripped onto the hallway.

"Surprise!"

"Jeese! Come in! Come in! I sure didn't expect to see you tonight."

"Pete closed the place early. Only a couple of die-hards there."

"Good for Pete."

He took her transparent raincoat and hung it up over the shower head. Meanwhile Holly had followed him and was ruffling her hair by the mirror.

"There's a robe on the hook. Why don't you take your stuff off. Let it dry out. I'll get some hangers."

When Holly reappeared her hair was pulled together in half a dozen relatively short braids. Gathering up the robe that could have covered two Hollys, she ambled over to him and kissed his chin.

"Would you fix me some coffee, Ed?"

"Sure you don't want a drink?"

"Coffee, please."

"How'd you get so soaked?"

"My car got stuck on Campbell. Too much water. I probably shorted out the electrical."

"Probably."

"Have you eaten?" asked Ed who was heating water.

"No."

"What about you?"

"Junk food. Got some chili."

"I'll share one."

Ed opened two cans and warmed the chili, stirring it occasionally. Soon the aroma of hot peppers filled the room.

"I'm going to be the lady and let you wait on me."

He tossed a book of matches to her.

"I know you've got your mind on the candle."

"You're learning," she laughed.

"I don't have any milk for your coffee. Sugar?"

"Plain."

"Want some bread with the chili?"

"Not for me. Just give me a little bit."

"Chili's good for your libido."

"Am I supposed to turn you on? I thought that was against doctor's orders at the moment."

"What he doesn't know."

"Weren't you supposed to see him today?"

"Closed."

"I'm not surprised."

He put chili on her plate and served her, then filled his. He spooned the last remnants out of the pot and licked the spoon.

"I'm glad you came, Holly. I was ready to climb the walls."

"What if you took it real easy? We might remedy that."

He leaned over and gave her a chili kiss.

"I like the sound of that."

Ed Kimball edged out of bed. He had fallen asleep right after Holly had made love to him. Slow and easy. She took the lead and straddled him. Because of his size

62

she was uncomfortable at first but then as she adjusted to his proportions she lowered herself further and further. Slow and easy, she teased him along until she felt his hands tightening on her buttocks. Ready to explode herself, it took only a few rapid thrusts till he pulled her as close as humanly possible.

He stood by the window looking out on the gray dawn. The rain had eased up for now, but the forecast predicted rain through Monday. The satellite photos showed a large mass of clouds spreading up from the Gulf of Mexico, bringing tropical moisture with it. Glancing at Holly sleeping on her back, he saw how her nipples were straining to penetrate the thin sheet. How her breasts had danced during their lovemaking. Delicious! Delicious! thought Ed. He decided to let her wake by herself although he was eager for her. It was strange how he had felt close to only two women before. Susan, back in New York. Comely Susan, but what a lay! Then Julia. Julia had been close once, but now? A rotted-wood splinter imbedded under his nail. No matter how many broken slivers you managed to get out, there was enough left to cause the finger to fester. Fester. How much would it have to fester before it had to be removed? Removed? He thought of the missing real estate man whose car was found by the airport. Removed? Had he been removed? Or had he skipped town to live his life out elsewhere under an assumed identity?

Holly stirred. He forgot about Julia, the irritation she was to him at the moment. The festering would have to be taken care of. Holly turned onto her side but didn't awaken. Kimball smiled down at her. Yes! Like his past feelings for Susan and Julia, he suddenly felt a closeness to Holly. She had proven herself to be a friend. A real friend. Looking after him. Giving all of herself last night. Dripping water like a drowned cat. He laughed aloud. She stirred again. He went into the living room and lit a cigarette. The light filtering into the room past the drapes brought the charging bull over the couch to life. Ed's eyes fixed on it.

Isn't that what he was all about? Heavy handed. Tough fisted like his old man. What did pa say? 'You've got to be ready, boy, to slam your way through life or they'll get you against the ropes. Don't give 'em an inch. Dance around light-footed, keeping them off guard. Let them swing at you from a distance. Then step in. Give them all you've got, boy. All you've got.'

The vinyl felt clammy against his skin. He put his legs up on the coffee table and inhaled deeply, letting the gray smoke ease out of the corner of his mouth. Two more puffs and some ash fell onto his thigh. He brushed it off and walked over to the window again. Feeling restless, he couldn't pinpoint it to anything in particular. The weather didn't help either. It pressed on the soft tissue that not too long ago had healed in his skull. When the barometer was falling, Ed always felt better. Now that it was climbing, his brain was in a vise. Thinking about Julia and the way she had said, 'I'll see' bothered him. He walked to the kitchen sink and shoved the cigarette butt into the disposal.

Kimball was pacing the living room unaware that Holly was standing naked in the bedroom doorway. "Hi! Is that what I do to you?"

His mood took a complete turnabout. He laughed.

"Like a caged animal ready to get at you."

"OK, tiger. I'm chilly. Come back to bed and see what you can do about it."

He walked over and pulled her close. Her skin felt

cool in contrast to his. Blood surged into his organ as he lifted her in his arms.

PART IV

The weekend storm which had begun on July 24th was two-week-old headlines, but the aftermath of damage by raging rivers still lingered, snarling traffic. During the past week Ed had been traveling back and forth to Yuma, coordinating supplies for a construction job at the air base. Two sections of U.S. 8 between Phoenix and Yuma had been undermined at the San Cristobal Wash and further to the west at the Coyote Wash. Detours caused aggravating delays and boiled-over radiators.

Today had gone wrong from the start. At the air-base a lieutenant had chewed Ed out for letting something get fouled up. Sure, it was his fault. He admitted it. Being made to look foolish by the lieutenant didn't help matters. When he returned to Phoenix, he was in a lousy mood. A letter from his attorney topped the day. It was over. The court had approved the divorce petition. The attorney in his covering letter spelled out that the court had stipulated that without the mother's consent, he would be unable to have the boy accompany him outside the state.

"Shit!" he shouted flinging the papers across the room, wishing he could have been in the courtroom to contest this decision. Why had he trusted Julia? Why had she sneaked this over on him? It wasn't in the draft copy.

He filled a water glass halfway with brandy. Tomorrow was Saturday. He needed to tie one on to forget Julia for the moment. To forgo his wanting to slap her around the way his old man used to slap his mother. He thought of that time when she had mustered all her courage and fought back. She kicked him in the groin and watched him double up. When his father recovered, he broke down the bedroom door and almost killed her.

Ed didn't like to think about death. His mother was the only dead person he had ever seen. He'd never attended a funeral since. Not a single one in 14 years. Strange. All the guys at work would ask for time off to attend funerals throughout the year. Maybe they had big families, lots of friends, or friends of friends. How the shit should he know? He didn't have uncles, cousins, all that crap. If somebody notified him that his old man had croked, he wouldn't bother going to his funeral. What if he, himself, died? Who in hell would care? Julia? Maybe for old times sake. Jeff? Sure. Jeff would cry. His only flesh and blood relative to shed a tear.

He became angry again thinking of Jeff and filled his glass. It wasn't anger directed at Jeff. Julia, that lousy attorney of hers and that stinkin' judge. They were the ones who needed to be shown.

The brandy was making him sweat profusely. He removed his shirt and tossed it onto a chair. From the refrigerator he took some cheese and ham and piled some between slices of bread. He hadn't eaten since noon.

Mike Perez had sat across from him at lunch. Mike was one of the foremen on the construction job. Wednesday night when Ed found it necessary to stay overnight, they had guzzled beer and talked. In fact Perez had talked too much. He bragged about ripping off construction supplies, falsifying vouchers, pocketing the profits.

"Why are you telling me?" asked Ed.

"You're my friend."

Ed patted him on the back. At this point everyone was Mike's friend.

"Yeh! I like you, too, Mike."

"You could make lots of dough."

"The way you do?"

"Sure. Nothing to it."

"Just rip off the stuff?"

"The next load. I'll get the vouchers OKd."

"Even if it doesn't show up at the base?"

"You learn easy."

Ed laughed. Guys like Mike were so many flies on garbage. They'd always come around. But stealing? That wasn't Ed's bag. Despite his failings, he was honest. He was one of those few who would return excess change given to him at the supermarket checkout.

"I'll keep it in mind."

Today as they were eating lunch, the atmosphere was strained. No mention was made of that conversation about ripping off the government, but Ed could sense that Perez felt he had left himself wide open, unsure of how much he had talked. This vulnerability

67

wasn't lost to Ed. In the jargon of World War II, 'loose lips sink ships', Mike's ship was awash in a sea of beer suds.

He dismissed Perez from his mind. Christ! It was hot. He put the dishes in the sink. A shower would wash off the stinkin' sweat from the drive. Jeese, how he hated that fuckin' drive. Seven hours of driving for a couple of lousy hours of work.

While showering he thought of Holly. The previous Sunday she had stayed over and had joined him in the shower. He laughed thinking how she had driven him half crazy by lathering him in all the right places. And then when she had everything going he had lifted her in his arms while she straddled him with her legs around his hips. The water was splashing over them both, but somehow he managed to step on the soap. Holly snapped half the curtain rings off as she prevented them from falling. The remaining rings were spread out on the rod.

"Buy some new ones, will you, Ed?"

"I'll pick them up."

He hadn't yet. Holly would give him hell. He laughed again. He liked her. Liked the spunk she had. Sort of complemented him, different from Julia. He and Julia were too much alike. When Julia got mad, so did he, and the other way around. With Holly it was all fun and games. A beautiful pixie. She had yet to make him angry.

A slight breeze was blowing when Ed drove from the apartment. For the past few hours he had been glued to the television waiting for the sun to set and the temperature to drop. He hadn't watched the program actually. He had seen what was happening, but his mind had been concentrating on the divorce decree which he read over and over. Why weren't legal papers worded so that people could understand what they contained without having to consult an attorney just to interpret the meaning of every sentence. Ed didn't consider himself to be dumb in any sense of the word, having majored in English. But this was a far cry from Shakespeare or any of the masters of English prose. Legal garbage, made by lawyers for lawyers.

Visitation rights were spelled out. Two days a month and the right to have Jeff spend two weeks during his vacation from school every second year. Shit! They even had school spelled out, even though Jeff wouldn't be starting regular school till September. And then there was that crap about permission to take Jeff out of state. Goddamned judge! He thought of what Tom Farrington had said. He sure was right. Not to count on anything until it was spelled out.

At the stop light he pulled out a cigarette. He tossed the match out the window and saw a familiar face. It was Mark, all smiles, sitting on the passenger side of an open convertible.

"Borrow your knife?" he joked.

"Son-of--a-bitch!"

"Where're you headed?"

"Just around."

"Wanna come along?"

The light changed. A driver honked.

"Pull over up ahead!" shouted Mark as the convertible leaped across the intersection and stopped at the curb. Ed pulled in behind them.

"What's up?" asked Ed when Mark walked up to him.

"We're tired of the stuff around here. How about raising hell with us in Nogales?"

"Tonight?"

"Shit, yes! We'll make it in three hours. Some good Flamenco ass? Come on!"

"Why not?"

He parked his truck on a side street and sat back as the Buick convertible rolled down the highway. The wind whipping through his unruly hair was hot, but he didn't care. For the first time in weeks he felt a sense of freedom. The smell of brandy was still on his breath, but with each passing mile the air forced into his lungs brought a cleansing effect. Occasionally he entered into the conversation, catching a word here or there above the sound of the wind.

Twice Paul, the driver, slowed when he spotted the highway patrol. Mostly he stayed around 60. In two hours they were passing through Tucson. The lighted city with the river flowing below the hills, shimmered in the clear air. As they drove beyond the city limits, darkness once more engulfed the highway. Ed lay back across the seat gazing into the sky. Stars glistened in the sky, not yet overpowered by the full moon barely visible, rising over the distant hills. This was what he loved. Space. The whole universe out there spoke of space. Room to breath. His anger that had goaded him earlier was gone. It was one of those rare moments when Ed was at peace with himself.

On the outskirts of Nogales, Ed sat up. He'd been to this busy border town on several occasions before marrying Julia. Thinking back, seven years had passed since the last time. It still looked unchanged. The cheap goods priced as bargains for the tourists, that could easily be found elsewhere for less money. Why were people so incredibly gullible. The moment they saw a sign saying bargain, they were eager to part with their dollars.

They were stopped momentarily at the border crossing, then drove slowly through the crowded streets on the Mexican side. Paul knew exactly where to go for the best action. He was also street-wise, knowing where to park. A guarded lot was necessary, otherwise a convertible like this would be many miles away by morning.

The men made a formidable trio as they walked along the sidewalk. All were over six feet tall, Ed the tallest at 6'3". Summer tourists were ambling past the shops, being hawked at by shopkeepers. Youngsters, high on cheap booze or illegal pot, were boisterous intrusions jostling pedestrians as they caroused about. One freckled teenager misjudged and spun into Mark. Instinctively Mark grabbed his arm to steady himself.

"OK mister, OK. Let go!" yelled the kid.

"Is that all?"

"All what?"

"How about a sorry?"

"Fuck you!"

The kid's girl friend pushed her way past Paul and Ed.

"Let him go!" she shouted, starting to pummel Mark.

Ed grabbed her arms.

"Easy, kiddo."

She glared up at him over her shoulder.

"Now why don't you say 'sorry' and it'll all be over?" Ed told the boy.

"Yeh. Sorry. OK?"

Mark released him and he ran down the street with his girl yelling back, "Fuck off, you guys!"

They laughed as the girl made a vulgar sign to

them. Ahead of them the street led to the bars and bordellos. That's what they had come here for, since prostitution was legalized and controlled to some degree by the government. Music blasted from the doorways. Some bars openly enticed tourists by letting them catch a glimpse of the nude dancers from the doorway. Others had a bouncer by the door. No viewing unless you came in and paid. Paul led the way to La Contina where the entertainers had the reputation for being the most beautiful. Paul had talked a blue streak about this place on the way down.

The timing was right for a ringside table between shows. The main room was dimly lit. Amber, red, and blue- green glass jars with wicks floating on oil provided candle light. A juke box off to one side played nostalgic music. Ed recognized the trumpet of Herb Alpert and 'Tijuana Brass'. He had always liked the clean, brassy sound.

By the time the third round of drinks was brought to the table, the juke box was turned off, stage lights came on, and a combo off to the side started tuning up. One after the other the girls appeared either to dance provocatively or to sing. Every table was now taken and Ed was amazed to see the groups of women who were leaning on the edges of their chairs watching the performers. Undoubtedly comparing their own bodies.

The latest singer spotted Ed alongside the stage and played up to him. Her jet black hair was braided in a single strand that hung to her waist. As she sang she kept pushing it back in place whenever it fell forward. When she come closer to Ed and bent over provocatively, he sprang to his feet. Her black eyes danced as she puckered her lips for a kiss only to pull back before he could make contact. Good-naturedly he played the game with enthusiasm. The patrons loved it. When the girl finished her songs, Ed told the waitress to ask her to join him for a drink.

Ed only knew a few words of Spanish, but Paul was there to interpret. Ed commented on her beauty and she smiled. When she was told that he wanted to spend the night with her, she cocked her head sideways as if to say, 'you do?' Before she could say anything, Ed told Paul to negotiate a price. They talked back and forth.

"OK", said Ed.

"OK?", the girl echoed.

Paul assured her that the price was agreed to and she smiled. Ed was all set to go off with her, but Paul told him the girl wanted him to watch her sister who would be on stage next. Ed sat back. The sister was a stripper. If at all possible, she was even more beautiful than the girl across from him. Her breasts were perfectly shaped. Long legged, flawless body. Not a single blemish anywhere on her creamy skin. Ed's erection began to press uncomfortably in his shorts figuring the sisters would be much alike. They looked like twins.

The bed had a rattan headboard in a fan shape. Its fragile appearance belied the sturdy framework supporting the mattress, which easily withstood Ed's onslaught. Only a 40 watt bulb lighted the sparsely furnished room. In a small closet-size area a toilet and sink provided some semblance of sanitation, despite the roaches that scurried around. For twenty minutes the girl had lain spread-eagled under him, as the alcohol he had consumed failed to curb his appetite. She lay there staring past him at the ceiling, vacant-eyed, expressionless. Like a cow being inseminated, standing patiently while the bull ravaged it, hooves pawing the hide on the back. Ed had expected more. He was proud of what he had to offer. Why didn't she feel anything? He was close to coming but suddenly he lost all interest in her. Perspiration dripped onto her breasts as he bent over her. She looked into his eyes.

In broken English she asked, "You like? You marry?"

He shook with laughter as he climbed off the bed. It was all such a farce. Marry? This computerized machine that didn't even go beep, beep, beep when programmed?

"You beautiful bitch. Marry?"

"More?" she asked not understanding him. She raised her buttocks and slipped a pillow under them, opening her wet cunt to him.

"Christ! No!" He waved her to get out of bed.

Neither Mark nor Paul had returned to the parlor of this bordello which stood directly behind La Contina. It was reached through a small courtyard, entered only through a door adjacent to the juke box near the bar. The flowering plants cascading from hanging baskets and red-clay pots were in stark contrast to the animalism that often tended towards depravity in the rooms beyond.

Ed sat down on one of two concrete benches. Above him he could see the stars. At the moment he felt nothing. It wasn't the girls fault in a way. Making herself available to hundreds of men. All shapes. All sizes. Young and old. Some acceptable, others possibly even repulsive. No wonder that she had long since been drained of emotions. He figured she was perhaps twenty.

It wasn't the first time that vacant eyes had stared at him. With Julia sometimes. That's why this girl had turned him off. That stare had reminded him of Julia. He couldn't understand why Julia had looked like that. With her, though, he had never stopped before satisfying himself. It didn't occur to Ed that perhaps he was at fault, that he could have said something tender, caring. Perhaps a kiss or just holding her. Thinking of her desires first.

He looked up as the girl walked out of the bordello. She said nothing but bent over and kissed his cheek, then went back into the bar from which loud music drifted.

"I heard that you were out here," said Mark coming from the bar. "How'd it go?"

"You'd never believe me."

"That great?"

Ed laughed.

"Where's Paul?"

"Still up there, I'd say."

"Guess he's enjoying himself."

"Sounds like you didn't. Wasn't she that good? Didn't she turn you on?"

Ed knew that Mark had a big mouth and Paul was sure to make some comment.

"The greatest."

"Yeh? Mine, too. Glad we came down. How about a drink while we're waiting? No sense sitting around. He'll find us."

Ed got to his feet slowly and stretched. Why not? Booze had a way of killing off things you didn't want to think about at the moment. But despite all the liquor, Julia had a way of cropping up again and again in his thoughts. Damn her, anyway!

Julia Kimball awoke from a nightmare. Her body was soaked with perspiration. She was terrified. Turning on the light she hurried into the second bedroom. Jeff was fast asleep. She adjusted the thin blanket so that he wouldn't be chilled by the blowing air conditioning. Relieved that the nightmare had only been that, she went into the kitchen and boiled water for tea. She needed to wind down. It was 2:30.

Her dream was conjured up from subconscious fears. Ed had abducted Jeff after having broken her legs so that she couldn't follow. Painfully she crawled to her car and somehow managed to track Ed to a deserted adobe structure in the middle of nowhere, only to find Jeff starved to death, his small body tied to a broken chair.

"My God," she said aloud as she dipped her tea bag into the cup. "What a ghastly nightmare."

Analyzing her fears she realized they were well founded. Ed's explosive temper was unpredictable. She didn't feel he would strike out and harm Jeff intentionally, but now that the divorce was finalized, how would he react? She still hadn't given him an answer as to Jeff going along with him. For the past weeks she had avoided returning his calls to her office. She had been busy with her move to the townhouse, surely Ed was aware of that. She had told him about the purchase.

This being Sunday made her nervous. Ed would have the day off. Would he try to contact her. There was no way for her to know that Ed had come out of the bordello and was sitting in the courtyard cursing her. It took a little time to regain her composure. Before going back to bed she looked in on Jeff. She was reassured, but the vivid nightmare still lingered in her thoughts.

Dawn came none too early for Julia. She heard the chirping birds as they noisily greeted the first light of day. She opened the blind and looked out to the back patio. Behind the privacy wall stood a unit similar to hers. Up at the roof line crouched the neighborhood cat silhouetted against the pale gray sky. The cat's tail switched as a bird flew close to her and then darted away. She felt glad that she wasn't one of the young birds she saw, facing the possibility of being pounced on.

The scene intensified her protective instincts of watching over Jeff. Thank God her parents no longer lived in San Diego, that she could count on their help at any time. They had been so helpful during her move, taking care of Jeff whenever she needed to be on her own.

She ate a light breakfast, fixed herself a second cup of coffee and organized her appointments and listed the things she had to accomplish during the day.

Around seven Jeff woke and came barefooted into the room. He rubbed his eyes, yawned sleepily and came over to lean against her as he was want to do in the morning She gave him a big hug and kissed him on the top of his head.

"How's my sleepyhead this morning?"

"Sleepy," he said yawning again. "Can I watch cartoons?"

"Sure you can."

"You going to be gone all day, mom?"

"Not all day, Jeff. I should be at grandma's around four. We're going to have dinner together."

"Will you go swiming with me then?"

77

"Sure, Jeff."

"Why doesn't grandpa want to come in the water?"

"I've told you before, he had a fright when he was a little boy. It made him afraid of the water."

"That's silly."

"It's not silly, Jeff. People have all kinds of fears."

"Do you?"

"I guess so."

"What?" he asked pulling on her hands as he leaned backwards.

"That you'll fall on the back of your head."

Jeff giggled. "Really, mom. Tell me'"

"All right. I'll tell you while I'm fixing breakfast. But first run and put on your robe and slippers."

She heard the flip-flop of his slippers as he ran onto the vinyl kitchen floor. He perched himself on a stool by the breakfast counter.

"OK, mom, tell me!"

"Looking back I wasn't much older than you. We were living in Spring Valley at the time."

"Where's that?"

"A little way outside San Diego. That was before we moved to Point Loma, where we used to visit with grandma and grandpa. You remember that house, I'm sure."

"Oh sure, mom."

"Anyway, I was sort of a tomboy."

Jeff thought that was funny.

"But you're a girl."

"That's what they call girls who try to do everything that boys do. I wanted to play their games, not dolls and house with the other girls my age."

"Oh!"

"There were some older boys in the neighborhood

who were building a tree house. They had already nailed braces onto the tree to hold the floor up when I first noticed it."

Jeff had his chin resting on his hands listening to every word.

"It was summertime and by next morning they already had the walls up. They had an opening for a door and even a small window. A 'lookout' one of them called it as I remember. Whenever I asked if I could help, they told me to 'beat it!', that this was man's work. No girls were allowed in their clubhouse."

"I thought you said it was a tree house."

"Both are right. The tree house was going to be their clubhouse, the place the boys would meet at."

"Oh!"

She stirred the pouch of instant oatmeal into a bowl of boiling water and placed it in front of him.

"Too hot," he said sitting back.

"I'll add milk in a moment."

She stepped over to the refrigerator and back.

"Anyway, to continue with my story, I didn't 'beat it!'. Instead I stayed and watched as they pulled lumber up the tree with a rope. With the last piece up there, the boy on the ground who had been tying on the lumber, climbed up to the platform.

Jeff hadn't started eating.

"Start your oatmeal, Jeff. I'll fix you a slice of toast."

Jeff sampled the oatmeal. It wasn't that hot anymore.

"Well anyway, the boys were nailing the roof boards on when their only hammer fell to the ground. I thought one of them would climb down to get it. Instead they all told me to bring it up."

"Why didn't they pull it up on the rope?"

"They had let the rope fall to the ground, figuring they wouldn't need it anymore."

"Did they make you climb the tree?"

"They didn't make me, Jeff. That's what I wanted to do all the time."

"Was it high?"

"Oh, I'd say ten, maybe twelve feet."

"That's high."

"It is when you're only a little girl."

She buttered the toast, walked around the counter and sat down next to him.

"I showed them I could climb their darn old tree." She started laughing.

"What's so funny, mom?" asked Jeff laughing with her.

"I fell."

Jeff looked at her open-mouthed, his spoon dripping oatmeal on the counter.

"Out of the tree?" he asked.

"I was holding a board and stepped back too far." She started laughing harder.

"Weren't you hurt?"

"I skinned my arm and leg against the bark of the tree. Luckily the ground was soft from all the walking around."

"Wow!"

"Wow is right. I was afraid to tell your grandparents what really happened. I told them I had been going too fast. That was true. I only left out the direction. I didn't want to upset them."

"Did that make you afraid of trees, mom?"

She smiled and put her arm around him and kissed the side of his face. "When I was hanging pictures the other day, remember how grandpa had to hold me on the stepladder? I'm scared the minute I get two feet off the ground."

"Oh," said Jeff unimpressed. He wasn't scared of climbing things. Even if he should fall, he told himself, he wouldn't be scared. "Can I have jelly?"

"Strawberry or grape?"

"Strawberry, please."

Julia cleared away the empty bowl. He spread the jelly on the toast and took a bite. He munched away.

"You're very quiet," she observed.

"I was wondering about daddy."

"What about him?" "Do you think he's scared of anything?"

"Let me think."

It was a valid question. If people had fears, why shouldn't his daddy as well.

"Mom?" he said impatiently.

"I'm trying to think, Jeff. Offhand I don't think there's anything. He's a pretty big fellow as you know. He can easily take care of himself."

"I didn't think he was," said Jeff pleased that his observation was confirmed. His dad wasn't afraid of anything. That was good. He turned on the TV and settled down to watch cartoons.

Julia cleaned up the kitchen, made the beds and laid out Jeff's things. When she was pencilling in her eyebrows to accent the light-blonde hairs, she suddenly remembered what Ed Kimball feared. Being confined in a small space. It happened in their fourth year of marriage. She had flown to San Diego with Jeff for a visit with her parents. When they were about to return to Phoenix, Ed suggested that he drive out and bring them back. He told Julia to expect him around four in the afternoon. When he didn't show up she feared he might have had a traffic accident on the way. He had been picked up for speeding in El Centro. When the officer smelled liquor on his breath he was taken directly to the police station where he underwent testing. Even though there was nothing wrong with Ed's coordination, the alcohol limit exceeded the percentage necessary for him being cited as a DWI. He was held overnight. Ed had told her that if it weren't for the open bars in the front, he would have gone out of his skull. She couldn't tell Jeff that his father, having been held in jail, was afraid of being confined.

At ten, Roger Hochstetter drove up and honked. Jeff was all set to go with his grandfather. Julia waved from the doorway, then phoned the office.

" 'morning, Ginny. This is Julia. Is Scott there?"

"He's got someone with him. Can he call you?"

"It's not important. I'll see him later. In case anybody asks, I'll be in around three thirty."

She had houses to check out for a prospective client. He needed a vacant one so he could move his family in quickly. Somewhere in the $80,000 price range. A house where the mortgage could be assumed with $30 or $40 thousand down. In the morning hours she had gone through her multiple book and had come up with four that met the requirements. All were on lock box.

By two thirty she had checked out the houses. After taking care of other matters first, she made her notes so that she'd be prepared when she met with her client the following afternoon. Before going to the office she managed to grab a quick bite.

"Sorry I was tied up when you called," said Scott Harrison when she entered his office.

"I've got a problem, Scott."

"Have a seat. Let's tackle it. I'm sure it can't be too serious.

Julia laughed. "It's only a matter of timing. I'm scheduled to have open house at the Hendersons tomorrow. There was a call I had yesterday from a man who needs a house in a hurry. I've never met him, but I've checked out houses this morning and think I have exactly what he needs. I'm supposed to meet him by the main entry of Saks at four tomorrow. It's the only time he could make it, and I hated to turn him down."

"Do you know where he's staying?"

"With relatives, but he didn't give me the number. He didn't want them getting involved in his purchase. I have his name, though. Saul Greenberg."

"Let me look at tomorrow's schedule," said Scott.

"If the ad weren't going to show it as open, I could close up and leave."

"I don't see Anne scheduled. I'm sure she'd be glad to help."

He buzzed the intercom. "Ginny, get Anne on the phone."

A moment later he was talking with Anne. He held his hand over the receiver. "She can take over around 3 or 3:30."

"Fantastic! Tell her many thanks for me. I'll buy her lunch next week."

"She heard that. She accepts provided it's at the Biltmore."

"You're late, mom," said Jeff.

"Remember, I'm a working mother. Come on! Only 20 minutes. That's no big deal."

Jeff was already in his swim trunks.

"Hurry up, then."

"What a mean fellow. I'll get moving"

He wacked her bottom with a magazine. "Giddy up!" and chased her towards the dressing rooms at the club house.

Julia was a complete contrast with earlier in the morning when she had awakened from her terrifying nightmare. She was a vivacious woman, not yet 30. In her lime and white striped bathing suit which clung to her well-proportioned figure, she could easily have passed for 22. She laughed gaily as she cavorted with Jeff at the shallow end of the pool. A child's laughter, an exception to the rules here at Sun City recreation centers, brought smiles and memories of their own youth to the senior citizens around the pool area. Betty and Roger Hochstetter were no exception. They idolized their only grandchild.

"Let me see your hands," said his grandfather approaching the edge of the pool and kneeling.

"Just as I thought."

Jeffs fingers were all wrinkled from being in the water.

"I think he's been in long enough, Julia," he said.

"All right, dad."

"No!" said Jeff stepping back from the edge.

"Your grandfather's right."

"No. Just because he's scared."

"What's that all about?"

"I'll tell you later, dad."

She waded after Jeff.

"Five more minutes. That's all, then, young man."

He knew from her tone and made the most of it. The breeze, despite the heat, had a chilling effect and

Jeff got goose pimples. His mother rubbed him dry with a large towel that matched her bathing suit.

"You're killing me," said Jeff as she kept rubbing.

"Only with love," she answered kissing his cheek.

Wrapped in terry cloth robes, Julia sat happily in the back seat of the car with her arm around Jeff. Roger was whistling off key in the front seat as Jeffs grandmother looked at him adoringly. They were all so happy.

How could they know that tragedy would strike the next day.

PART V

Ed Kimball's eyes opened slowly. The drinking bout had continued till four in the morning. Paul had protested the bar closing down and he and Mark had half dragged Paul out. When he smelled the stench from urinating merrymakers on hitting the street, he pulled away from the others and vomited until he was doubled over with cramps.

"He'd better sleep it off," said Mark.

Their night on the town ended in a fleabag hotel. Half bombed himself, Ed didn't take notice of the room assigned to him, but threw himself down on the bed.

He now glanced around, aware of the stale-smoke odor. The dirty tan walls were cracked and thick layers of paint hung loosely from the ceiling. They seemed to be reaching towards him.

"Good God!" he said sitting up with a start and grabbed under the metal-framed bed for his other shoe. Apparently at some stage he had kicked it off. Several roaches scurried out from the shoe as he picked it up. He had trouble with the laces in his hurry. The room was closing in on him. Other than the bed, there was nothing in the room except a coat hook on the door. If he had laid on the floor with his arms out-stretched he would have easily touched the walls. The instant claustrophobia he experienced panicked him. Was he in a Mexican jail? He grabbed at the door handle and found it opened easily.

Lunging into the hall, he glanced around quickly and made for the stairs. Once through the lobby on the main floor and out the entry, the light reflecting from the white buildings blinded him. He ran into the street gulping air. Deep breaths to clean his lungs of the smell and the fear. When the feeling of panic left him, he began to wonder about the others. Were they still in their rooms?

The woman behind the desk in the lobby looked at him curiously when he re-entered the building. Crazy Yankee! What did he want now? His money back?

"My friends?"

She shrugged her shoulders.

"They came in with me last night."

"No here at night," she muttered and returned to what she was doing.

He wasn't about to look for them. A man could get stabbed to death opening the wrong room. In all likelihood Paul wouldn't be in any condition to drive. However, he decided to check on the car.

Shops were doing an active business. Up to now he hadn't paid attention to the time. Checking his watch he realized it was after eleven. Spotting the convertible in the parking lot, he backtracked to a stall where the smell of coffee had caught his attention. From a small table where he sat, he could survey the street leading to the fleabag hotel. He washed the Mexican equivalent of a dunking donut down with coffee, then a second cup while he watched for Mark and Paul to appear. Waiting proved futile.

With another donut in hand he walked slowly back towards the hotel. Finding a young man behind the desk he asked about his friends.

"What do they look like?"

Ed described them while the clerk looked through a lined entry book. There were no names shown, only some kind of description of what they were wearing and some thing about their features or peculiarities, for easy identification.

"Sounds like them. Rooms 6 and 7."

"Where was I?"

The clerk looked at him and referred back to the record.

"Five."

"That's them."

He hoped he wasn't making a mistake as he climbed the creaking stairs. Opening the door to room 6, he found Mark sitting on the edge of the bed.

"Hi," said Mark, "where's the pissery?"

"Down the hall, I think."

"Jeese, how do you feel?"

"Fine."

"You son of a bitch. You must have the constitution of a water buffalo. Do you know how much rock gut we drank?"

"Lots."

Mark shook his head as he slipped his trousers on.

"How about you? Hung over?" asked Ed.

"Not bad as long as I don't bend over too long."

He stood up and tucked his shirt in. Fastening his belt, he checked his wallet. Satisfied that his money was still there, he went out the door.

"Be right back."

"I'll check on Paul."

Paul was lying face down breathing heavily. Ed waited in the doorway to the room.

"Let him sleep it off," suggested Mark.

Ed took him to the coffee shop and joined him over more coffee.

"When do you need to get back?"

"I'm in no sweat. It's up to Paul, I'd say. You in any hurry?"

"No."

Finishing their coffee they spotted Paul wandering about in the street. He looked terrible. His legs were rubbery, his actions sluggish. When Paul saw them, his face lit up.

"Jeese, I'm glad to see you guys," he mumbled.

"Think we'd leave you here?"

"Leave me? Shit! No."

"You look lousy. Can you make it?" asked Mark.

"We on the make again?"

Both Ed and Mark laughed. They each took an arm and led him to coffee.

By three o'clock Paul was feeling better. He started taking a closer look at every good looking prospect that walked by.

"I want to get laid," he sputtered.

"You really up to more action?" asked Mark.

"I don't know if I'm up to it, but I'll sure as hell try. Isn't that what we came for?"

"OK," said Ed. "We're in no hurry to get back today."

Paul rubbed his chin. "Should we get shaved?"

"What the hell for?" asked Mark.

"You're going to fuck them, not slobber all over them."

"Guess you're right," agreed Paul. "We can be the three mustacheers."

They all laughed as they locked arms and wandered along the street.

The Saturday night special was more drinking and whoring. Ed wound up with a fiery-tempered redhead who wanted to sit on his face and he had a hard time convincing her that she was being paid to please him, not the other way around. When the bars closed at two, Mark and Paul were both fairly sober. This night they found an inexpensive hotel with airy, spacious rooms.

When they left Nogales after lunch the next day, Paul asked Ed to drive.

"You're the soberest, Ed. You get us home safely, will you, guy?"

The sun was mostly hidden during their drive back. Fleecy white clouds clustered together, then separated to let the sun break through momentarily. It was going so well after a time that Ed forgot to keep check on the speedometer. They were approaching the greater Phoenix area near the South Mountains, and had passed Williams Field Road. Hidden behind one of the wide the cement columns that supported the overpass at Warner Road was a police car and Ed was picked up on the radarscope.

"Shit!" said Ed angrily when blinking lights pulled up behind. He slowed and pulled off to the side. Watching the officer making a note of the license and calling it in, he waited patiently for him to approach.

"Your license, please."

"What's the trouble, officer?"

"About 70 miles worth."

"You're kidding?"

"This isn't my day for it. License?"

Ed handed it to him and he went back to his vehicle. When he returned he had the citation all filled in. He showed Ed the scope with 72 showing clearly on the LCD.

"I'm being generous. Those 2 extra miles per hour are costly."

Ed took the citation and signed his name.

"This car's registered in another name," said the officer. "Borrow it?"

"My car," said Paul who was spread out on the back seat with his legs up.

"I want to check it," said the officer.

"Bottom of the pile," Paul told Mark who was opening the glove compartment.

Mark handed over the registration and the officer compared it with the name he had gotten over the radio. He tore off Ed's copy of the citation.

"Wednesday, the 18th. Two o'clock. Tempe Traffic Court."

The officer stepped away from the car. "Drive safely!"

"Mother fucker!" said Ed contemptuously as he pulled into the mainstream of traffic.

There was no getting away from it. It was his

own stupidity, especially right outside the city limits. He should have known better. He was in a real stinking mood when he pulled up to where his pickup was parked. He would have driven right to his apartment if Mark hadn't reminded him.

"Take care, guy!" said Paul moving up to the driver's seat.

"Yeh! Hang in loose!" added Mark.

Ed unlocked the doors of the Ford, rolled down both windows to air out the built-up heat. When he reached home he found the Sunday paper lying against the door. Once inside the apartment he dropped it on the coffee table. The divorce papers were still scattered about on the floor. Except for the girl's vacant look on Friday night, he hadn't thought of Julia all weekend. Now his pent-up anger surged. He blamed everything that was going wrong, including his speeding ticket on her.

Sunday was a big real estate day with many companies having open houses. Perhaps? He flipped through the pages of the special section devoted to real estate advertising. On the third page he found the display ad for Scott Harrison's company and on the upper section the boxed-in listing of homes that were being held open today. Among them was one to be held open by Julia Hochstetter. He thought of cleaning up and changing, but it was already after four. The house would only be open till five. Julia had seen him unshaven before. What in hell did it matter? The important thing was to get things off his chest, make her listen once and for all. He tore the ad out and drove over to the house in Glendale. He parked further down the street from where he could see the open house sign. He didn't want her to see his truck drive up.

Maybe she'd lock the door on him.

The front door was pulled wide open. He quietly pressed the latch of the screen door and let himself in. Crossing the room he noticed Julia with her back towards him standing by the kitchen counter writing something As he stepped up to her, she turned and was about to scream. Ed's hands coiled out and grabbed her neck to prevent it. His heavy thumbs pressed hard on the carotid artery leading to the brain. All his pent-up anger lodged in those hands which relentlessly pressed tighter and tighter. As her body sagged he stepped back and released his grip.

"Good Christ!" he gasped.

It wasn't Julia who slumped to the floor. She was blonde like Julia, about the same size. Who in hell was she? Why did she start to scream? Why wasn't Julia here? She was supposed to be? She had done it again. Tricked him. That's what she had done. She had tricked him into killing somebody else. He had only come to talk. Now he had killed somebody. It was all her fault.

"Goddamn you, Julia!" he shouted as he bent over the body. There was no pulse as he expected. Who'd believe it was a mistake? It was murder. Plain and simple murder. Prison cells flashed in his mind. His flesh crawled and he began to sweat nervously. No! No! He couldn't get caught for this. He had to think. He looked around and spotted her handbag. He picked it up with his sweaty handkerchief, turned it upside down and dumped the contents on the kitchen counter where she had been writing. He put her wallet into his pocket, then decided to take the keys as well.

Ed knew this street of houses. One of Julia's best friends had lived further up the street. Maybe that's how she got the listing. There was an alley in back of all these houses, shaded by mature oleander bushes. Letting himself out the back door, he carefully stepped on the round cement pavers that led to the alley where the trash was picked up by the city. He had to avoid leaving a careless footprint in the grass or anything that could tie him into this killing.

There was nobody in sight when he walked from the alley onto the side street. He was glad he hadn't parked in front of the house. Fortunately his engine didn't sound like most trucks, more like an ordinary car. He pulled the door open and avoided slamming it shut until he came to the corner and made his turn.

When he reached home he checked the identification in the wallet. Anne Pearson was her name. Age 28. Christ! Why was she there? Julia was the one the newspaper ad had shown as being the hostess for the open house. Julia wouldn't have screamed. Why would Anne Pearson scream, anyway? Suddenly it dawned on him. He went into the bathroom and looked into the mirror.

"You're a sad looking son-of-a-bitch!" he said when he saw himself. Three day growth of beard. Dirty smudges on his face. His hair matted and wind blown from the convertible. Jeese! He must have frightened her half to death thinking some vagrant was about to rape her. He looked like a giant size version of a wino from Jefferson Street. Of course she'd scream.

He went back to the kitchen. No sense tossing out the $30 he found. Everything else had to go. One other thing caught his eye. He slipped the lock box key off her key chain. Wiping prints off everything, he placed the wallet and keys in paper toweling and headed downtown to Washington Street. He drove west from 7th Avenue to 12th Avenue, circled Carnegie Park, turning east on Jefferson. On this one-way street he edged over to the curb and let the wallet and keys slip out of the paper towel into the gutter. Seeing all the bums lying around on the lawn and sitting on the benches with paper bags that hid their bottles, he knew somebody would stumble onto these.

Standing under the shower, he tried to wash away his guilt. As he was about to shave he had a hard time looking at himself. For the second time in his life he had faced somebody who had died. His father, in his own way was responsible for his mother's death. But this? Nobody other than himself had robbed Anne Pearson of life. Anne Pearson! Age 28! His face was still covered with lather. He put his razor down. He needed a brandy.

Julia parked so that she could see the main entry at Saks. The Biltmore Fashion Park Shopping Center, despite the heat, was moderately crowded with people looking into store windows and others going to and from the several choice restaurants. Anne had relieved her a little before 3:30, giving Julia ample time to make her appointment.

This type of contact was never assured. Several times in the past she had waited for people who didn't show up. She hoped that her efforts of the previous day wouldn't be in vain. Parked under the shade of an ironwood tree, she had shut off the engine and let her windows down. A slight breeze was keeping her moderately comfortable.

When the car clock said 4:10 she became apprehensive but then a man wearing brown slacks and an open sport shirt rounded the corner of the building and walked over to the entrance. Julia left her car and went over to him, smiling. She extended her hand. "Are you Mr. Greenberg?"

"Yes, Miss Hochstetter. Sorry I'm a little late."

"Please call me Julia."

"I'm Saul."

"I'm glad you could make it. Is Mrs. Greenberg coming along?"

She led him to the car.

"She's still in Chicago. I'm staying at her sister's, but I didn't want them along to influence my decision."

"Is your wife leaving it up to you to decide?"

"Rose will go along with me. I always pick the house and leave the decorating to her."

"You said you needed something right away. Am I right that it's not contingent on your selling your home in Chicago?"

"That's already been sold. We have till the end of the month to move out."

Julia pulled onto Camelback Road, turned north on 24th Street. This was an ideal situation. If she had done her previewing right, she might be able to write up a contract offer today. She was in high spirits.

As they moved from house to house, she realized that he'd be difficult to satisfy. Not familiar with the prices, he was expecting to find a $150,000 house selling in the $80,000 category. He showed his frustration after seeing the fourth house she had screened.

"Is there anything else you can show me? I only have to be back by seven."

"Why don't we stop for a cup of coffee?" she suggested. "Or something cold to drink?"

He agreed and paid for her ice tea. While they sat in Wendy's on Glendale Avenue, she looked through the multiple book. Further north on the west side there were two possibilities. She told him about each. He wanted to see them. It turned out he liked one of them, wanted to think about it. The price was $10,000 more than he had wished to pay, but he liked it.

"Are you sure you don't need transportation?" she asked when they drove back to Saks.

"My sister-in-law and her husband went to Ciné Capri. The show's over around seven. They're planning to take me to that Café Casino."

"Want me to drop you there? It's right across the intersection."

"Thanks, but they said Saks."

"So Saks it is."

When she dropped him off, she parked and phoned Anne Pearson's house. She had never met her husband who answered the phone."

"She's not home yet. She said she might hold it open till 5:30. Is there a phone?"

"No. Service was cancelled when the Petersens moved out. I'll drive by. Maybe she's got an interested party."

"If she walks in, I'll have her call you later at home."

"Thanks. Nice talking to you."

"Likewise."

The open house sign was at the corner, another still in front of the house. Anne's car was in the driveway, but no other car. That of a possible client. Maybe they had only now driven off and Anne was locking up the place. She opened the screen door and stepped inside.

"Hello! It's Julia, Anne."

She entered the kitchen and saw Anne slumped on the ground.

"Anne?" she said anxiously bending over her. Anne didn't respond. She took her limp wrist and felt for a pulse. None.

"Oh, my God," she cried out in a terrified voice as she rose and saw the contents of Anne's pocketbook spilled over the kitchen counter.

She ran out the front door over to the neighbor's and pounded on their door. A man opened it angrily.

"Please! Call the police! She's dead."

He ran across the yard and into the house. Julia found him bending over the body.

"She's dead all right. Strangled from the looks."

"Oh, God, how terrible," said Julia, tears forming. "She was doing me a favor."

"You'd better sit down." He glanced around for a place.

"By the fireplace," he added pointing to the raised hearth in the family room off the kitchen.

It was only a few moments before they heard sirens converging from opposite directions, then heavy footsteps as the first officers walked in.

"Out here!" said the neighbor in a loud voice.

"Call in, Jim," said the officer after kneeling and feeling for a pulse.

"What happened?" he asked the man.

"This lady got hold of me. She found the body."

The officer turned to Julia. "Can you tell me about it?" He took out a pad.

She told him how she had come by to check on Anne and finding her dead.

"Have you touched anything?"

"No. Only her wrist and neck."

"What about you?" he asked the neighbor.

"Touched her neck to see if she was really dead."

"She's dead all right. OK! I'll want your names and information."

Two other officers had come in. "What's up?"

"Don't know yet. Probably foul play." He said having taken note of the spilled contents of her pocketbook. Seeing his partner he asked. "What'd they say?"

"Sending right over."

"What happens now?" asked the neighbor.

"Crime lab people. A detective will be over."

"Oh, my God. What do I tell her husband?" said Julia.

"Better leave that to us. Will you give me her name and address? Phone number?"

"In her wallet?"

"Doesn't seem to be any on the counter."

"Stolen?" asked the neighbor.

"Who knows?" He turned to Julia again, "Her name?"

"Anne Pearson. I can't remember her address. Can I phone my office?"

"Would you, lady?"

Julia turned to the man living next door. "Can I use your phone?"

"Sure. Anything you need."

He steadied her on the way over.

"What is it, John?" asked his wife standing in the door way looking at all the police cars.

"Real estate lady got strangled."

"Good Lord. No neighborhood's safe."

"Don't worry! It's all right."

"Worry? I'll do nothing but."

"Sandy, get some whiskey!" he ordered looking at

98

the pallor of Julia's face as she dialed.

"Scott! Julia," she said in a quaking voice when she was put through to him. "It's Anne. She was killed in the house."

There was a pause.

"Yes, at the Hendersons. You are. I'll tell them."

"You look as if you could use this," said John, handing her a glass.

She looked at it, hesitated.

"Try some. It'll help."

She sat down next to the phone, took a sip and broke into tears. Her hand trembled holding the glass. She took another sip and handed back the glass.

"I better get back."

"I'll go with you."

"John! Don't leave me alone."

"Come on, Sandy. Stop worrying now. I'll be right back."

Other police vehicles had pulled up. The officers were milling around the house. Outside on the street neighbors were standing by speculating as to what had happened.

"What's going on, John?" asked one of them.

"Woman's dead inside." He hurried back into the house with Julia.

People from the crime lab were checking over the body, taking photos, and making notes of everything. Shortly afterwards Scott Harrison arrived as did a detective who drove up in his unmarked car.

The detective took charge when he had been given the rundown. "Anybody check out back?"

"Waiting for you."

"Don't miss anything. Looks like we've got a murder."

Julia had seated herself on the hearth again. Scott Harrison walked over to her with the detective. Scott sat down next to her and put his arm around her to comfort her.

"This is Detective Benicki, Julia. He'd like to talk to you."

Julia looked up at Detective Benicki. He had a kindly face. "Yes?"

"Would you tell me exactly what happened? How you happened to come by?"

She told him about talking with Anne's husband. Why she had driven over. "I was supposed to be here," she started crying. "It's not fair. She was only doing me a favor."

"She saved your life," said Scott. "You might have been killed."

"I know. But why her?"

"There's no way this situation can be changed, Miss Hochstetter," said Benicki. "Be grateful you're alive."

He waited for her tears to let up and continued. "Is there anything you noticed when you drove up? Anything? Any cars parked around?"

"No. Not that I remember."

"This is an orderly neighborhood, Detective Benicki," said Scott. "People usually drive right into their garages."

Word got around quickly and a video team from Channel 10 arrived. An officer barred their entry.

"Detective Benicki. Media!" he shouted.

"Excuse me," said Benicki. "I'll be right back."

He walked to the front door.

"Can you let us in?" asked the video team.

"No pictures."

"Tell us what happened?"

"Real estate lady was found dead."

"Murdered?"

"That's up to the medical examiner."

"Can you give us her name?"

"We haven't notified the husband yet."

"Can you tell us how she was killed?"

"No comment. That's all, guys."

"Thanks! Thanks for nothing"

"Anytime," said Benicki grinning. He turned to the officer at the door.

"Nobody gets in."

He returned to the family room and continued talking with Julia and Scott Harrison.

"I'd say you were real lucky that she took your place. There's no sense blaming yourself. Fate has a strange way of working things out."

"Was it robbery?" asked Harrison.

"Hard to say. Is that her car in the driveway?"

"Yes."

"Strange. There were no keys on the counter. Whoever took her wallet and keys could have driven off in her car."

"Maybe the killer had his own car."

"We'll check that out."

"Do you need us any longer?" asked Harrison.

"No. You can both go."

"What about her husband?"

"I'll take care of that. He'll have to come down and identify her."

"Here?"

"The morgue."

"Why the morgue?"

"Routine. All unnatural deaths."

"The officer said she was strangled," said Julia. "If he's right, that's murder. Murder's unnatural."

Scott put his arm around Julia and walked with her to the car. "I'll follow you. See you home."

"That's not necessary."

"I insist."

"Thanks, Scott."

When they reached the town house he entered with her and waited till she phoned her parents.

"Something's come up, mother. Will you keep Jeff overnight. I'll call in the morning."

PART VI

Ed Kimball's ashtray was full of cigarettes. The empty brandy bottle stood next to an unopened pack of cigarettes. He sat there in his shorts, bare feet dangling over the coffee table. The woman's face, eyes bulging occupied his thoughts. Christ! Stupid. Stupid. Stupid. Why in hell hadn't he realized he had frightened her? There was no need to shut her up. What if a scream had brought a neighbor running? He could explain his presence. He had come there to talk with his wife. Ex wife. There was no denying he was angry with Julia, needed to talk with her. That goddamn officer ticketing him? Had that anything to do with this? Now he'd have to tell Mel about the ticket, that he needed time off for a court appearance on the 18th.

He relived those moments at the house. What if somebody had noticed him? He was linked to Julia. A police investigation would tie him in with the truck, place him at the scene at the time of the murder. It would be only a question of their piecing it all together. There was something in his favor, however, something that Julia had once mentioned.

It was before Jeff was born. She had continued in real estate through the 5th month. One Sunday after getting a new listing she held an open house. It was the first time it was open to anyone without the necessity of making an appointment.

"How'd you make out?" Ed asked her when she came home.

"Nosey neighbors."

"Nobody else?"

"It's funny, Ed. There's always somebody on the block who's never been in a house. Maybe they aren't that friendly to have been invited for coffee or something. They can't wait to come the first time it's held open like this to satisfy their curiosity, to compare it with their own house. A few weeks after a house is on the market, people pay no attention to what's going on. They're never conscious of the cars stopping there at all hours of the day or night. They've satisfied their curiosity. I don't think they even bother to look out their windows when they hear a car. People are funny, aren't they? "

He hoped that was the case now. He opened the fresh pack and lit another cigarette. Without thinking of what he was doing he blew out some smoke rings. He started laughing to himself and his groin tensed as he thought back.

That particular day the damned thing wouldn't go down for some reason. Julia was sore from all their lovemaking and more sex was the furthest thing from her mind. Ed lay in bed propped up against several pillows. He lit a cigarette and a smoke ring formed and floated near his erection.

Julia started laughing and grinned at Ed.

"Can you?"

"What?"

In reply she formed a circle with her thumb and forefinger. Playfully she made believe it was floating and slowly settled it on the tip of his penis. Ed started laughing.

"Watch this."

On his fourth try a large puffy smoke ring formed. As it floated down he shifted his hips.

"That's not fair," said Julia.

A second later it slid partway down the shaft before breaking up.

Somehow it excited Julia so much that she climbed in bed. Shaking with laughter they rolled around together locked in each other's embrace. Yes, thought Ed, they had shared some fun times.

The ringing phone brought him back to reality. He picked it up. "Yes?"

"It's Holly."

"Hi."

"Where've you been all weekend?"

"Nogales."

"With whom?"

"Couple of the guys. Why?"

"Are you watching the news?"

"No."

"You know, your wife might have been killed."

"What do you mean?"

"Channel 10. Some real estate lady was choked to death. Pearson. That's the name. The reporter said that a Julia Hochstetter was scheduled for an open house. Isn't that your wife's maiden name?"

"How'd you remember that?"

"You told me once. Anyway this Pearson lady took over for her. They think it was some wino."

"That's terrible."

"Maybe you'd like to call her."

"Guess I should. She was surely lucky. I'll call her office in the morning."

"Stop by at the club."

"Tuesday, maybe."

"See you, handsome."

A wino. So that's what they thought, just as he had figured. He was pleased with himself for having thought to dump her things in the gutter. He flipped on the TV and switched to the other major networks to see if they had any coverage. Nothing. He had missed that portion of the news. In the morning he'd have to buy a paper since only the Sunday edition was delivered to the apartment. He emptied the cigarette butts into the trash and got ready for bed.

When he lay down he stared at the ceiling. The light from the parking area streaked through the parted drapes. He didn't like the room to be completely dark. Anne Pearson's death was uppermost in his mind. Finally he wrote it off as a mistake. A stupid mistake, but there was no way that thinking about it or regretting what he had done could bring her back. Tired from the crazy weekend, he quickly fell asleep.

The casual observer driving by the pale brown

building at 120 South 6th Avenue would think that it was an industrial park renovation beginning. Its clean lines on the site by the railroad track bespoke of an upgrading of the area. Certainly they wouldn't suspect that its one story contained the facilities of the Maricopa County Medical Examiner. A more careful look, however, would reveal the small identification sign located by the entrance to the parking area.

At eight o'clock Karl Vincent Benicki approached the glass door which was opened to him by remote control.

The previous evening the body of Anne Pearson was brought here and rolled into the viewing room. After leaving the murder scene, Benicki had been faced with the unpleasant task of notifying her husband, who accompanied him to the morgue and made a positive identification. He had to be sedated and Benicki later went back to the apartment with him and sat talking awhile, letting the dead woman's husband reminisce. Finally the sedation began to take effect and Benicki knew that Pearson would be all right for the night.

"Blake come in yet?" he asked the girl.

"Yes. He's in back."

Karl walked through the swinging stainless steel door. From here on all equipment was also stainless steel aside from the spotless white walls. Making his way into the room where the autopsies were performed, he glanced around at the familiar surroundings. Along the wall bowls containing specimens from various organs were grouped together along with the particular case number to which they referred and the coroner's findings. This was required by law. On one of the walls an exhibit contained bullets, classified as to the size, origin, and type of gun from which a similar bullet would be fired, and served as a ready record for the laboratory personnel. Bullets removed from shooting victims were quickly classified by comparing them.

Anne Pearson's body lay on one of the two autopsy tables. Dr. Blake put down the red report to which he was referring as Benicki approached. He looked up.

"Have you started yet?" asked Benicki.

"Just about to, Karl."

"Shouldn't take long, should it?"

"I've looked over the preliminary. It looks simple."

"I'll go back to the office. An hour?"

"Better make it ten o'clock."

"OK, Charlie."

Benicki stood there a moment and glanced at the red tag that had been placed between her toes. Pretty girl. What a goddamned shame. At the moment he desperately wanted to nail the killer. As he walked out the door he heard Blake dictating into the recorder. "Case 83 dash 609. Name Anne Pearson. White Caucasian woman, blonde hair....." The words faded as he reached the end of the hall.

He walked over to 7th Avenue so that he could cross with the light. The Medical Examiner's building was separated from Phoenix Police Headquarters by a short block of open space used for parking. The headquarters building occupied the corner of Washington Street between 6th and 7th Avenue. An imposing 4-story building, its facing consisted of light tan prestressed concrete panels. 12 sets of narrow windows appeared as thin vertical strips to break the surface between the 2nd and 3rd floors. The entire 4th floor was glass enclosed with a heavy cement-faced overhang.

Karl Vincent Benicki would be classified as a serious sort of man, a loner. Even as a Green Beret in Vietnam, though he worked smoothly in conjunction with others, floating down to the jungle by parachute gave him the freedom of action that made his blood course with excitement. In those anxious moments whenever he first hit the ground, he knew that all hinged on his instincts and reflexes. That's what made him a good cop in civilian life and now he was considered one of the best detectives in the department.

His 6'1" frame was muscular. He worked out systematically in the police gym, especially with weights, trimming off every ounce of excess fat. He wasn't sure exactly what his ancestry was. His father claimed their forebears came from what used to be Estonia, a mixture of German, Polish, Russian, or whatever. Certainly the name Karl was German. It was his grandfather's and he was close to his grandfather who lived in Cottonwood. Strangely, his parents had both died a few years ago within a year of one another. Karl had been born in Phoenix, gone to Union High and later to A.S.U. in Tempe. His short-cropped, light brown hair, flashing blue eyes, gave him a look of authority. Military like. When he looked at you, the eyes sometimes seemed to bore into your brain as if he were trying to rob you of your innermost thoughts.

His wife, Elizabeth, found him to be a warm, considerate human being. They were childless and she worked for the mayor's office. Often she could see how troubled he was by a case he was working on, but somehow he never let the despair, so often a part of his job, interfere with their relationship.

He looked every bit the professional this morning

as he entered the building, crossing the white terrazzo floor to the elevators, then pressing the button for the second floor. He wore light-weight dark blue slacks, a short-sleeved pale blue shirt with an open collar. The snub-nosed pistol by his right hip pocket and the cuffs attached by the belt on the other side to the rear spoke with no-nonsense authority.

Benicki, instead of going to room 242, went to the crime lab and talked to the man working on this case.

"Come up with anything?"

"Couple of things. First a question of prints. Looks like everything was wiped clean. Only prints on the billfold were those of the guy who turned it in and the desk sergeant."

"I didn't think it was a simple robbery. Otherwise this stuff would have wound up at the bottom of a dumpster where it never would have been spotted. What else?"

"This key ring. Bent out of shape. Somebody was in a hurry, I'd guess."

"The car keys?"

"No. They're here."

"So, he didn't need her car. Had his own wheels and dumped this stuff where it would be readily spotted. Why?"

"I'm sure you're going to tackle that one."

"Damn right."

"I'll get the report to you, Karl."

Benicki busied himself cleaning up loose ends. At ten he was back in the autopsy room. Charles Blake had taken all the required specimens from various organs.

"Let's go into my office, Karl," said Blake.

Blake sat down behind his desk and referred to his clip board. Karl leaned forward to listen.

"First of all, she wasn't molested. Whoever attacked her had strong, powerful hands that easily wrapped around her throat. Large thumbs from the bruised tissue by the arteries. Shut off the blood supply to the brain as easily as turning off a faucet."

"Anything under her nails?"

"Nothing. She didn't have any chance to fight back."

Benicki didn't think so either. He had observed the murder scene and this morning referred to the photographs that had been taken. Anne Pearson was undoubtedly surprised by the intruder. She was in the middle of writing a sentence when she turned around, dropping her pen when she was caught off guard. Why? It didn't make sense to murder for so little money and his gut feeling told him that theft hadn't been the motivation for this killing. Rick Pearson, on questioning, said that his wife never carried much cash with her. Usually $20 or $30. Never more than $50.

"Were there any other marks?" asked Benicki.

"Minor. When she fell, one arm was pinned under her. Means nothing."

Benicki recalled the photo. Yes. It was her left arm.

"Anything in her organs?"

"Nothing. No drugs or anything."

"You're all through, then."

"Ready for them to pick her up."

"Thanks, Charlie. I'll notify the husband."

Benicki was glad that Rick Pearson wasn't alone. Pearson introduced his minister, Dr. Hensley.

"Tragic," said Hensley. "I wonder how you manage to cope with all the violence we read about, Detective Benicki."

"I could answer with the cliché that it's all part of the job, but I won't."

"I've been praying here with Rick. I know its of little comfort to say it's God's will, but if we do turn to Him in our hour of need, He'll lead us by the hand and show us the way."

"I'm glad you're here, Dr. Hensley."

"Coffee?" asked Rick Pearson.

"Thank you. I wouldn't mind."

"Milk? Sugar?"

"Black, please."

Rick set the cup down. "Any news?"

"I've come from the coroner. You can be grateful she wasn't molested."

"Thank God for that," said Pearson.

"Is the paper right?" asked Hensley. "Some wino?"

"Too early to say. Our investigation's only started."

"Of course. Of course."

Benicki set the cup down.

"Your wife's key ring. Would you look it over."

Pearson hesitated. "Apartment key. The one for the mailbox. Car keys. This is her office key. Why do you ask?"

"The key ring was distorted. Somebody forced it open. Can you think of any other possibilities?"

"We have a safe deposit box. She usually kept her key in the jewelry box. Let me check."

He returned right away. "It's there."

"What about a key to the house where she was? Could she have brought that from the office?"

"The house is vacant according to Julia Hochstetter. She told me that's why there was no phone service. It was probably on one of those lock boxes."

"Did your wife have her own lock box key?"

"I'm sure. They all get one."

"That must be it, then," said Benicki. "Her lock box key."

"So whoever robbed her can use that to rob somebody else," suggested Hensley.

"Unfortunately," said Benicki finishing his coffee. He stood up.

"The main reason I came here was to notify you that the medical examiner has completed his report. You can go ahead with your arrangements."

"Thank you, Detective Benicki," said Hensley. "I'll be helping Rick with that."

"I'm glad," said Benicki shaking his hand. He reached out to Rick Pearson. "I'll be in touch."

This case had troubled him from the start, from the moment that he saw the victim's pocketbook lying on the counter, contents spilled out. He put himself in the position of the thief. Wouldn't you grab the purse, go out the back way and run like hell? Especially if you had perhaps accidentally killed someone? With the open house sign out front, there was the possibility of a prospective buyer walking in at any moment. Would you stand there in the kitchen and casually go through her things? And having taken the money out of the wallet, why stop there? Why not sell her credit cards? They were worth money. A simple theft was out of the question as a motive for this killing. Whoever had done it was determined to have the blame placed on some innocent wino.

"It's not going to work, mister," said Benicki as he pulled into a Kentucky Fried Chicken outlet for lunch.

Julia Kimball, or Hochstetter, since she was now using her maiden name, had spent a terrible night. Her eyes were reddened and puffy from crying on and off. At times she had dozed, only to waken, picturing Anne lying on the kitchen floor. She couldn't get out of her mind that she was somehow responsible. It was her listing. She should have been there instead. At the same time she became clammy at the thought that she herself might have been attacked and become the victim. She'd be dead instead. Thinking about Jeff, she thanked God that she was alive.

When the morning paper arrived a little before six, she found a short paragraph on the front page identifying the victim and where the murder had occurred. No mention was included of any articles having been turned over to the police, having been found only a few blocks from headquarters.

Her dad was likely to catch it on the morning news. She wondered what he'd have to say. Her mother was bound to be terribly upset.

Sure enough, right after eight, her father called. "Thank heaven it wasn't you, girl."

"I know, dad. I'm all confused. I should have been there, yet I'm thankful I wasn't. Is mother terribly upset?"

"She's still asleep. She was up with Jeff last night."

"He's all right, isn't he?"

"Oh, sure. Just some cramps. Maybe he was in the water too long."

"That's probably it, dad."

"Should I call your mother?"

"Let her sleep. Can you take care of Jeff? I really should be available in case the police have anything."

"Sure, girl, don't worry about a thing. We'll take

good care of him."

"I'll check with you later on."

"You do what you have to."

"Thanks, dad."

People in the office were terribly upset. Those not busy on the phone came right over to say how glad they were that she hadn't been injured. A little after ten, Saul Greenberg phoned. He wanted to make an offer on the Randall house. Julia controlled her emotions until she had made arrangements to meet with him. When she put the phone down she broke out into hysterical sobbing.

"It's not fair! It's not fair!" she kept repeating.

The others crowded around her.

Harrison came out of his office and tried to comfort her. "Why don't you come into my office, Julia?"

He nodded to the others to move away to go about their business. He led Julia to the conference corner in his office and eased her into one of the comfortable chairs.

"Want to tell me about it? Bad news?"

Her tears subsided. She took out a tissue from the box he offered to her and blew her nose. "It's not fair, Scott."

"What's not fair?"

"That was Mr. Greenberg. Remember? My appointment yesterday."

"What about him?"

"He wants to make an offer on the Randall house."

"That's wonderful."

"But it's not fair. Can't you see, I'm benefiting from Anne's death."

"Oh, Julia, you can't think of it that way. There's always give and take in life. One man's benefit is another's loss. If Greenberg hadn't shown up for the appointment you might have gone back to the house. Think of that. You, too, could have been injured or killed by that maniac."

"You're right, of course, Scott. It doesn't take away the pain."

"Is he coming to the office?"

"No. I'm meeting him at the house where he's staying with friends."

"Why don't you let me mark it down for the record?"

Julia passed her daily diary to him in which she had marked the address next to the time. He looked at his watch and back at her diary.

"Is this the time you're meeting him?" he asked pointing to the time opposite her notation.

"Yes. In twenty minutes."

"Good luck, Julia. Would you want one of the others to go with you?"

"I'll be all right, Scott. Thanks for the use of your shoulder."

He watched as she gathered up her contract forms and all the things she needed. As she drove off he couldn't help but see her point about gaining financially from Anne Pearson's misfortunate death. He shrugged his shoulders.

Shortly after one o'clock Benicki walked into the office of Scott Harrison & Associates. "Mr. Harrison, please."

"Do you have an appointment?"

"Please tell him Detective Benicki is here to see him."

Scott Harrison came out to meet him. He offered

his hand. "Please come in."

The office was spacious and well appointed. Apparently a successful firm. Decorative shelving contained an assortment of books, Indian pottery and pieces of sculpture. Western art hung on the walls interspersed with real estate awards, memberships in various professional organizations including FIABCI, the International Real Estate Federation. Scott led him to some comfortable cinnamon-colored leather chairs that surrounded a glass-topped conference table. Julia's body impression was still in the cushion where she had sat earlier.

"Cigarette?" asked Scott offering one.

"Don't use them."

"Mind if I smoke?"

"Quite all right."

"This thing about Anne's death has my nerves all frayed."

"I don't doubt it." He waited for Harrison to light up.

"Did Mrs. Hochstetter come in this morning?" Benicki continued.

"She was here earlier."

"How's she taking it?'"

"Terribly upset. This morning heaped coals on the fire."

"How so?"

"Her appointment yesterday afternoon. The client wants her to write up an offer. She was terribly upset, feeling that she was benefiting financially by the fact that Anne took over for her."

"I'm sure that would upset her."

"Do you have any news, Detective Benicki?"

"Let me pose a question first while we're talking

116

about Mrs. Hochstetter. What does her husband do?"

"They're divorced. Last week in fact. Her name was Kimball, but she's been using her maiden name for about six months."

"What's he like?"

"I've never met Ed Kimball. Julia mentioned that he works for a construction supply company."

"Would you know the name of the company?"

"I believe it's Claybourn Supply. They're down the access road off the freeway around McDowell."

"I know the place. What about his home address and phone?"

"Let me find out." He walked over to his desk and buzzed zed his secretary. "Ginny, do we have a home address and phone number on file for Ed Kimball?"

He came back to the conference corner and sat down. He handed the slip of paper to Benicki.

"Only the phone number."

"Thanks. I can get the address easily." He slipped the number into his wallet and asked, "Do you expect Mrs. Hochstetter to return soon?"

"I'm not sure how long it will take."

He extinguished his half-smoked cigarette by grinding it into the ashtray and looked at Benicki.

Benicki read the body language.

"I realize you have important things to do. I appreciate the time you're giving me, but I have one more question that's very important. It's really why I'm here."

"What's that?"

"Would you fill me in about lock boxes and the keys that are issued?"

"Sure. The lock boxes are all numbered. The keys are strictly controlled. Only licensed real estate people are able to obtain keys to fit the boxes we all use."

"What kind of records are kept?"

"Each person pays a deposit, signs a contract before a numbered key is assigned to them."

"What if one is lost?"

"That creates a problem. There's no real way to track down a key. Hopefully, the person finding one might think it's for one of those special padlocks rather than a lock box. The agent who loses a key has to pay a fine. That's a deterrent against carelessness."

"You say each key is numbered. I'd like the number of Mrs. Pearson's."

Scott Harrison picked up his phone again. "Ginny, bring me the record for issued lock box keys, please." She came and handed it to him.

"Anne's keys were missing yesterday. I see what you're driving at."

"Exactly," said Benicki.

"Maybe the keys will be found and turned in."

"They were turned in last night, in fact along with the missing wallet. They were found by Carnegie Park."

"Then that wino bit is correct."

"Don't count on it."

"If you have the keys, why are you asking about them?"

"The lock box key is missing"

"Christ!"

He handed the list of names to Benicki.

"Third name from the bottom. The number is alongside."

Benicki jotted down the number in his notebook.

The phone rang.

"Yes, Ginny."

"Julia's back."

"Ask her to come in, please."

Benicki got to his feet as she entered. Julia looked surprised to see him.

"Oh!" she started to turn around and leave.

"No! Come in, Julia," said Scott Harrison.

"Detective Benicki, isn't it?" she asked although that name would be forever etched in her mind.

"Yes, Miss Hochstetter."

"Please sit down, Julia," said Scott.

"I don't want to interrupt anything."

"You're not. Detective Benicki was just about to leave. He was telling me that Anne's lock box key is missing"

"I thought they all were."

Benicki interrupted and told her about the keys.

Julia grew pale. "Then he..." She didn't fill in the words out of fear.

"There could be a problem. Whoever took that key knew exactly what it was for," said Benicki.

"Oh, God. Not again."

"We'll do everything we can to prevent a recurrence of what happened yesterday," said Benicki, knowing full well that nothing could be done if some madman were determined to use the key to gain access and commit murder. If only he had a suspect. He decided to follow up the line of questioning he had begun with Harrison.

"Are you up to answering a few questions, Mrs. Hochstetter?"

"Yes," she said with little or no conviction.

"I understand that your divorce went through last week."

"How'd you learn that?"

119

"It's my business to learn as much as possible about everyone involved."

"Yes, of course. I didn't mean it to sound that way."

"How does your former husband feel about the divorce?"

"He didn't contest it."

"Is he, let's say, damaged financially by it?"

"There's no alimony to be paid. Not even child support."

"Children?"

"Only one. Jeff's six."

"Good relationship with his father?"

"Doesn't see much of him. The decree spells out visitation rights, but I don't know."

She glanced at Scott.

'Would you like me to leave the room?" asked Scott standing up.

"No, Scott. It's all right."

"You were saying."

"Yes. This visitation business. Ed's rather angry because I've been putting him off. See, he wants to take Jeff with him to New York City during his vacation. I stalled him at first because I was moving into a new house. So he's postponed his vacation till the end of the month. I don't know," she said looking off to the side deep in thought."He drinks heavily and gets into all kinds of fights. In fact he was shot recently."

"Could you tell me exactly when?" asked Benicki.

"It was a Friday night three weeks ago, I believe."

"He's been phoning the office, hasn't he, Julia?" asked Scott Harrison.

"Now that he's recovered from the gunshot wound, he wants me to give him permission to take Jeff along."

"Will you continue to stall him?" asked Benicki.

"You sound as if you're not in favor of it."

"I don't know if I can keep stalling him. I left him because he hit me once too often. He's got a violent temper."

"How will you handle it?" asked Benicki.

"Try to work out a compromise, I guess. I have friends who own a lodge in the rim country. Ed could take Jeff up there. Then I wouldn't worry so much."

"That might be a solution," said Benicki. "Is your husband a big man, Miss Hochstetter?"

She looked at him. "How tall are you?"

"Six one."

"He's a little taller. Maybe heavier as well."

"Have you heard from him since last night?"

"Should I?"

"If he heard about what happened, don't you think he might be concerned? For old times sake?"

"I don't know."

"I won't take any more of your time. I thank you both."

"Did you get the key number?" asked Scott. "I believe you marked it down."

The men shook hands and Benicki left.

He drove to the nearest gas station that had a pay phone. The connection was poor and the heavy street traffic didn't help provide clarity as he listened, but he learned that Kimball should be in around three. That gave him more than an hour. He swung onto the freeway and took the Jefferson Avenue exit ramp. Minutes later he was back at his desk at headquarters. The crime lab report as well as the coroner's report lay under a highly polished paperweight made of petrified wood. He glanced at them before setting them aside.

Eventually they would be placed in chronological order in his case report dossier. He added into his investigation report what had just been covered in Harrison's office. The number of the lock box key that had been assigned to Anne Pearson was fed into the computer. Julia's description of her former husband fitted the physical characteristics of the assailant from what the coroner had implied. Would there be witnesses who could place him at the scene? But motive? What motive would he have to kill this woman? It didn't make sense, but then many killings needed no motive. Acts of passion, sudden anger, and other triggered responses. Strike one? He went over to the crime lab again.

"Did a search of the grounds show anything?" he asked.

He was shown a photo made that morning when the sun was at the right angle to cast a faint shadow.

"We noted this in the alley by the gate. It's recent. Possibly made by the assailant."

"Enough for a cast?"

"No, Karl. We'd have lost it. There's no way of identifying what kind of a shoe he was wearing, but it gives us an idea of the man's approximate weight."

"Can you really tell from that?" asked Benicki.

"I tried a comparison and put my weight on some similar dirt. It's hard packed from the sun, but when you shift your weight sideways, the way this other print was made, you get a similar depression. I weigh around 175 and the mark I left wasn't as deep. The soil conditions wouldn't have changed overnight enough to make any difference, even with a little humidity. They guy had to be heavier. I'd say he's probably over 200."

"Thanks, sergeant."

At 2:45 Benicki's cream-colored 4-door Chevrolet was parked near the office entrance at Claybourn Supply. The two red flashers mounted inside the rear window gave away it's law-enforcing capacity. A similar light was also mounted on a pivoting arm by the windshield on the driver's side. Benicki had checked inside the office and learned that Kimball drove a light-blue Ford pickup. Benicki decided to catch him off guard. Kimball was late. Twenty minutes later than expected. By this time, Benicki was ready to head for the shower. Even in the shade where he had parked, the temperature was 110. When he spotted Kimball he switched off the music which was keeping his mind off the heat, and watched as the truck was parked in the reserved space marked Kimball. The forty feet between them gave the detective ample time to take stock of him and intercept him.

"Ed Kimball?" asked Benicki approaching him.

"Yeh!"

"I'm Detective Benicki with the Phoenix Police Department."

"Didn't I pay a parking ticket?"

"Not that serious, but I'd like a word with you."

"Sure. Let's go inside."

"Do you have a private office?"

"No."

"Let's stand over there in the shade, then. It'll only take a minute," he said holding up his arm as if to guide him off to one side.

"What's this all about?" asked Kimball when they reached the spot.

"Your wife had a lucky escape yesterday."

"So I heard."

"Have you tried to call her?"

123

"Is that police business?"

Benicki laughed.

"I met with your wife earlier."

"Ex wife," he snapped.

Benicki noted his tone of belligerency.

"Yes, so I learned. Ex wife. In the discussion there was some suggestion made that you might be concerned. Your son might have been motherless under different circumstances."

"She was lucky, wasn't she?" he answered puppeting the expected answer.

"Would you mind telling me where you were yesterday afternoon?"

"Not at all. What did you say your name was?"

"Benicki."

"Oh, yes. Well, Detective Benicki, I was on my way back from Nogales."

"In your truck?"

"No. I was driving a friend's car."

"Would you give me his name."

"Paul. I don't know his last name."

"I thought you said that he was your friend. Am I wrong about that?"

"He's Mark's friend. Mark asked me along."

"This Mark. What's his last name?"

"Why don't you ask him? He's pulling in."

Benicki watched a small white Fiat pull into the space marked Garrity.

"Garrity."

"You win the Kewpie doll," laughed Kimball. The sarcasm wasn't lost to Benicki. Under the carefree exterior was a razor edge. Mark walked in their direction.

"Hey, old buddy. I see you survived."

"Mark, this is Detective Benicki."

Turning to the detective he said, "You already know his name."

"Got you already?" kidded Mark.

"For what?" bristled Kimball.

"Afraid you wouldn't show up in court."

"Oh, that?"

"What's that all about?" asked Benicki.

"Some son-of-a-bitch ticketed me as we were coming home."

"Going too fast," volunteered Mark.

Benicki didn't add that the officer was only doing his job. He had seen Kimball tense at the suggestion that he had already been caught. Guilt conscious? Strike two?

"The detective's got a question for you," said Kimball trying to make light of it.

Mark Garrity faced Kimball. "Yes?"

"Mr. Kimball said he was down in Nogales with you."

"Boy, were we ever down there. Down and out. Wouldn't you say that, old buddy? Especially Paul. You, you fucker, I don't know where you put it. Even when you're stoned, you seem to be sober."

"When did you get back to town?"

"Jeese, I don't know. I'd say around four. Wasn't it, Ed?"

"Much later," said Ed emphatically.

"Paul dropped me off at home. What did you do, Ed? Drive off and sock it to some other broad?"

"Shut up, you jerk."

"Hey! I was only kidding"

"What did you do?" asked Benicki.

"Drove home, took a shower and washed off all

125

that Mexican dirt."

"I have your phone number. I need your address, Mr. Kimball. What is it?"

"What's all this questioning for, anyway?" asked Mark

"Some real estate woman got bumped off yesterday," answered Kimball. "She was sitting in for my ex."

"You mean Julia almost got herself killed?"

"That's what's in the papers. Isn't that so, Detective Benicki?"

A real smart ass, thought Benicki. "That's right. Sometimes people get the wrong impressions of us when we're asking all sorts of questions. They think we're throwing our weight around. Like that officer who ticketed you, Mr. Kimball. You referred to him as a son-of-a-bitch." His eyes zeroed in on Kimball's and challenged them to a dueling match. Not blinking, he continued. "We're listening to what's said and how it's said. We've got these little computers in our brains that assemble all the input of information. And before you know it, we've put it all together and the guy who thought he was so damned clever hears those iron bars clang shut. A little cubicle becomes his entire world."

Ed's eyes suddenly faltered. Benicki detected fear in them as he pounded his fist into the palm of the other hand to emphasize the 'clang'.

Strike 3?

There was silence all around. Benicki reminded Kimball by repeating the last question. "Your address?"

"710 West Turney, B-6."

"Thank you for your time," said Benicki.

"You bet. Anytime," said Garrity moving towards the office.

"See you," said Kimball.

"You can count on it," said Benicki walking to his car slowly. He could feel Kimball's eyes boring into his head. He smiled. He had done what he set out to do. Catch him off guard. He hadn't realized that he would also shake him up. That was a bonus.

Karl Benicki arrived home a few minutes before his wife. She saw he was still wearing the belt with the revolver and cuffs, went over and kissed him.

"Looks like your day's just starting."

"It's not that bad, Liz. Could you fix me a couple of eggs?"

"Over easy?"

"Please."

"Want some coffee?"

"I'll take care of that."

"Let me fix it, hon. Put some bread in the toaster for yourself."

"For you, too?"

"I'll have some salad later. I'm not hungry at the moment ."

"Why don't you let me fix the eggs, then?"

"Karl! Sit down and stop fussing!"

"OK, Liz," he said laughing

"How's everything going?"

"Going."

Karl never discussed his cases with her. Sometimes she got the news from the morning paper, reading that Detective Karl Benicki was working on the case. That's how she got the news today. In the afternoon Gazette. He was mentioned as having been put in charge of the Pearson killing. She sat with him while he ate.

"Shall I save out some salad for you when you come home?"

"I don't know how long I'll be. You better not wait up if it gets late."

He gulped down his coffee, kissed her and drove off to the Henderson house where Anne Pearson had died. He started his questioning in the neighborhood with the next door neighbors, John and Sandra Blake. Neither of them had paid any attention to vehicles on the street at the time that Julia had rushed to them for help. Had they seen a blue pickup parked anywhere in the neighborhood? Negative. The same answer came up elsewhere down the street. Several of the people hadn't been at home. Those who were had gone about their business oblivious to the world surrounding them. What Ed Kimball had counted on had actually taken place.

PART VII

Ed Kimball was fuming when he arrived home around five. The confrontation with Benicki had come as a complete surprise. It had put him on the defensive and that was something he disliked. Loathed in fact. He was a man who had to be on top, or not at all. He realized quickly that Benicki was nobody's fool, an adversary as dangerous as a cave full of rattlesnakes. Thinking of that idiot Mark's stupid reference to the court appearance and the 'got you already' bit annoyed the hell out of him. Why didn't people keep their goddamned mouths shut?

In rationalizing the killing of Anne Pearson, he blamed it in part on that speeding ticket. The lousy mood it had put him in. He was ready to confront Julia, argumentative, ornery if he had to be.

This detective bothered him. He bet there were little computers flashing their stupid lights like crazy. Why in hell did they all have blinking lights anyway. Nobody could keep up with them, if for some reason they had a meaning. And the man's eyes! The way they bored right into him. He wanted desperately to stare him down, but he couldn't. That reference to the iron bars scared the shit out of him. He had to admit that to himself. The way Benicki pounded his fist, saying 'clang'.

"Shit!" he uttered.

Benicki had no proof to go on. He was guessing, or was he? He wished Julia had been the victim. Now she could cause trouble. How much had she told Benicki? Certainly she wouldn't hang out their wash for him to see all their dirty linen. The arguments, the fights. Sure. One sided fights where he had bullied her. She wouldn't divulge their private affairs, their differences, or would she? So they expected him to call and see how she was. Maybe Holly was right. Woman stuff. Holly would know. Good Christ! She sure as hell was all woman if he ever saw one. Yeh! Holly was right. He should show some concern for her safety. That should put him in good light with her. He dialed Julia's office.

"This is Ed Kimball. Is Julia there?"

"You're in luck, Mr. Kimball. She was on her way out." Julia came on the phone.

"I was sorry to hear what happened. This guy, Benicki, came by the office."

"Thanks, Ed."

"I'm glad you weren't there at the time. Might have been you." His hand tightened on the receiver as if it were her neck.

"You say Detective Benicki saw you?"

"Yes, Julia. What did you tell him about me?"

"Nothing much. He knew we were divorced. Scott must have told him."

"That's something we need to resolve. This business about Jeff."

"I've been doing some thinking. I'm sure we can work something out."

"We have to. I looked over the papers. I get to see Jeff twice a month on Saturdays. I'd like to take him to the park this Saturday. OK?"

"I don't see why not."

"What's your new address? I'll come by for him at ten."

"It's 1510 West Hayward. Below Northern."

"What's your phone number in case something goes wrong?"

995-0062."

"Thanks. Glad you're OK."

He smiled as he put down the phone. Pretty good actor. Sometimes he wished his start in life had gone differently. If economic survival had at all been possible, maybe an acting or directing career would have opened up. He would have been a good director. That he knew. He liked telling people what to do, but hated being told what to do. That was one reason he didn't like the idea of having to tell Mel about the 18th. Maybe he could get over to Tempe without saying anything to Mel. It was a thought.

Karl Benicki's phone rang in the office. Since eight he had been adding pertinent information to the case file. He had written down the statements of people he had interviewed from the sparse notes he had made at the time or directly afterwards. There was one area of contradictory testimony that he was checking into. Mark Garrity had said they arrived in Phoenix about four. Kimball had stated it was much later. Why this emphasis on the time? He picked up the phone as it rang.

"Lopez. DMV."

"Yes, Ray."

"Sorry it took so long to track down. It only now showed up on the computer."

"Go ahead."

"Edward Kimball was stopped by Officer Frank Cook of the Tempe Police Department. The citation for speeding was issued on I-10 and Elliot Road at 3:40 p.m. on the 8th. Sunday."

"Thanks, Ray. Send me a copy."

He went into the map room. From where the car had been stopped to downtown Phoenix was little more than 12 miles. A fifteen minute drive at most. Allowing for time to issue the citation, Kimball could easily have reached the area where he picked up his truck fairly close to 4 o'clock. Why much later? Benicki's gut feeling was that the man's instinctive desire for self preservation had surfaced defensively and subconsciously.

131

Once again he went over his notes. He toyed with the assumption that Kimball had killed the Pearson woman, but try as he would, a logical motive was missing. Without a motive to probe, collaborating testimony, even if circumstantial in scope, or concrete evidence, he had nothing.

Something occurred to him and he dialed the office of Scott Harrison. He identified himself and asked to talk with Julia Hochstetter.

"Good morning, Detective Benicki."

"I hope things are looking a little brighter to you."

"They are. Thank you."

"It's getting near lunch time. Do you have any plans?"

"I have to present a counter offer at one. May I ask what you have in mind?"

"Would you have a quick sandwich with me if I come by?"

"I'd be happy to."

"I'll be there shortly."

He took her over to the Metrocenter, the huge shopping mall west of the freeway and north of Dunlap, and one of the restaurants on the lower level. They had only to stand on line for a minute before being seated in one of the booths. The waitress poured coffee and took their order.

"Hearing from you was a surprise," she stated.

"It shouldn't be. I'm sure we'll be talking on and off."

"You were right, by the way."

"About what?"

"Hearing from Ed. He called."

"What did he have to say?"

"He was sorry about what happened. Glad it wasn't me."

"Is that what he said? He was sorry about what happened?"

"Not exactly. What he said was, he was sorry to hear what happened."

"Anything else?"

"We talked about Jeff. He's planning to come by on Saturday and take him to the park."

"Did he say anything about his vacation plans? Did that come up at all?"

"No. He said there was something to be resolved. The business of Jeff. Then in the next breath he talked about visitation and Saturdays."

"What time is he coming by?"

"He mentioned ten. Why do you ask?"

He laughed and her seriousness also melted.

"I'm just a crazy, asking guy. I can't help myself. Guess I've gotten into a rut over the years."

The waitress brought their order and refilled their cups. They ate in silence for a moment.

"You seem to be staring at me," she commented. "Something wrong?"

"You have your hair different today."

"I let it down. I had it pinned up yesterday."

"You girls are lucky, all the things you can do with yourselves. We poor guys either let it grow or shave it of?"

"Kojak style? Are you feeling that sorry or fishing for compliments?"

"Both, at the moment."

She smiled over her cup.

"I assume you're married."

"To a wonderful woman."

"I'm sure she is. Do you have children?"

"No. We couldn't have any. My wife now works in the Mayor's office. Loves her job."

"How about you? Do you love yours?"

"When I succeed, yes. When I run into dead ends, I'm completely frustrated and wish I had made the army my career. I could sit back, have fun and games and win a Kewpie doll."

"I haven't heard that in ages. Ed used to use that expression. I never knew what it meant till I asked him one day."

"He likes to put on an act, doesn't he?"

"Is that the impression you got when you talked to him?"

"I felt that he likes to be in the center of things, exercise control. Doesn't like to be off guard."

"That goes back to his college days. He majored in English Lit, Shakesperean drama in particular. Took part in their theater group. He's always felt pride in the fact that he played the lead in both Hamlet and Macbeth. Guess he's a frustrated ham."

"You say frustrated ham. You don't consider him a frustrated actor?"

"I don't. Living with him, I got to see through him all the time. You can immediately tell what he's got in his mind. A good actor would be able to hide his emotions."

The waitress came by with the check.

"Would you like desert?" he asked Julia.

"No, thank you. How's the time?"

"Guess I should drive you back."

"Thanks very much for lunch."

"It's my pleasure."

She walked ahead of him and he paid the cashier.

Her height and figure were very much the same as Anne Pearson. With her hair let down, they would look very much the same, it occurred to him. Their features were different. Julia's face was oval, whereas the victim had a rather prominent square jaw with a small pointed chin. Brown eyes compared to Julia's blue. He recreated the murder scene in his mind. Anne Pearson had her back to the murderer. She was busy writing. Whoever killed her didn't see her face at first.

"Good God!"

"I beg your pardon," said Julia who was standing nearby as he pocketed his change.

"I'm sorry. A thought occurred to me."

He dropped her off and hurried back to headquarters. He wanted to act something out.

"Could you come in a moment, Carol?" he asked one of the police women as he passed the report stations. Carol had shoulder-length hair and was the right height.

"Do me a favor. Stand over by that cabinet with your back to me as if you were writing. When I clear my throat, turn around. I won't hurt you."

The look of surprise in Carol's face as he grabbed her by the throat was as he had expected. He also realized that her height in relationship to himself required him to keep his elbows down. His face maybe a foot away from hers. He let go and apologized.

"What was that all about, Karl?"

"Just testing my theory. Thanks for your help. Sorry I startled you."

He walked to the narrow slit of window that overlooked the government mall to the west. A mile away the sun beat down on the copper-clad dome of the capital building. The way the dome glistened accented the realization that he had hit paydirt. He could swear that Anne Pearson had been an innocent victim of mistaken identity, that the killer had expected Julia Hochestetter to be at the house. He also felt that Ed Kimball was the murderer. Maybe he hadn't intended to kill. Perhaps something went wrong at the time. But from the experiment he had conducted with Carol, Kimball couldn't have known right away that he had killed the wrong woman. That would account for the clumsy cover-up, dumping only certain of Anne Pearson's belongings by the park.

He tried putting himself in Kimball's place. If the killing had been accidental, he would have backed off. Tried to put himself as far removed as possible from being implicated. But that's not what the killer had done. The killer clung onto one strong link with the murder. He had pocketed the victim's lock box key. Why? There was only one explanation. Somewhere in the back of Kimball's mind lingered the intent to kill his wife. But with the police investigation at the moment, he would have to refrain from any attempt. Wait for things to cool off. Then try again? Is that what he had in mind?

Benicki wondered what it was all about. What was there to gain by the death of his former mate? Certainly not financial gain. The recent divorce ruling would negate the joint property aspects of Arizona law. The boy? For all Kimball could know, the boy's grandparents might be awarded custody. The only thing Benicki could come up with was that the murder was one of passion. Statistics showed that 75% of homicides are done by relatives and friends. Only 25% fell under the 'who done it' category, done by a complete stranger. If his theory about Anne Pearson's death was correct,

Kimball would fall under both categories. He had no connection with Anne, and yet he was acting like a relative, thinking that she was his former wife.

Proving it was now the problem uppermost in his priorities. He needed to know more about the man, to crawl inside him. Find out what made the strings on this puppet to be pulled and why. Looking back at his notes of the previous day, he decided to follow up on the recent shooting that had put Kimball in the hospital. In the computer room he entered the name and date. The information appeared on the tube. He glanced at it and pressed the print out button. As he listened to the matrix chatter away it reminded him of automatic rifle fire in theVietnamese jungle. Flashbacks of tense situations raced through his mind, ending only with the silence of the print wheel. He reached over and tore off the sheet. It was all there. He pictured the scene. Play-acting all the way. The offended damsel. The brave hero coming to her rescue. Fighting off the bad guys. The ambush. The damsel grateful to the wounded hero.

There must be a happy ending to this scenario, thought Benicki. Surely the damsel lavished her affections on her hero. If so, had she seen him relaxed? Off guard? Maybe she could fill in some of the pieces that contributed to the overall puzzle picture of Ed Kimball. Holly Jones. Not a very glamorous name for a stripper. With the time factor when the shooting took place, he figured she worked the night shift. He looked at his watch. If she got home in the early morning hours after the club closed, she would have had plenty of time to sleep during the day. By now she should be up and around. He figured there was no time like the present.

The apartment complex where Holly Jones lived lay beside the Grand Canal where Osborn Avenue crossed over it. The canal was one of two that carried irrigation water through the city under auspices of the Salt River Project. The location wasn't too far from the prestigious Phoenix Country Club and the glistening high-rise towers that comprised the midtown financial district. Stately palms cast shadows across Osborn Road as he approached the entry off Osborn. The security guard stepped out of the gate house.

Benicki showed his badge despite the fact that his car could easily be recognized as an official vehicle.

"Which building is F?"

"Go past the first building, turn right till you come to the canal."

"Thanks."

Each building had covered parking assigned to the tenants. He pulled into the visitor area and walked over to the cars parked there. He noticed the sporty metallic-brown Cougar parked in space 205. Holly Jones was at home.

Multiple staircases partitioned the building like a sliced cake into a dozen apartments. 205 was on the second floor next to the end. He took one of his cards from his wallet before knocking.

"Yes. What is it?"

He looked straight at the little peephole in the door and held up his badge. "Like to talk to you, Miss Jones."

"What about?"

"Would you put the chain on and open, please."

She did as she was asked and peered at him around the door. In a low voice he continued.

"You were at the scene of a shooting three weeks

ago. I'd like to talk to you about Ed Kimball."

"Oh, is that all?"

He figured she thought he was from the vice detail. She partially shut the door, removed the chain and let him into her apartment.

"I was fixing some iced coffee for myself. Can I make some for you?"

"I'd appreciate that."

"I won't be but a minute. Then we'll talk."

Holly was barefooted, wearing tight-fitting white shorts and a sleeveless white and pink striped jersey. She wore no bra and as he watched her stirring the ice into the glasses, her breasts bobbed provocatively. He glanced away and walked over to the sliding door that lead to a narrow balcony.

"You've got a nice spot overlooking the canal."

"I like it. Nights when I'm not working, I often sit out there. It seems there's always a breeze, even with so little water."

She placed the glasses on coasters she carried with her. "Why don't you sit here with me?"

She seated herself at one end of the textured cotton sofa, resting one knee on the cushion. Thinking of Ed Kimball, Benicki wondered what this ravishing girl with her dark hair and black eyes saw in him. Then he remembered the damsel in distress scenario. He took a sip from his glass and handed his card to Holly.

"I'm Detective Benicki, Miss Jones."

"Everybody calls me Holly," she said looking at the card, then setting it on the coffee table.

"OK, Holly. This iced coffee hits the spot."

"You sit tight a second. I'll pop some cinnamon buns into the microwave."

"Please don't bother."

"No bother. I want one. If you don't, I'll eat them all."

He laughed.

While she was in the kitchen, he glanced around. He liked what he saw. She had good taste, combining modern and antique furnishings. A grandmother clock stood next to a Mondrian print framed in glistening brass molding. The sofa on which he was sitting had two companion chairs. The modern dark oiled oak framing offset the upholstery material which was probably hand loomed in India. A bookcase was constructed of shiny brass tubing with greenish glass shelving. Artistically-placed books were displayed, set between various objects such as an Acoma pot, and other interesting collector's items. One shelf was devoted to glass paperweights. He got up from the couch to examine them. He selected a special one that contained intricate spirals blown into a square cube of reddish Venetian glass.

"This is beautiful," he commented holding it up for her to see.

"Isn't that lovely? I picked it up last year. I treated myself to a trip to Venice and the Mediterranean. I wanted to see how the other half lives."

"That must have been exciting."

"Refreshing's the word."

She entered carrying the buns on two Japanese Imari plates, along with silver forks and linen napkins. "Get them while they're hot."

He set the glass paperweight down carefully and joined her.

She used her fork. "These get pretty sticky, but please pick it up if you wish."

He also used his fork.

"As I was saying," she continued, "it was a marvelous experience. I've been dancing at the club for two years now. The money's real good, but the characters leave much to be desired. Some are so crude they turn your stomach. Eventually I plan to write a book. We have to be nice to all of them, of course. Only at the club."

"I know what you mean. Your private life is your own."

"It may surprise you, I rarely go out with anyone."

"I'm not surprised at all. The excellent taste you have, from what I can see surrounding us, isn't something you turn on and off. It's part of you, I'm sure. You'd be equally selective in your dating, picking out the characters for that book you just mentioned."

"With one exception."

"Do I read you correctly?"

"The reason you're here."

"Ed Kimball."

"He's been coming to the club for about a year. Guess about the time his wife walked out."

"Has he told you about her?"

"Ed's a little rough and gets carried away."

"So I imagine by what happened three weeks ago."

"I know." She took more of the bun and coffee.

"He apparently was very gallant according to the report I read."

"These two were giving me a bad time."

"Don't you have a bouncer?"

"I saw Pete try to get his attention, but I guess he was talking with customers at the door."

"Pete?"

"The bartender."

"You say you made an exception of Kimball. May I

ask why?"

"I feel it was my fault that he was shot."

"Only indirectly, perhaps."

"Anyway, at the time I felt responsible. He has nobody to look in on him, so I did."

"Do you still see him?"

"I've gone up to his apartment a few times."

"Like looking after a stray cat?"

Holly laughed. "You might say that."

"When you're with him, do you see another side of his character? Does he get carried away?"

"Do you wonder if I have sex with him?"

"That's none of my business. What I'm referring to is how he treats you generally."

"He has his gentle moments."

"Few and far between?"

"You could say that. I figure this divorce business has him up tight."

"That's not unusual. Divorce is an emotional trial."

"Would you like some more iced coffee or another bun? Only take a second."

"Thank you. This is just right."

"Getting back to Ed, I'm sure he's upset about that real estate woman. Lucky for his wife that she wasn't there at the time."

"You can't imagine how lucky."

"When I talked with Ed on Sunday night and told him about it, I suggested he might want to phone her. He wasn't watching the news when the killing was first learned of."

"He followed your advice. He called Mrs. Hockstetter yesterday afternoon."

"I'm glad," she said smiling.

Benicki wondered about this girl. Beautiful to look

at. Striking figure. Exquisite taste. And apparently having sensitive and decent values. Why in the world would she wish to dance in front of gawking, ogling men and display all her charms down to a flimsy G-string?

"Will you be seeing Kimball soon?"

"He thought he might drop in at the club tonight to catch my act."

"What time do you go on?"

"Around 8:30. Hey! Why don't you catch the show, too?"

"If he's going to be there, perhaps I will."

He figured the timing to leave was right. He had established good rapport with Holly Jones. That was important. He felt that she could be a small window through which he could view another part of Kimball's soul. He stood up and extended his hand.

"Thanks so much for seeing me, and a special thank you for the iced coffee and bun."

"I'm glad you came by." She opened the door to let him out.

"Goodbye, Miss Jones."

"I thought we agreed on Holly."

"Goodbye, Holly."

"Goodbye, Karl."

He turned and saw the twinkle in her eye. He smiled and waved as he made his way down the stairs. "Phew!" he said. He was reminded of the interview with President Carter, which was reported in a national magazine. He admitted to himself that he had lusted in his mind where Holly Jones was involved. Quite a woman. From the twinkle in her eye he figured that she was going to resort to a little mischief tonight.

On this Tuesday, Ed Kimball spent the day in Yuma again. Everything went smoothly and on schedule. He managed to have lunch with Mike Perez.

"How's all your dealing going" he asked Perez.

"Whatcha mean?"

"Common, Mike. Don't play cozy. You told me all about those sweet deals you've been making."

Perez frowned across the table from him.

"You shot your mouth off one night," he continued.

"So?"

"I'm not looking to be cut in, Mike. Trust me! Don't worry."

"So what's your bag?"

"I might want a favor sometime."

"And?"

"You'd like to keep a free hand in what you're doing, I'm sure."

"I get the message."

Kimball could feel the hatred in the man's eyes. It didn't bother him in the slightest. He was in control and that was all-important. At the moment he didn't know exactly how he could make use of Perez. The feeler had grown out of his subconscious.

When he drove home at the end of the afternoon, he felt good about things. In fact, he was whistling, something he hadn't done in years. Remembering he had told Holly he might drop in at the club, he decided to do exactly that.

Around eight he sauntered into the dimly-lighted bar. A number of people were lined up at the bar. Only a few tables were occupied. Having sat for 7 hours during the drive to Yuma and back, he felt comfortable standing. He hadn't been back since the night he was shot. He spotted Pete at the far end and went over to him.

"Pete," he said, "I want to thank you for taking care of my truck."

"No sweat. Doing OK, now?"

"In good shape."

"What are you drinking?"

"I'll have a Coors."

"How about a shot, on the house?"

"Thanks."

Pete poured the shot and opened a can of Coors, pouring some into the chilled glass he had set up on the bar. Kimball emptied the shot glass and washed the whiskey down with some beer. Turning towards the stage he spotted a familiar face.

"Fuckin' bastard!"

Pete was drying some glasses close by. "What's up?"

"That guy who's about to sit down over there."

"What about him?"

"What the hell's he doing here?"

"Same as all of you, I'd guess," as he walked away to fill an order for one of the waitresses.

What was Benicki doing here? It was as if a man had walked into his bedroom while he was making out with a chick. Wasn't there anything sacred to this mother-fuckin' cop? The elation he had felt all afternoon had suddenly been dashed to earth. Like Icarus, who flew too close to the sun and drowned in the sea when his waxed wings melted, Ed found himself submerged, fighting for air. This guy was pushing. Had he followed him here? Was he under surveillance? He felt anger tinged with fear. The gauntlet had been thrown down by Benicki. Damn the man! OK, Benicki, he said to himself, I'll show you.

145

He watched as the girl serving him placed a beer on the table. Shit! Only beer? He turned to Pete.

"Give me a double shot and another beer." They'd see who the better man was.

The music had been blasting as a honey-colored blonde with a boyish haircut went through her final gyrations on stage. The spotlight following her spilled over where Benicki was sitting. Ed saw him smiling at the girl. Damn him! The dirty bastard was enjoying himself. The bright orange color of the spot dissolved to a blue. The tempo changed to a plaintive tone, the words speaking of love as the recording continued.

In Love? In love with love? Which shall it be?
A warm embrace, a caring smile, held tenderly?
Or just a dream of love itself,
Of something that will never be?
In love? In love with love? Just the idea?
Oh, tell me please sweet love of mine
Those words I long to hear.
That dreams of love have given way
To wondrous times together spent.
In love with you, and you with me,
No longer dreams...
REALITY.

As the opening theme repeated, Holly stepped on stage. The raucous chatter at the bar suddenly stopped as all eyes turned in her direction. Her body swayed and gracefully writhed to the music. You could feel the pulse of the audience quicken as the dark blue light brightened to a pale green. The transparent toga draped over one shoulder was gossamer resting gently on her upswept breasts. At first her eyes seemed caught in a dream, gazing upward, unaware of where she was or the spell she was casting. Then her eyes found Karl Benicki and a smile beamed in his direction. She pouted her lips in a provocative kiss and moved into the next phase of her dance. To the quickened tempo of the same theme, accompanied by her spinning movement, the gossamer fell from her body and her breasts sprang forth to renewed freedom.

Again her attention was given to Benicki who watched spellbound as this creature of sensuality glided around above him. Benicki noticed that her nipples were becoming aroused, something not lost to Ed Kimball.

The sound of shattering glass caught everyone's attention. Holly turned in the direction of the sound but couldn't see what had happened in the dark outer fringe of the room. Distracted momentarily, she swirled to the quickening refrain. The green dissolved into a warm yellow revealing her peachy, unblemished skin. Teasing the audience a moment longer, she moved closer to the edge. Then her dance ended and applause rocketed.

Benicki's waitress stepped over to get his reorder.

"What was that all about?" he asked her.

"One of the men at the bar broke a glass in his hand."

"Cut badly?"

"Pete's trying to take care of it, but I think it's bad the way he's bleeding."

Benicki walked over to the end of he bar where Pete was with the injured man. There was something familiar about the back of him despite the fact that he was doubled over.

"Bad?" he asked one of the bystanders.

"Looks that way."

"Anybody call in?"

"Think so."

The sound of sirens suddenly coming to a halt outside the building signified the paramedics' arrival. Benicki walked behind several men grouped around with their drinks in hand. Now he saw why he had recognized something about the injured man.

Ed Kimball looked like a zombie. He wasn't moving, or speaking. A medic was examining him now, removing the bar towel from his left hand to determine the extent of his injury. He began to pack heavy wads of sterile gauze over the wound and wrapped gauze bandage around to hold it in place temporarily.

Benicki found Kimball staring at him all the time during the medic's attempt to stem the bleeding. There was no avoiding the hatred in the man's eyes. If Kimball could have, he would have hacked Benicki into small pieces according to the impression he conveyed.

One of the patrons offered to run Kimball over to the emergency room at Good Samaritan Hospital.

"He'll need a tetanus shot. Remind them!" said one medic.

Benicki watched the men leave and returned to his table. After a few minutes Holly appeared and joined him.

"What were the sirens all about?"

He told her what happened.

"You mean Ed literally crushed the glass in his hand. Whatever for?"

"I'd say, because I was here."

"And I played up to you?"

"That's the only way I can figure it."

"But that's sick."

"He's a dangerous man. I've seen the symptoms before. "

"I know he's hot tempered, but crushing a glass like that and getting badly hurt? Whatever for? What's he trying to prove?"

"That's a good question, Holly. I'll stick around until he comes back and picks up his truck."

"Will he be able to drive?"

"It was his left hand. I'm sure he can manage."

"After your warning about him being dangerous, I appreciate your staying"

"Let me call home and I'll buy you a drink"

He telephoned Liz. "Problems, hon. Don't wait up."

Holly was deep in thought when he joined her. All her light heartedness seemed gone for the moment.

PART VIII

Karl Benicki nicked himself shaving. The previous evening he had waited around the club till twelve. Holly appeared on stage again, but didn't flirt the way she had earlier. She was all seriousness now. Her dancing was sensual but it lacked the fiery provocation he had witnessed .

Her body seemed more tense and he attributed it to the warning he had given her, that Kimball was a dangerous man. When her performance ended, he checked the parking lot. Kimball's pickup was no longer there.

"I've got to run," said Benicki to Holly before leaving. "I'll give you a call tomorrow. Are you in the book?"

"243-1600."

"Around four."

The bleeding didn't stop with pressure using a tissue. He reached into the medicine cabinet and applied a styptic stick. After a few seconds it was under control and he finished shaving.

The blood reminded him of Ed Kimball. The man was even more dangerous than he had figured. A man whose tendency towards violence was unbridled.

"You were pretty late last night," said Liz.

"Problems came up, my love."

"I noticed from the match book there was some fun mixed in."

He laughed. "You know I'm a collector."

She kissed him. "I'll have breakfast in a minute."

As his first order of business he drove to Good Sam and went to the emergency entrance. In a matter of minutes the doctor on duty reviewed Ed Kimball's admission chart with him.

"How bad was the cut?" asked Benicki.

"The tendons around the thumb required more than a dozen stitches. The fleshy pads by the last three fingers required six and all the fingers were cut in various places. I'd figure it would be quite a while before he can make use of that hand. Not having been on duty then, it's hard for me to speculate on the extent of the injury."

"Might his hand be permanently crippled?"

"It would depend on the exact number of tendons that were severed and how well they heal together. He might require therapy to get full use of the hand back. But we're talking 8 months to a year."

"Thanks, doctor."

All that self-inflicted agony, for what. Was he a sadist? Or was this another instance of passion? An unthinking act over which he couldn't exercise control? Similar to the killing of Anne Pearson? Sitting at his desk he made new entries in the case history elaborating on the psychiatric aspects of the subject. A staff meeting and lunching with several of his colleagues, then more paper work, and it was four o'clock. He phoned Holly. A muffled voice answered.

"This is Karl Benicki. Are you all right?"

"Not really," came her soft reply.

He raced down the stairs to his car. With lights flashing and the siren screaming, his car hurdled through intersections narrowly avoiding a collision at Osborn and 3rd Avenue. When he passed over the canal and turned into the apartment complex, he went right past the guard and made for Holly's building. He mounted the stairs three at a time. There was no need to knock.

Holly was waiting and opened as he appeared.

"Oh, my God!" he said when he saw her face. She had been struck on the right side of her face. Her cheek was terribly swollen, her lips puffy. The blue bruised skin discoloration spread across her nose and blackened swelling half closed her right eye, which was all bloodshot.

"Kimball?"

She nodded.

After she closed the door he put his arms around her and sobs erupted as her cheek rested on his chest. He walked her over to the sofa.

"Have you seen a doctor?"

"Nothing's broken. It'll subside."

"That bastard. I'll put a warrant out."

"No!" she said firmly.

"You mean you're not going to file a complaint?"

She started to cry again.

"That animal should be in a cage," said Benicki.

"I know that."

"Well let's put him where he can't harm anybody again."

"He'll kill me. I know he will. The minute he gets out."

Benicki sat silently. Holly was right. Charge him with assault? How long before he'd walk out? He'd even be wilder if put away. Holly's fears were justified. He swore to himself that he'd put Kimball away permanently. The savagery of the assault on this beautiful face made him more certain than ever that Kimball was Anne Pearson's killer.

"OK, Holly. I'll go along with your request, but I swear to you I'm going to nail him once and for all."

"I phoned the club."

"To tell them?"

"I talked to Nick, the owner. Ed won't be allowed to set foot in there again."

"Good."

"Oh gosh, Karl, I'm scared."

"I'm going to keep tabs on him. He'll never be quite sure what to expect, but I'll make sure he knows I'm after him."

He got up. "Is there anything you need?"

"Can't you stay?"

"You know I can't"

"I know," she sighed and walked him to the door. "Thanks for looking in on me."

He winked encouragement to her before heading down the stairs. There was little likelihood that Kimball had worked today, so Benicki decided to pay him a visit.

The buildings were earth-tone stucco over wooden frames. Probably built in the early 70s. A sign by the manager's office showed there were several vacancies. Benicki decided to check with him.

"Yes, sir?" asked the manager, a thin-faced man in his mid sixties wearing a sweaty T-shirt.

Benicki showed his badge.

"Yes, sir!" he said straightening up. "What can I do for you?"

"Your tenant in B-6."

"You mean Kimball?"

"Yes. How long's he been here?"

"He hasn't been out all day, far as I know?"

"I don't mean that. How long has he been a tenant?"

"I could look that up. We've been here six months only, but I think he's been here about a year."

"On a lease?"

"No. Month to month. We don't require leases on our furnished units. People like to come and go."

"You say he's been in all day. Do you keep tabs?"

"We try to. They had several burglaries before Marge and I took over. We don't snoop. Only try to protect our tenants' property."

"I'm sure they appreciate that."

"Yup! Most of them do."

"Guess there're a few who like their privacy more."

"B-6 is one of them. Marge and I try to stay out of his way."

"Which apartment is B-6?"

"I'll show you." He stepped outside and pointed.

"That one up there. The end door. Can't miss it. Right off the stairs."

"Thanks."

"Anytime."

Pink oleander bushes hid some of the shabbiness of the compound. It was in sad need of repair and maintenance. Paint, crumbled by the Arizona sun, showed two previous paint jobs that had been covered over. Going up the stairs, he found the railing loose. On the second floor, a hall perhaps 50' in length served three apartments on either side. A fire exit at the far end had a lighted sign over the door. B-6 overlooked 7th Avenue and the visitor parking area. He wondered if Kimball had noticed him from the window. Deciding to take no chances, he unbuttoned the short strap that held his revolver in its holster. He knocked.

"You!" snarled Kimball.

"Yes! It's me."

"What the fuck you want?"

Benicki decided to play it cool.

"How's your hand?"

"Why in hell should you care?"

"You've got me wrong. I'm not talking about the one you messed up. I mean the one you used to mess up."

"I don't get you."

"But I'm going to get you one of these days. For

sure!"

"What the hell are you talking about?"

"I came here directly from Holly Jones's apartment."

"So?"

"You worked her over pretty well." Benicki's tone was quiet, deliberate and firm all the while.

"Who says I did? Maybe she fell."

Benicki laughed. "You've got quite a sense of humor. You should be a comedian. On stage. You know, Kimball, I've been psyching you out. You put on a pretty lousy act."

"Bug off!"

"When I'm through."

"So, there's more?"

"I'd like to be telling you that I have a warrant for your arrest, but the young lady's afraid to press charges."

Kimball laughed.

"You can laugh all you want to right now, but I promise I'm going to be on your tail. One false move on your part and I'm going to nail you. And when I do, I'm going to make sure they lock you up so tight, you won't know what fresh air smells like or hear any sound except the jailor's footsteps."

With that Benicki turned and walked down the stairs. He thought the door would come off the hinges the way it was slammed in B-6.

Ed Kimball grabbed for his throat and gulped air. His heart was pounding, his chest tight like an asthma sufferer having an attack. The vivid picture Benicki had hurled into his mind had temporarily paralyzed his trachea. It was psychosomatic, triggered by his fears. He broke into a cold sweat as he walked over to the window in time to see Benicki drive away.

When he regained some composure, his next move was predictable. He made for the pickup, edged his way across the heavy traffic heading uptown, and drove to the nearest drive-in liquor store. The brown bag containing a quart of Southern Comfort gave him some feeling of relief as he followed the flow of traffic as far north as Dunlap before heading west to the freeway.

His chest was less tense now. He still had some difficulty in breathing. The thought of confinement made his skin itch. Benicki's words kept repeating over and over again in his mind.

> *"...lock you up so tight, you won't know
> what fresh air smells like..."*

Those were the key words that terrified him and had him on the run. If it ever came to that he preferred to die. Simple as that. This Benicki would go down with him though, straight to hell if he had his way. At the same time, his gutter-fighting instincts cried out for survival. He had to get the upper hand. Fight his way, tooth and nail, if need be. He couldn't figure why Benicki had told him he would be tailed. Why had he warned him? Was he that sure of his case? Could he have some evidence? Kimball couldn't imagine anything having gone wrong in his killing Anne Pearson. The only thing that had gone wrong was the fact that he hadn't intended to kill her. Oh, jeese? Why had they sent a replacement that day who looked like Julia. Why couldn't it have been a man?

He kept glancing at the brown bag on the seat. There was no way he could stop in freeway traffic and take a swig, which he desperately wanted. He thought of pulling off on one of the intersection ramps, then returning to the freeway. That was stupid, though, he figured. Hang on, Kimball, he told himself. It wouldn't be much longer.

He had driven past Bell Road. Traffic had greatly eased. Soon the jail facility at Union Hills would be behind him. Glancing at that, he sped up to get past it as quickly as possible. Then the ramp warning for the Carefree Highway appeared. He slowed for the stop sign after leaving the highway and continued east. The row of small hills he circuited were familiar. He was heading to a spot he called his own.

On two other occasions he had spent the night out here. At the foot of a dip he turned north onto a dusty trail that wound over a few boulder-strewn hills leading to a steep bluff overlooking the desert. The view opened out for miles, unobstructed except for the desert growth that clung to mountain sides. On the horizon, one group of mountains sat behind another, and another, ad infinitum. They looked like cardboard scenery positioned by a master stage designer. The colors fading with the distance to add perspective. He remembered as a child playing on the beach and lining up pails of wet sand, inverting the pails to dump out the small mound. Then later trampling down the effort in a vindictive, destructive mood. At the moment he wanted to trample down everything in sight.

The beach. Christ! He hadn't seen the beach or ocean since leaving New York. The people around here opted for hunks of sand lining lake fronts. Shit! They didn't know the first thing about a beach. He pictured himself sitting on the sand, listening to the surf, feeling the fresh air blowing in from the ocean. He breathed deeply, but the air was dusty and hot. Dusty as his wheels spun and sent up clouds of it in the last 50 feet of the trail. When he parked and the dust settled he unscrewed the bottle and washed the dust down. Where he sat, the late afternoon breeze blew over the ridge and through his open windows.

He was far enough away from the freeway that the sounds of cars became hushed whispers as they raced along. Spread out before him, barrel cacti, saguaro, palo verde and desert broom, as well as an assortment of scorched, yellowed plants glowed orange in the reaches of sunlight. An occasional cactus wren's chirping reminded him that life abounded in the vast stillness.

The panic had subsided. So had the fear. Bravado replaced it with each swig from the bottle. He climbed out, stretched, and then urinated down the steep embankment. His voice broke the stillness as he stretched out his penis. "Piss on you, Benicki!"

Hearing it made him feel even better. Sure! He'd piss on Benicki and the whole stinking police force, including the guy who had ticketed him. It suddenly occurred to him that a week from today he would have to appear in court. He wondered what kind of fine the judge would sock to him. Mel would give him a hard time if he told him. Somehow he'd have to get around it. Hell! Mel had lectured him this morning.

"You're not?" Mel asked when he learned Kimball wouldn't be coming in.

"Cut my hand. They stitched it up last night."

"What'd you do. Smash your fist through somebody's car window?"

Ed kept his temper. "I broke a glass."

"Another barroom brawl?"

"Hell, no."

"I can't picture you washing dishes."

Ed felt like saying, fuck off! "A beer glass broke. That's all. No fight, no nothing."

"It's getting to be quite a habit with you. You were just in the hospital for a week plus the time to get back on the job. I'll give you a piece of advice. Watch your step if you like the feel of those paychecks."

"OK! OK! I was planning to come in tomorrow, anyway."

Yeh! Mel would fire him at the drop of a hat. He'd seen it coming. That report from the air base at Yuma when he screwed up last month, hadn't helped Mel's disposition. One more stupid stunt and he'd really be out on his ass.

He walked back to the truck and left the doors open so the wind would blow through. He turned on the radio but the reception out here, blocked by hills, gave only static. He settled back and tried to think things out.

What would Julia say when he picked up the kid on Saturday? She'd take one look at his bandaged hand and know he'd been in another brawl. It wouldn't be work related. Julia knew that. He drank more from the half empty bottle. The hours passed quietly. The liquor was gone and he watched as stars speckled the sky, some twinkling in the night air. He felt like a whole man again. The open space had been like an injection of adrenaline given to a troubled heart that was failing.

Around ten, he flung the empty bottle down into the gully and heard it smash against the rocks. It reminded him of Holly's excited nipples and Benicki eyeing her. Damn them both! High in the sky a last-quarter moon shown serenely.

The next morning Benicki was parked so that he could see when Kimball left his apartment, and after Ed finished his working day, followed him home. The hours in between he added to the Kimball file and consulted with the staff psychiatrist. He gave him a synopsis of his observations about the suspect. The psychiatrist twirled a pencil, held between thumbs and forefingers, by his lips as he listened to Benicki. Benicki noted his habit with amusement. What would Freud make of this? When his observations were completed Benicki sat back in his chair to listen to the doctor.

"You've got an extremely dangerous man on your hands. There's a paranoiac instability interlaced with extreme claustrophobia. He must feel constantly threatened by his fears of confinement. His aggressive characteristics, his acts contrary to accepted norm, open the way for social criticism. Delusions of grandeur probably surface protectively, to place him above this social criticism. He reverts to the rolls he portrayed in college, the leading characters in Hamlet and Macbeth. He finds kinship to their tragic rolls and becomes caught in their web of bravado and fear. His aggressive daily behavior is an outgrowth of this roll playing. Because of his penchant for tragedy he's willing to strike out at those who oppose him in what he considers is his blueprint for survival. Even his self-inflicted pain is tolerable since it became a necessary implementation to put himself into the spotlight. You posed a threat, Karl. He had to upstage you. The way he struck at the girl proves his sadistic nature. I'd say the sooner you can build your case and bring him to trial, the safer it will be for all whose lives he is likely to threaten."

The psychiatrist again twirled his pencil by his mouth.

"He scares me, " said Benicki. "Not me, but the problem he poses. We can't keep him under 24-hour surveillance without more evidence to link him to Anne Pearson's death."

"That's the dilemma," said the psychiatrist.

Back in his office, he gave Holly a call. Her ability to speak without mouthing her words was improved.

"I'm doing much better, Karl."

"I'm glad."

"I've decided not to worry about Ed."

"Good. Don't worry. His moves are being watched."

"Come by for lunch, tomorrow?"

"Let me call around eleven."

"Please."

He felt glad that she was better. Fortunately Kimball hadn't broken any of her teeth. The swelling would go down and the discoloration would disappear over a three or four week period.

Benicki wondered how Kimball would react finding himself barred from the club. Would this trigger additional violence against Holly? From what Dr. Andrews, the psychiatrist, had said, the latent instability of the man could erupt at any time. Benicki figured the best way to discourage him was to keep him off base. Guessing. The one obstacle, however, was the weekend. He knew what Kimball's plans were for part of Saturday. But Sunday? He'd have to see if Liz had anything going. Play it by ear. Judge the next move by what occurred on Saturday.

His instincts told him to talk with Julia before Kimball picked up Jeff. She was sure to question him about his hand and Benicki felt she should be told exactly what happened. There was no telling what

Kimball was likely to concoct. Undoubtedly it would be directed to arousing her sympathy rather than revulsion. He made a note to call her the next day.

Friday the 13th was typical for such a day as far as Benicki was concerned. His morning started badly when he found a dead car battery, and by the time he got hold of his neighbor's jump cable, got the car started and drove to Kimball's apartment, he was gone. Not taking any chances where Holly was concerned, he cruised the area around her apartment but didn't spot the light-blue truck.

Security at the complex was primarily geared to vehicular traffic, to make sure nobody came in with a truck and then drove off with a load of stolen furniture. There was a tall chain-link fence between the westerly apartments and the canal, with an open gate and a guard house at the north of the complex. However, this was left open during the day, and only manned at night till eleven for joggers living in the complex who enjoyed running along the water's edge. It would still be relatively easy for anyone bent on mischief to bypass these safeguards.

At this time of the morning, with people on their way to work and others up and around, it would be difficult for anyone to enter the grounds, unless they posed and acted like one of the residents. Kimball's size ruled him out as someone who would be unnoticed. Anyone seeing him would remember. What was the old quiz question that gained such popularity in the early days of television? Oh, yes! Is it larger than a bread box? Ed Kimball certainly was. Big fellow. Rough opponent even with a useless hand. Right now, he certainly was handicapped. Strange word. He remembered looking it up one time. It was originally the name of a lottery game in which the players held forfeits in a cap. Odd, the worthless scraps of knowledge that cluttered up one's brain, thought Benicki.

The way he was concerned about Holly's welfare made him feel like a guardian angel, or since they shared in secrets, a father confessor. But Holly wasn't his chief concern. Julia Hochstetter was standing directly in the center of the cross hairs of a gun sight. There was no doubt in his mind that she was targeted.

When he phoned her house, there was no answer. Either she had taken Jeff to the grandparents for the day or, if his grandfather had picked him up, she was on her way to the office or an appointment. He kept calling the office and shortly before nine was able to contact her.

"How's it going?" he asked.

"You missed a beautiful service yesterday afternoon. The flowers at the chapel were magnificent."

"I'd like to have attended, but my presence would have been an unpleasant reminder."

"That's thoughtful of you."

"Many there?"

"Lots of Board members, and countless friends."

"Family?"

"Only her husband."

"How's he holding up?"

"As might be expected."

"The reason I'm calling, Miss Hochstetter, relates to your former husband. I know he's picking up your son, tomorrow, and there's bound to be a question raised."

"I don't follow you."

"Something bothered him the other night and he

crushed a glass in his hand. Got cut rather badly. You won't miss the bandage. I'm sure your son will ask about it."

"That sounds like Ed. What was he trying to prove?"

"It was basically a display of anger."

"Do you think Jeff is in any danger being with him?"

"None. There's no reason for him to direct any anger towards him."

"Thank God I don't have to put up with it anymore. I sometimes wonder why I did for so long."

Benicki wondered if Kimball had ever struck her the way he had injured Holly. He refrained from asking. It would only increase her fears.

"You're not planning to go along with your son, are you?"

"No. Ed has the right to be alone with Jeff. Since they'll be in Encanto Park, I'm not going to worry."

"If I'm in the area, I'll take a look."

"How thoughtful of you."

"Mrs. Benicki enjoys the park, too. She won't mind my buying her a hot dog."

"Thanks for telling me what happened to Ed's hand."

"Thought you should know. I'll be talking with you."

Around eleven, after checking his schedule, he phoned Holly.

"Do you like Eggs Benedict?" she asked.

"Love it."

"Then that's what we'll have. What time can you be here? You can always look over my shoulder while

I fix it, of course."

"If I do that, I might learn how to do more than boil water."

"You're joshing."

"I'm all thumbs in a kitchen."

"And elsewhere?"

"I have my moments."

"I'll bet you have," she said lowering her voice.

"Quarter of twelve?"

"Aye, aye, sir."

He stopped on the way and picked up a small bunch of flowers.

"For the patient," he said with a smile.

"Thank you, doctor," she said curtsying. "What a lovely bedside manner you have."

He laughed.

"Why don't you sit down at the table over here, Karl. I'll put these in a vase."

Her table top was modern with heavy plate glass set on amber-tone anodized aluminum. The chairs, however, were early American ladderback with rich brown velvet cushions. Place mats of genuine cowhide rubbed to a soft patina, had hand-tooled borders in a twisting vine design. The ivy leaf napkin rings, which he recognized, since Liz had bought eight from the Metropolitan Museum of Art, were inspired by an early 19th century French ormolu mount. They looked like gold, but were cast in pewter with 24 kt. gold electroplate. The napkins were Irish linen in a color matching the chair cushions. A solid brass drip-pan candlestick, probably English, held a scented dark violet candle, which burned while the blowing air conditioning made the flame flicker.

She placed a canary yellow glass vase on the table.

"Very sweet of you to bring these flowers."

"My pleasure."

"I thought we'd have hot coffee, if that's agreeable."

"I'd like that."

A moment later she served them.

Holly was wearing a cotton dress today with pale pink and lime green embroidery bordering the square neckline as well as the short-length sleeves. A belt of the same material with embroidery at the end ties was fastened in a dangling bow pulling the dress in at the waist. She looked fresh and summery.

He wore gray striped slacks with gray and white summer-style shoes and a short-sleeved white shirt open at the collar.

As they ate she smiled. "We go well together, except you're so tan and I'm so pale."

"It's becoming to you."

"You should see how golden brown I can get, but I can't be on stage with bikini patches."

"That's true."

"Some of the girls use liquid makeup, blending in those areas. But I don't like that. I don't think it's particularly good for the skin."

"Then you're one of those girls who uses nothing but Boraxo," he said with a straight face.

"No, not Boraxo. I like Liquid Comet better."

They both laughed. He admired this girl. Beauty and brains.

"This is delicious," said Benicki. "My compliments to the chef."

"Thank you. Pass me your cup."

She filled it from a Silex that was warmed by a small candle flame hidden under a trivet.

"I have some lime sherbet available. That would take away the Canadian Bacon taste. What's your pleasure?"

"I will, if you will."

She cleared away their dishes and served the sherbet in heavy glass dishes on matching plates, also in the shape of an ivy leaf.

"You don't smoke, do you?" she asked.

"Never have."

"Neither have I. Shall we sit over there? You don't have to rush, do you?"

She got up from her chair and he moved it away for her.

"I can stay a little while," he answered.

"Yesterday when you called, you said something about Ed's moves not escaping you."

"I let him know on Wednesday, after I left you, that I was going to put him behind bars. He seems to be toeing the line. With his hand undoubtedly bothering him, he's restricted in what he can do. But I'll keep the pressure on."

"Are you superstitious, Karl? This being Friday the 13th?"

"You bet I am. Would you believe it, my car battery was dead this morning?"

"Really?" she laughed heartily, grimacing a little.

"Still hurts, doesn't it?" he observed.

"I'm getting used to it. In fact it felt much better when Dr. Benicki showed up. Do you know him?"

"I've run into him on occasions, like the face on the other side of the medicine cabinet."

He glanced at his watch.

"The doctor has more calls to make?"

"Sad, but true."

He got up. "Thanks so much, Holly. I enjoyed every moment."

"Me, too. We'll have to do it again."

He bent over and kissed her lightly on the left cheek. "I'll be checking up on you."

Friday the 13th finally closed in on Ed Kimball. The day had gone smoothly. In fact his boss was all smiles when he returned to check out around 3:30.

"Had a call from that new customer of ours, O.G.I. They're very pleased the way you've been handling their logistics. They're running ahead of schedule which translates into cost savings. Very complimentary. We don't often get calls like that. With their expansion plans, it won't hurt our business any."

That was the first time Mel had ever done anything but complain. He was in high spirits when he drove towards home. Along McDowell Road, an accident took place up ahead at a major intersection. He could see the way the cars were crawling, that it would be best to cut into a side street. When he finally inched up to the corner, he swung out of the lane of traffic and cut over to the next street heading in his direction. Midway down the block a U-Haul truck was being unloaded. What caught his eye were the children fooling with an upright freezer that was standing off to the side. One of them opened the door. Ed could see that the shelving had been removed for the move. It all happened in a split second. One of the youngsters climbed in and the other closed the door on him.

Ed floored the brake bringing the truck to a skidding stop against the curb. With half-closed eyes, his good arm shielding his face as if he were emerging into a blinding hell, he raced off in the other direction screaming gibberish at the top of his lungs. His child-hood fears blotted out everything else for the moment. He was the 8-year old hiding in a discarded refrigerator while his playmates looked everywhere. Their deadly game was hide and seek and would have resulted in tragedy if it hadn't been for a girl who had noticed him climbing in from down the street. She opened the latch just in time.

The sunlight was blinding. With lungs aching, heart pounding, he raced aimlessly for several blocks. Then his pace slowed to a stumbling trot. Finally, soaked in perspiration, gasping the while, he came to a stop and sank to his knees. Perspiration trickled down his face and drops formed on the tip of his nose, falling onto the sidewalk. He felt it running down inside his armpits. The bandage on his left hand was getting moist.

The memory that had triggered flight was now relegated back to the childhood past. The sound of Friday traffic replaced it. Once again he was rational, remembering the detour he had made. He glanced over his shoulder and figured his truck was parked somewhere behind him.

It took him twenty minutes to spot the U-Haul and his truck off to one side. A bare-chested man in his forties approached as he came nearer.

"You, OK mister?"

Ed nodded.

The man reached into his pocket and handed Ed's keys over. "You left your motor running. My kids shut it off."

"That freezer?"

"David got out OK. You know how kids get to fool around. Dumb stunt, though."

Ed knew. The panic from not being able to open the refrigerator door from the inside would haunt him all his life. Ed held up the keys.

"Tell the kids thanks."

When he reached his parking space he noticed a light colored car in the common area. The way the sun was reflecting on the windshield, he couldn't make out the occupant. Then he realized whose car it was.

"Goddamned bastard!" he mouthed. Of course. Who else but Benicki? The hair on the nape of his neck felt as if it were rising. He didn't glance back. Once in his room he closed the drapes against prying eyes that couldn't see in regardless. Why? Why was he being constantly spied upon?

Daylight filtered through the drawn drapes. He went around turning on all the lights. As the air conditioning blower came on, he felt better. He wanted nothing to remind him of the inside of that dark, air-less box that had precipitated the harsh memories.

Taking a beer from the refrigerator, he kicked off his shoes, removed his shirt and sat back with his feet up on the coffee table. Fuck Benicki! Let him sit out there in the scorching heat. He sipped the foam, licked his lips. Better than the salty sweat that had trickled down his face to his lips only a short time before. Let Benicki lick his own salty sweat! He laughed. They all thought how goddamned smart they were. He'd show them. All in good time. He'd keep them guessing, running around like a bunch of half-assed amateurs.

He switched on the TV. The girl in the picture reminded him of Holly. Goddamn cunt! Beautiful cunt, but cunt anyway. Not so beautiful at the moment. He pictured how the blow he had struck would mar her looks. He knew how soft fragile skin turned black and blue. He remembered how Julia looked after she told him she had been careless, that she was pregnant. Shit! He never wanted a kid. A kid who could fit into a refrigerator or freezer.

PART IX

Scattered clouds moved into the valley Saturday morning. Rain was predicted for later in the day and possibly on Sunday.

Ed was prompt as usual. Despite many shortcomings, you could count on him being on time for an appointment. When Julia opened the door, Jeff ran up to him but was distracted by the bandaged hand.

"What happened, daddy?"

"Detective Benicki told me all about it, Ed," said Julia. He frowned and turned to Jeff.

"I cut it on a glass. I should have been more careful. All set to go, sport?"

"You bet! Are we going to ride in your truck?"

"We sure are."

"Have fun, fellows!"

Jeff stepped over to his mother and craned his neck. She bent over and kissed his mouth.

"Would you try to get back by four?" she asked Ed.

"We'll be back."

Jeff climbed aboard the pickup and Ed let him close his own door.

"Fasten your seat belt, Jeff."

"Why don't you?"

Ed fastened his for a change.

"How do you like your new place?"

"Neat! You should see my room."

"Nice?"

"Mom got me some super furniture."

"That does sound neat."

Ed was amused by the way Jeff chattered incessantly as they drove along. He was at that stage when he was coming into his own, a real little magpie. As they turned into Encanto, Jeff asked.

"What are we going to do first?"

"How about going out on the lake."

"In one of those boats?"

"You can help me row."

"That's keen!"

The lake was small but ample for the dozen or more boats that slowly moved about. Stately palms and grown trees near the water's edge provided a shady setting. The lush lawn of the park and countless bushes and flowering shrubs were in stark contrast to the desert that spread beyond the fringes of the city.

"I'm glad you're letting me row, daddy. You wouldn't last time."

"You were a year younger then, Jeff. You're getting to be quite the little man. I'm glad you are able to help. We'd be turning in circles if I were rowing with only one hand."

"Can I try? Please daddy?"

172

"Sure. I'll stop rowing"

Jeff laughed loudly as he splashed the water with his oar and the boat made a small circle. After turning the boat around completely several times, Jeff tired of doing it. He feathered his oar like his father's. He looked at the bandaged hand.

"You can't use it, can you?"

"Not right now."

"Will it be OK again?"

"The doctor said it would take time."

"You'll be able to bat a ball to me again, won't you, dad?"

Sure. He hoped he'd be able to do everything again with that hand. He realized that the boy had a soothing effect on him. He was enjoying this more than he had anticipated. Up to this morning, his only reason for seeing Jeff was to deprive his mother of something dear to her, even if only for a short time.

"Daddy, grandpa's afraid of the water. Did you know that?"

"Your mom mentioned it to me once."

"What about you? Are you afraid of anything"

"Me, afraid?"

"Mom didn't think so. I'm sure she'd know."

"She's right." Ed changed the subject.

"Do you have kids to play with?"

"I'll have more when I go to regular school after the summer."

"I was thinking about now."

"No. There're no kids except one girl. She's fourteen."

"That's pretty old."

"Is for me."

"What about giving your old man a break? Head

173

for shore?"

"That's OK. I'm thirsty, anyway."

Ed held the boat steady while Jeff climbed up on the dock. As they walked over to the concession stand, Jeff put his hand in his father's. How could he know that hand helped to drain the life out of a human being. At the moment it meant security to Jeff. The simple trust of a child who someday might learn the terrible truth about his father. Now it meant cokes, hot dogs, cotton candy, popcorn, ice cream cones. Things that made a park unique. Nearby the music of the small carousel kept time to the clang of the metal wheels of other rides bumping along their tracks. The happy laughter and shrieks of joy as children whisked around at fast speeds, echoed from the amusement area.

Jeff rode them all while his father watched patiently. Kimball threw popcorn into the air and caught it in his open mouth. At the moment there was nothing on his mind but sharing in the joy expressed by Jeff's happy expression as he waved to his dad.

Around noon on this Saturday, Karl and Liz Benicki parked and walked towards the playground by the lake. He was wearing heavily-framed dark sunglasses. Without his revolver and handcuffs, he looked much like others spending the day off with their families. It didn't take long for an experienced observer to spot Kimball throwing popcorn into the air by the rides. He seemed to be relaxed like others in the area who were watching their children on the rides.

"Karl."

"Yes, dear?"

"Am I reading you right? Is there a special reason for our coming here?"

"You're too smart for me."

"Then I am right."

He didn't answer.

"Anything to do with the case you're on?"

"Which one?"

"The match book cover the other night."

"You know, lady, I've run out of prizes. How about a hot dog instead?"

"I had my heart set on a stuffed giraffe."

"Why? You have me."

"You're a stuffed ox," she said laughing. "OK, lover. Be a big spender."

"Hot dogs, here we come."

Out of the corner of his eye, as he was squeezing mustard onto his hot dog, he noticed Jeff standing by his father who was reaching into his pocket. Jeff took the money that was handed to him and ran towards one of the rides. There was no point in staying around after they had eaten. His main concern was Kimball actually taking the boy where he said he would.

The predicted rain had moved into the valley on Saturday evening. A thunderstorm brought a brief period of hail that pelted the city. This morning the intermittent showers continued. The Sunday paper had been delivered late and Ed Kimball now fingered through the real estate section frantically until he found those under Scott Harrison & Associates. He glanced down the list of houses that were being held open today. None showed Julia's name.

Hell. What did it matter? Today was a lousy day, anyway. He picked up the editorial real estate section. One of the stories caught his eye. The badly decomposed body of a real estate agent, missing for more than three weeks, had been found in a gully among boulders near Pinnacle Peak. Ed remembered reading about the man not having been heard from after presumably meeting a prospective client. He read on. Dental records established positive identification. The Scottsdale Police were still searching for a man who had called himself David Spencer. The police artist sketch accompanied the article. Scottsdale Detective De Morro was to be contacted by anyone having information that could lead to an arrest.

Seeing De Morro's name, Ed thought of Benicki. He conceived a brilliant idea, a flash of genius to get Benicki off his back. Divide and conquer. He laughed as he picked up the section he had earlier discarded. He found a red felt pen in one kitchen drawer and sat down at the kitchen table. Carefully reading the listings shown by Julia's company and several of the others who worked more expensive homes, he organized and numbered certain ones.

Monday morning Benicki waited patiently for Kimball to drive off in the direction of the freeway and his place of business. Satisfied, he headed south on 7th Avenue to headquarters. He was thankful for Sunday's rain since the overtime spent on the Pearson case had deprived him of Liz's company during the previous week. After church services he had taken her for their usual brunch and had spent the remainder of the afternoon browsing through the paper and watching TV. The article about the discovery of the agent's body also had caught his attention. De Morro was having problems of his own.

At his desk he managed to catch Julia Hochstetter before she left home this morning.

"How'd the outing go?"

"Jeff had a good time."

"What about his father?"

"He's stark, raving mad."

"Can you talk?"

"Dad's already picked Jeff up."

"What happened?"

"He was all smiles when they came home. He told me that he arranged to change his vacation to start the 28th. He planned to come back on the 12th. Jeff starts school in two weeks. I thought he was going to have a stroke. The veins in his neck and temple actually stood out. I was so frightened I didn't know what to do. I didn't want Jeff to see him strike me, if that was to be his next move, so I sent Jeff to his room. I'm sure Ed wished to see me dead at that moment."

"Did he strike you?"

"No. He starred me down. He accused me of deliberately stalling this past month and lying to him. He said, 'Julia, I'll see you in hell'."

"Is that the threat he used."

"Yes."

"What happened next?"

"He slammed the door as he went out. I've gone through difficult times with Ed, Detective Benicki, but I've never seen him so furious."

"I'm glad you're unhurt."

"I don't know how to handle this. What about the next time he meets with Jeff, and the next after that? Will it always be like that?"

"I wish I could assure you that it could never happen again."

"Thank you for your concern. I know you're doing everything you can."

"If he should bother you again or threaten you

with bodily harm, call me. Will you do that?"

"Right away."

Benicki rarely chewed on the end of a pen. Only at times when he was completely frustrated. He didn't know what he could do. If his theory were correct and Kimball had murdered Anne Pearson by mistake, this latest setback would intensify his resolve to kill Julia. Dr. Andrews, the psychiatrist, had verified the assumption that Kimball would of necessity strike out at anyone who opposed him. Now that Julia had openly opposed him, what would keep him from carrying out his threat to see her in hell?

What goaded Benicki was the fact that he was actually helpless to prevent Kimball from killing his former wife. You couldn't arrest him and lock him up for wishing somebody dead. There were times when he thought the whole judicial system stank. He had seen men convicted of selling heroin sentenced to 30 years, while psychotic killers became eligible for parole after two or three years. Thrown back at society to commit the most horrendous atrocities. Who was to say that an unstable human being should be free to roam at will? Why couldn't law abiding citizens be protected from the rapist, the sadist, and the determined murderer?

Karl Benicki agonized over the situation. In his years of police work he had run into many difficult situations, had felt compassion for victims of crime. But this case had affected him differently. He found himself involved personally. He had a special warm feeling towards Holly. The blow to her face had given him pain as well. Not because of some future involvement possibility, although he admitted to himself that he could easily be aroused, but because he liked and respected her as a warm, intelligent, caring human being.

The fears he had felt immediately for Julia, once he realized that she had been the intended victim, were fears and concerns that you would have for a family member. He found a need to protect her and Jeff as a family. What was one without the other? It was only a matter of time before he'd be able to have Jeff's father indicted for murdering Anne Pearson. At least, that's what he hoped for. It became especially poignant since he and Liz were childless. The child in the park seemed so happy with the man who casually snatched popcorn out of the sky, mouth open. The irony of it all. Jeff's hand in his fathers. A bloodstained hand that intended to strike down the closest human being Jeff would ever know.

The middle of the week came unexpectedly. You would think that Tuesday would follow Monday and Wednesday would be the day after Tuesday. Like the lunar tides, seasons of the year, all the cosmic orderliness that is paramount in nature. But since Tuesday was so uneventful, Wednesday came as a complete shock to Ed Kimball. It was mid morning before he realized this was the day he had to appear in court in Tempe at 2 o'clock.

Mark and he were planning to grab lunch together at a nearby Burger King around 11:30. When Mark arrived, Ed had already been waiting for ten minutes.

"How busy are you this afternoon?" asked Ed when they had picked up their orders and found an empty table.

"Why?"

"I've got a problem and need somebody to cover for me."

"I'm tied up till around three, maybe three thirty."

"Shit! Is there any way one of the guys could cover for you?"

"Jeese! I don't know," he said chewing away on his double cheeseburger.

"There's a twenty in it for you if you can work out something."

"Twenty?"

Ed put his burger down and fished out a $20 bill.

"What do I have to do?"

"I'll be at that new Honeywell job. Come by no later than one thirty. I need half an hour to get where I'm going. And, Christ! No later than one thirty. Think you can handle it?"

"Then what?"

"I'll have my checklist all filled out. When you go to the office, hand it in. If Mel asks about me, tell him you saw me fixing a flat on the way. I gave you my sheet so he wouldn't be tied up. He'll buy that."

"Sure! I can handle that," he said taking the $20 and shoving it into his wallet.

"Thanks."

Mark earned his money. At twenty after one he showed up at Ed's site to give him a head start. Ed drove by way of I-10, turned off at 48th Street over to University. He knew this area having been involved in construction supplies to a couple of projects in the industrial parks, but as far as Police Headquarters and the courts, he only had a general idea that it was somewhere around the A.S.U. stadium. Going east on University he crossed Route 60, then got messed up in the side streets. Finally he spotted the Tempe City Hall. Who could mistake it? The building was an inverted glass-sided pyramid. He'd seen pictures of it, but this was some hunk of engineering he had to admit. It was like a kookie stage set. Unique! Dramatic! He approved. The court buildings, he found out by questioning, were across the street from the City Hall. He followed the directional arrows to court parking.

It was a good thing Mike had taken over early. Ed had only a minute to spare when he checked in with the traffic clerk. The girl told him to sit down anywhere in the courtroom. He learned from the man sitting next to him, a habitual offender with parking violations, that latecomers had their cases put at the bottom of the pile before the judge.

Ed was no stranger to traffic courts, but this room was packed. Those bastards, he observed to himself, are working overtime to pay for their goddamn pyramid. All rose precisely at 2:30 p.m. when the judge walked in. There was no frittering around, clerks fumbling for papers or unprepared, and all that jazz. This judge ran a tight operation. All business and efficiency looked over thin gold-framed glasses. An equally thin white mustache perched over a firm mouth. Ed listened to his staccato verdicts. The fines he was socking to certain offenders gave Ed concern. Most were double the rate of speed. That would cost him $140. Jesus Christ! A few, however, he gave an option. Ed wondered if that might apply to him as well? Finally the judge called out his name and asked him how he pleaded, guilty or not guilty to driving seventy. There was no point in avoiding the issue.

"Guilty, your Honor?"

"Have you taken the Defensive Driving Course in the past 18 months?"

"No, sir."

"OK, I'm requiring you to take this course. Eight

hours of instruction. A Wednesday and Thursday night from 6 to 10, or all day Saturday. See the clerk. If you pass the examination your violation will be suspended and it won't go on your record. Or do you prefer to pay $140?"

"I'll take the course, your Honor."

He selected the all day session. The first available date was the 28th of August. In 10 days. The 28th. What a fuckin' way to start his vacation.

When he returned to his truck he checked the glove compartment to make sure he had placed the ads from Sunday's paper in there. He felt sure he had done that on Monday. They were there. It was only three o'clock. What better time than now, especially since Scottsdale was an easy drive from here.

He went south to University, but instead of heading west he drove east towards Scottsdale Road. There were plenty of students meandering around the campus as he drove past some of the dormitories and other buildings. Few, however, compared to the 38,000 enrolled for the fall semester.

Crossing the bridge over the Salt River he noted the flow of water coursing through the deepest portion of the riverbed. The runoff from the weekend's heavy rains, which had dropped several inches in the watershed to the north and east, was causing water to be released from the dams upstream.

When he reached the Scottsdale area, he methodically followed the numbers marked on the house ads. Ed was methodical by nature. When he planned something, he organized it well. If an end result were to be effectively reached, you had to consider each step along the way. His math professor in high school had emphasized the importance of setting up algebraic equations properly. One entry in the wrong place and the solution was shot to hell.

The fifth house he drove to was ideal for his purpose. It was newly constructed, built on one acre at the end of a cul-de-sac. A six foot high wall on either side provided privacy from the neighbors. Desert planting covered the grounds and curving from the street, a circular drive led to the main entry and the attached double garage on one side of the house. What made it ideal was the rear yard which overlooked the Mountain Preserve. It was also not more than a 500' walk along a gravel road, no longer in use, that led to a wooden barrier and a paved road by other houses. Oleanders in a rear yard partially screened this road from view.

He peered through the windows and got a preliminary idea of what he'd encounter inside. Making sure that a lock box was hanging on the door handle, he returned to the pickup and drove home. There was no need for him to check out the other houses he had marked.

The ad mentioned it was a spec home built by Greg Brothers, a San Diego developer, and available through your local broker. The price of the house was $450,000. and entailed a healthy 6% commission to any broker making the sale. It was exactly the bait he needed.

When Ed arrived at the apartment and he spotted Benicki, he cursed the womb that had carried him. Why hadn't Benicki's mother had a miscarriage and spared him? The man was becoming a leech that clung and sucked. The anger evoked by the sight of the man was energy-draining.

That night, when he watched television, he paid

particular attention to the weather forecast over the coming days. His plan had crystallized. He had to have a weekday. Saturday or Sunday were out. Benicki was making him impatient. He wanted to get this over with. What if the house should sell in the meantime? Would he be able to find another house so unique to his purpose? He doubted it. He found himself blessing the weatherman as he showed viewers the satellite photo and the course of the jet stream. It was swinging in from the north bringing with it clear weather that would cheer the Chamber of Commerce's heart. This area, touted as the Valley of the Sun, would live up to its name for the next few days.

His hand bothered him, but in his planning it could prove a blessing in disguise.

Elizabeth Benicki was doing some mending. Looking over the rims of the glasses she needed for close-up work, she watched Karl. They had eaten at home after going to mass because he hadn't felt like having brunch out today. At home he picked over his food, leaving most of it untouched. Even the Sunday paper which he usually enjoyed reading, hadn't merited his attention. He had flipped through it hastily. When she got together the things that needed mending, he turned on a baseball game. That lasted only five minutes in his attention span. Now he was pacing around the house in an aimless fashion. She noticed his frown.

Since Monday night when he came home, she noticed he had appeared tense. It wasn't his mannerisms alone, but also his body movements. She had lived with the telltale signs before. From past experience it signified that the investigation he was occupied with wasn't going well.

"Karl," she said, "why don't you go out for a walk or a drive?"

"I hate to leave you alone."

"Don't be silly. I'm not alone. I've got my needle and thread to keep me company for some time. If you stick around, I'll feel I should drop this and pay attention to you. I've put off this mending long enough. Give me a kiss and run along."

"Maybe you're right, Liz. It might do me some good."

He needed to talk about the case, to air his fears, sound out his premises. There were times when he desperately wanted to talk over a theory, or something that bothered him, with Liz. But he had made this a rule early in their marriage, not to get her involved with his police problems.

Without realizing it, he found himself at the intersection of Central and Osborn making a left turn. Subconsciously he had decided to see Holly. He had talked with her several times since the Eggs Benedict luncheon, but he hadn't seen her since.

Not wishing to arrive unannounced on a Sunday afternoon, he stopped at the security gate first.

"Miss Jones says to come right up."

Holly stood at the head of the stairs watching as his car drove from the gate. She was all smiles. For a moment his problems vanished as he took the stairs two at a time.

"I was thinking about you," she said as they entered the apartment. "Now I believe in wishes."

"What were you wishing?"

"That I wouldn't be alone. You answered a maiden's prayer."

"Did Kimball call you?" he said bristling.

"No. Nothing like that. I was thinking how nice it would be to see you. Can I get you anything to drink?"

"Not at the moment, Holly."

"My, you sound serious. Sit by me."

"I need to talk. I've made a point of never discussing my cases at home."

"I'm a good listener. More trouble?"

"I don't know what to make of Kimball. All of a sudden he's become a model citizen. Leaves for work in the morning. Comes home about the same time. I see him carrying grocery bags. I've checked with the manager. Tells me that Kimball hasn't gone out at night since he cut his hand. No more bar brawls. Nothing. I can't figure what's going on. But he's shrewd. I know he's got a plan in mind. I could swear he's going to kill again, but Holy Mother of God I don't know how to stop him. I can only keep surveillance on him so much, otherwise he'll scream harassment and I'll have some attorney breathing down my neck with a court order to show just cause."

"Are you so sure he's going to kill someone?"

"He made a threat on Saturday. I've talked about him to our psychiatrist. He agrees there's a ticking time bomb walking around. I wish I were the demolition expert to defuse him, but I feel helpless. There's no way I can be right behind him every second."

"Is he trying to put you off guard by being a model citizen?"

"I've wondered about that. I don't think so. He knows I'm keeping an eye on him. I've heard his door slam a number of times after he's spotted me. He even draws the blinds to blank out the sight of me. He could just as easily be establishing another routine by visiting some night spot during the week. Isn't that what he used to do? All of a sudden our hell raiser is probably sitting with his feet up on the coffee table, drinking beer and watching a night game in Philly or somewhere else."

"Could it be his hand? Does he want you to feel he's not capable of violence at the moment?"

"That's a good thought, Holly. Go on." This is what he had hoped for. To get a different perspective. Perhaps play devil's advocate with him.

"Well, it was easy enough for him to strike me. I wasn't strong enough to fight back effectively."

He looked at her face. The swelling had gone down completely, but he knew it would be another two or three weeks before all the discoloration disappeared. Holly continued.

"But somebody like yourself, Karl, would be a formidable opponent. You'd fight back hard. Right now, though, Ed can' t risk a fight because of his hand. He's at a disadvantage. He'd need both hands to take you on."

Karl agreed with Holly that this could be the reason for Kimball settling down. Two hands had clamped down on the carotid arteries in Anne Pearson's neck. If this were the way he planned to kill Julia, he'd have to play it cool for the time being. But on the other hand.

"The way he broke the glass, Holly, he could have as easily choked you to death with one hand."

"Me?"

"Figuratively speaking."

"I guess he could have. But a grip like that can be broken. In college I took some classes in self defense against muggers and that kind of stuff. We were taught that if somebody grabs you by the wrist, you use all your defensive counteraction away from the thumb.

187

Let's say you had me by the throat with one hand, I'd only have to twist out of the crotch made by your thumb and fingers to break the grip."

"You're right in that."

"With two hands there are opposing forces. I'd have to seek some other way of breaking away."

"OK, then he's faced with a similar problem. He has to seek another way."

"What if he's already got one in mind, Karl? Is it possible that he wants you to think otherwise? Is he trying to say, 'Karl Benicki, I'm out of action for six or eight months till my hand's OK again. So, copper, bug out.' Is that what he wants you to think?"

"I believe you're right, Holly. He wants to lull me to sleep, put me off guard."

"Now that we've got that settled, I'm going to fix you something. What can I get for you? Brandy and soda? A wine cooler. I don't have any beer."

"You're too much, Holly."

"I'm having a wine cooler. Shall I make it two?"

"I'll gladly join you."

Up to now he had been wrapped up in a cocoon. Holly had taken one end of the silk thread and unrolled it. Somehow the burden that had confined him had vanished. Like the winged insect emerging, he felt ready for a new world of flight.

He walked into the kitchen area and suddenly discovered what Holly was wearing, or not wearing. Her crocheted dress was one of those see through variety. The skin could be viewed, but in the areas calling for some semblance of modesty, the skillful arrangements of knot patterns gave only a conceptual view of what one might wish to see. She wore nothing underneath. He was amused at himself. Ed Kimball had dominated his every thought, that somehow the finer things in life were escaping him. "I like your dress."

She laughed. "You noticed. "

"Cops are clods at times."

"I have to admire you, Karl."

"Why is that?"

"I try my level best to be seductive and all that's on your mind is saving my neck or someone else's. That takes real will power on your part."

"I sound like a real bore."

"You have your charming moments. Let's drink to your old school tie."

He laughed.

PART X

The temperature had reached the low 100s all week, but by noon on Wednesday a mass of gray clouds blotted out the sun dropping the temperature five degreees.

Before leaving for the day, Ed Kimball talked to the boss and postponed his vacation plans a second time. Mel went along gladly since Kimball was needed on the job at the moment.

He turned on the radio in the pickup, listened to western music and caught the latest local news and weather report. At last. He was in a jubilant mood when he reached home and almost disappointed at not finding his nemesis parked there. Maybe he had finally given up. Once inside the apartment, he stripped down to his shorts, took a cold beer out of the refrigerator and polished off the can to quench his thirst.

The previous afternoon he hadn't come home at all. Instead he bought one of those throw-away razors, drove to the motel at Bell Road and I-10 and spent the night. It was all part of the plan to catch Benicki off balance. The early evening he spent down in the lounge eating peanuts at the bar and washing them down with beer. A bit of television and he put in a call for five thirty. This morning on the way to work he had grabbed coffee and a donut at Dunkin' Donuts. He chuckled to himself at the time wondering what Benicki would be thinking. Not that he gave a shit, really. The broken routine would surely have him guessing. Where would he start to look? What would he figure on doing?

Just for kicks, Kimball sauntered over to the window, pulled aside the drape and looked out. Benicki hadn't showed up. Maybe he was watching from another vantage point. If so, what of it. It didn't make a hell-of-a-lot of difference.

Picking up the phone he dialed the number he had memorized, having repeated it over and over again as he drove in the pickup. It went...

> 'When I phone you'll soon be dead
>   got your number in my head
>   you'll no longer be alive
>   two six four three two oh five'

When the secretary answered he spoke with certain inflections characteristic of the Midwest.

"Do you have a Miss Hochstetter?"

"I believe she's in, sir. I'll ring."

"Julia Hochstetter. How may I help you?"

"I'm sure you can from what I've heard about you. You came highly recommended by a friend of a friend in Chicago."

He knew that Chicago was supplying a lot of newcomers who were tired of snow and ice. The law of averages would be in his favor. Surely she would have had a client from that area.

"Could they be the Greenbergs? Saul and Rose?"

He had been right in his assumption. "I'm sure that they're the ones my friend mentioned."

"Lovely people. Sold them a house recently."

"That's what I was told."

"May I ask your name, sir?"

"Krause. George and Jean Krause."

He figured that with the adverse publicity in the recent deaths of real estate agents, Julia would be less apprehensive in dealing with a couple.

"Exactly what are you looking for, Mr. Krause?"

"I think we've found it. We were driving around the Scottsdale area and came across a house by the mountains. Jean fell in love with it the moment she saw it. We kind of peered through the windows, but you can't tell too much that way. The sign said to contact our local broker. Could you show it to us tomorrow?"

He was enjoying his play acting. She would never connect the Krause voice with his. A smile spread across his face in expectation of her answer. Her company would be getting the entire sales commission with no marketing expense whatsoever.

"I'd love to show it to you. What is the address."

Ed gave it to her.

"Where can I pick you up tomorrow?" asked Julia.

"That's not necessary. We'll meet you there at four thirty. All right?"

"Four thirty," she said confirming the time. "I'll look forward to meeting you and Mrs. Krause."

Ed replaced the receiver slowly. The fly had taken the bait, the sugar coated commission. With a quick movement he banged down the plastic receiver.

"Gotcha!"

He admired his performance. He had roll played exactly what he was going to say. Having lived with Julia, he was fairly certain of her responses and had made dialogue allowances in the event that her answers were contrary to what he expected.

Ed crumbled the empty beer can in his hand and tossed it in the trash. He was about to make an out-of-town call but changed his mind. They were bound to check with the telephone company if it came to that point.

Morning came none too soon for Ed Kimball. He had waited a long time for this day. In his mind he had covered every aspect, every contingency. Nothing would go wrong. He smiled with satisfaction when he noticed Benicki two cars behind. From the freeway access road he turned into the parking area at the office, all smiles. Ed Kimball was a jubilant man. The sky was threatening with only a slight possibility of rain before nightfall. After all these days of sunshine, the desert soil would be packed hard, defying any imprint to mar its surface.

His day was routine. At three thirty he checked

out at the office and drove north on the freeway, taking Thunderbird in the direction of Scottsdale. He watched anxiously to see if by any chance he was being followed. He knew Benicki wouldn't give up on him, but he was accustomed to finding him waiting at the apartment. That was close to headquarters. But, Christ! the man couldn't devote every second to him. His driving speed varied. Cars passed him when he slowed below the speed limit. In short order he knew he wasn't being tailed.

By four he had arrived at his destination and parked the truck in the shade of some huge Queen Palms. He walked around the wooden barrier and took the gravel road to the back yard of the house. Making sure that he wasn't being observed by any neighbor, he moved up to the front of the house, took the house key from the lock box, and let himself in the double-door entry. Replacing the key in the box, he adjusted the latch inside so that the door would be locked. He had but to wait. Ten minutes later he saw Julia's car drive up. She held her briefcase under her arm while removing the lock box key from her pocketbook. He heard her first try the dead bolt which he hadn't locked.

Julia made her way to the kitchen, her footsteps echoing. Then he heard her coming back to the front of the house to open the shutters in the living room. From there she stepped into the family room, intent on letting more light in .

"Ed'" she gasped, startled by the sight of him.

His good hand grabbed her throat. He had caught her completely by surprise. With all his strength he forced her back until he was able to push her head against the lava stone wall behind the fireplace. In rapid succession, before she had a chance to slump, he repeatedly pounded her head against the stone. His grasp hadn't been that tight. Tight enough to hold her head up, but not enough to suffocate her or blacken her out. In his hip pocket he had the hunting knife taken from the glove compartment. He plunged the knife into Julia a half dozen times. There was no question now that she was dead. Wiping the blade on her skirt, he replaced it in the leather sheath. He then removed the car keys from her bag and using his handkerchief to wipe off the door knob, he let himself out and drove her car to where he had parked.

He had a sense of urgency now and made his way as quickly as possible to the west side to link in with I-10, heading towards Buckeye and finally to Yuma. At eight fifteen he walked over to Mike Perez who was lined up at Ernie's bar, where he usually hung out after work. Perez turned away.

"Hey! I want to talk."

"What about?"

"Not here. Over by the juke box."

Perez reluctantly followed. "Well?"

"You owe me. It's time to collect."

Perez scowled at him. The music stopped and Ed put some coins in and pushed buttons at random. As the music blared up he stepped closer to Perez.

"In case anybody should ever ask, I've been with you since seven. Seven o'clock, mind you!"

"Seven o'clock," repeated Perez.

"If you stick to that, you're off the hook."

"OK, it's a deal."

"Good. I'll buy you a drink."

As they stood by the bar, Ed thought of his drive to Yuma. At the second construction detour he had a chance to throw the hunting knife into a ditch that was being bulldozed over. In the morning when they started up again. that knife would be buried forever.

After two beers, Ed drove back to Phoenix arriving around eleven thirty. When he pulled into his parking spot, he purposely leaned on the horn until the manager appeared in his doorway. "Sorry!" shouted Ed as he climbed out and made his way upstairs. A perfect day. He had accomplished everything he had set out to do. And best of all he had all the bases covered. When he lay down in bed he set the alarm and was fast asleep in a matter of minutes.

Scott Harrison was usually in the office by eight, a half hour before Ginny came in and changed the switchboard over from the night lines. When he was unlocking the front door he heard the phone ringing. Whoever was calling was not letting the answering machine pick up, was hanging up and ringing again. Now the urgency became a staccato of irritating sound. He reached for the nearest phone with its telling red light flashing and picked it up. It was the quiet before the storm.

"Scott Harrison," he answered.

"Is that you, Harrison," came an older voice.

"Yes. Who is this?"

"Roger Hochstetter "

"Oh, good morning, Mr. Hochstetter."

"Would you know where my daughter is?"

"She hasn't come in yet. Can I have her call you?"

"That's not what I mean. She never came to pick up Jeff last night and we haven't heard from her. That's not like Julia. Her mother and I've been up sick with worry half the night."

"If she had car trouble or anything last night,

she would have called, I'm sure."

"What can we do?"

"Let me make a couple of calls. Give me your number and I'll get back to you."

He wrote down the number and suddenly felt clammy. The flower-bedecked casket bearing Anne Pearson flashed before him.

"Oh, my God. Please, God. No!"

In panic he dialed the direct line for Karl Benicki shown on the card he had been given.

"Detective Benicki."

"This is Scott Harrison. I just hung up on Julia's father. She never showed up last night. He's frantic and I'm very worried."

Those words battered Karl like a champion heavyweight throwing a final haymaker at him after staggering to his feet from an eight count. The blow caught him squarely. His teeth almost jarred loose despite the mouthpiece. Amidst a skull full of imaged stars streaking in all directions at incalculable speed, the black hell of unknown void descended. From somewhere a whisper in the distance blasted like the whistle of a train emerging from a mile-long tunnel.

"Did you hear what I said, Detective Benicki?"

From years of experience in fighting losing battles, he recovered his equilibrium.

"Yes, I did. I'm just letting it sink in. When did you last talk with her?"

"She was in and out yesterday trying to clear things up for a four thirty showing"

"When did you talk to her?" he repeated.

"She called in from Scottsdale around four, I believe."

"Do you know where this showing was going to

196

take place?"

"I don't. I'm sure she left word with Ginny."

"Would you ask her?"

"She's due any minute. I'll call you back."

Benicki's worst fears were realized. The target he was trying to protect was unaccounted for. He groped for words that could best express what he felt. None surfaced. There were no clear-cut words that encompassed his emotions. The doubts, the fears, the terrible shattering inadequacy that drained him of his energies. He knew what was required of him, but he was clay at the moment squished by the hand of Ed Kimball. That was the only thing he had no doubts about. Somewhere in this city Ed Kimball had struck and he had not been able to prevent it.

He snatched up the receiver. "Yes."

"Harrison. Ginny has no record of it."

"Could she have told someone else?"

"Possibly. We'll check, but it'll take time."

"Do whatever you can."

Benicki checked the case file on Anne Pearson. In with other information were facts regarding Julia Hochstetter. The make and license plate of her car. He called it in to the communications dispatch, to be on the lookout for her vehicle. Since they were hooked into the County Sheriff's Office computer, police departments in the adjacent cities were also fed this information. For the moment there was nothing else he could do.

By noon all the people at Harrison's office had been canvassed about Julia's appointment. She hadn't spoken with any of them about her plans. The secretary mentioned that Julia had been excited by a call received the previous day, but nothing more.

Once again Karl Benicki parked in front of Kimball's apartment area waiting for him to return from work. When Kimball arrived at the usual time, instead of him frowning or cursing, he had a smile on his face. A self-satisfied smirk. He even refrained from slamming the door and left the drapes open.

Benicki knew the signs of the sadist pulling the hind legs off a grasshopper, saying, 'OK, get off your ass', knowing you can't move. He was throwing down the gauntlet, sure of his own victory.

He had already driven back onto 7th Avenue on his way to the office when he got word on the dispatch that Julia Hochstetter's car had been spotted, parked by the Mountain Preserve in North Scottsdale. He raced up to Lincoln Drive, over to Tatum and Mockingbird. He had called through that he was on his way. When he arrived at his destination two Scottsdale Police cars were there as well as one from the Sheriff's Office. He identified himself.

"You the one who spotted it?" asked Benicki.

"Yeh! Found the keys in the ignition. Haven't touched anything. Is the car hot?"

"No. The driver was reported missing. Have you checked any of the houses?"

"Detective De Morro's on his way. We were told to wait for him."

Benicki knew DeMorro. A couple of years younger than himself. Prone to carrying a little excess weight around the paunch, but a man who could hit a horsefly on a fence post at fifty feet with his 38. A good, intelligent detective. While the men were standing by Julia's car, De Morro drove up.

"Hello, John," said Benicki.

"Karl! What brings you out here?"

"Case I've been working on. Anne Pearson, killed three weeks ago."

"Read the bulletin. What's this car got to do with that?"

"Belongs to the agent whose place Anne Pearson took."

"Good Christ! Don't tell me we're having an epidemic on our hands."

"Scares the hell out of me, John. I've been keeping tabs on a guy who's capable of starting one."

"Have you checked around?" De Morro asked the officers.

"Waiting instructions."

"OK! You two, take each side of the street. See if she's in with any of them." He told the other officers to search the desert area by the foothills.

"Take care, guys!" said the driver of the Sheriff's car as he drove off.

"Do you really expect foul play, Karl?" asked De Morro. "This guy you say's capable of it?"

"You know how these things go, John. He was recently divorced from the missing woman. Off the record I believe he killed Pearson by mistake, not realizing at the time she wasn't his wife."

"So, with her missing, you fear the worst?"

"He's psychopathic. The worst kind of sadist."

"But you've got nothing on him?"

"Theory, John. All the pieces fit. But nothing to hang on him, yet."

"I know what you mean."

Ten minutes later the officers gathered. No woman had rung their doorbells asking for assistance or anything. Neither had they noticed any unusual activity in the neighborhood.

"That's the trouble nowadays," observed De Morro. "Nobody ever uses their living room overlooking the street except as a showplace for expensive furnishings. They're all back in the family room or out by the pool. They don't know or couldn't care less what's happening out here in this goddamned world."

De Morro got a small Ziploc bag from his car and with his handkerchief removed the ignition keys from the parked vehicle, dropping them into the bag. He locked the car doors. "I'll get the lab on it in the morning if she doesn't turn up."

Jean Schaeffer of Whitehead and Winters, Realty pulled into the circular driveway of the Greg Brothers house. Seated beside her in the Mercedes diesel was Herbert Edly, a Philadelphia industrialist. His wife, Jennifer, sat in the rear.

"It's even lovelier than the photo you showed us. I love it already. Don't you, Herbert?"

The Edlys had decided to see what Scottsdale was like during the worst time of the year. Now they were prepared to pay cash for a second home in this price range, knowing that the climate would be ideal during the long winter months. Jean Schaeffer was a Million Dollar Club producer, a very capable Realtor. The past hour had been spent looking at homes that would have been acceptable, but she had held back on the pièce de résistance. It was like serving flambé after a gourmet dinner.

She noticed that the dead bolt on the upper lock hadn't been locked and thought nothing of it as she used the key taken from the lock box. After all, the house was vacant and anyone determined to enter could break a window at the rear of the house. Unlocking the door, she pushed it open, closing it after the Edlys.

Jennifer Edly loved the large living room directly off the spacious entry hall. She glanced up at the vaulted ceiling with its heavy beams and smiled at Herbert. One of those knowing smiles.

"I like the fireplace," announced Herbert.

"There's also one in the family room. Let me get the shutters."

The double doors to the family room stood ajar and sunlight was trying to stream through the closed shutters.

Making her way to the windows, she adjusted the louvres on the first pair and then moved to the next. Her back was turned to the fireplace. The Edly's followed her into the room. As sunlight streamed through the windows, Jennifer turned in the direction of the fireplace. Her scream of terror echoed through the empty rooms. She screamed again and her husband prevented her from collapsing to the ground. He focused his eyes on the woman's body lying against the black lava stone. The opened shutters let in stripes of light which followed the curves of her body. The dead woman's eyes stared vacantly into the blinding sun. Across her blouse the matted blood looked unreal, like a macabre setting in the wax museum.

Jean Schaeffer was still carrying a portion of the lock box in her hand. It dropped to the floor. The attached key lay on the plush mist green carpeting like a compass needle pointing at the body. "Oh, God! Oh, my God! Oh, my God!" she kept repeating over and over again.

Edly guided his wife, half paralyzed by fear and shock, out the front door to the car. Jean Schaeffer, clutching her clipboard, backed out of the family room and ran.

"Stay with my wife! "he ordered."I'll be right back." He started to walk, but broke into a run instead to the nearest house. Moments later he was accompanied by members of that household who had called the police. Within minutes half a dozen law enforcement vehicles converged on the scene.

The news reached Benicki at his home. He was about to have lunch. His fist pounded his palm repeatedly. "He killed her! He killed her! He said as much. Good Holy Christ, what's it all coming to?"

Since the murder had taken place in Scottsdale, the investigation became the province of the Scottsdale Police Department. Benicki had no jurisdiction. There would, of course, be some form of cooperation between the Scottsdale and Phoenix police departments, but as far as the murder of Julia Hochstetter was concerned, it became Detective De Morro's ball game.

Benicki grieved over her unnecessary death and be came more determined than ever to nail Ed Kimball. He drove over to Kimball's apartment and spoke with the manager when he didn't notice Kimball's truck.

"He drove out of here around seven thirty. That's pretty early for a Saturday. He usually sits around mostly on Saturdays during the day, then doesn't get back here till the early morning hours on Sunday. I'm a light sleeper and recognize the sound of his pickup. Wakes me up every time."

Benicki knew this latest murder wasn't his case, but he wanted to know where Kimball was this morning. Julia's body had been discovered a little before noon. From 7th Avenue you could figure a fifteen or twenty minute drive on a Saturday to the murder scene. Where had Kimball been this morning

De Morro agreed to let Benicki notify the Hochstetters about their daughter. Instead of telephoning, he drove out to give them the news. Roger Hochstetter broke down and began sobbing when he learned about Julia. Fortunately, his wife and grandson were out shopping at the time.

"Would you be able to come with me for an hour or so?" asked Benicki.

"Why's that necessary?"

"I'd like you to make a positive identification. I know how difficult it will be, but it's necessary."

"I'll leave my wife a note."

"Not about your daughter."

"Oh, God, no! I'll tell her when I come back."

The drive from Sun City to the morgue was as painful for Benicki as it was for Hochstetter. He listened as Julia's father reminisced about her childhood, the joys and sorrows they had experienced. Hochstetter wondered how God could condone the evils in this world. Why, he asked, was good always counterbalanced by evil in this life. Was it necessary for each person to bear a cross? Hadn't Christ done that for all of us? His energies gradually ebbed as the shock of his daughter's murder spread in his body like a malignancy.

Benicki led the way when they reached the Medical Examiner's facility, which just twenty days earlier had held Anne Pearson's body. He checked with one of the lab assistants who led them to the viewing room where the body lay on a gurney covered by a sheet. Roger Hochstetter, who had summoned all his strength upon arriving here, stood by the shoulders as the sheet was pulled away revealing only her face.

He stood there rigidly in disbelief, then lost control of himself. His shoulders heaved, and in asthmatic-type breaths his sobs continued to shake his body.

"Is this Julia Hochstetter?" asked the lab assistant.

"Yes," he whispered in a choked-up voice.

Benicki put his arm around his shoulder as he gently led him out of the room. The painful task of identification was over. Now it was up to the medical examiner to determine the cause of death.

Roger Hochstetter sat back in the seat without uttering a word on their return home. He was a man defeated. The way his head clung limply with his eyes open, he was lost to a world of oblivion where neither joy or sorrow ever penetrated. A world devoid of feeling. A refuge. An escape from reality. It was the comatose existence sought by alcoholics, drug addicts, and those for whom a painful experience was too overwhelming to cope with.

When they reached the house, Betty Hochstetter took one look at him and guessed. She paled. "Julia?"

"I'm afraid there's bad news," said Benicki. "Your grandson? Where's he?"

"He's next door watching Mr. Simpson working on his train setup."

Roger Hochstetter then told her.

The effect was predictable and Benicki waited till their family physician arrived and sedated her. Finally, Roger saw him to the door.

"Get the murderer!" pleaded Hochstetter.

"That I promise you. We'll get him."

"Do it soon," he held his hands in prayer.

It was after four when Benicki perched himself on the top step leading to Kimball's apartment. Like a vulture waiting to grasp the carrion with its claws, to tear away the flesh with its hawk-like beak, he waited patiently. If he had to wait all night he was determined to confront Kimball with Julia's death. He wondered what kind of an alibi he would contrive. Whatever he came up with, Benicki was prepared to shoot it full of holes. He was sure that Kimball had done it. Tomorrow the medical examiner would have made all the determinations including the approximate time of her death.

Benicki didn't have to wait long. A few moments after five the light blue truck appeared turning into the complex and Kimball, with a handful of literature, came up the stairs. He stopped in front of Benicki who was blocking his way.

"Why don't you get off my back?"

"Would you like to tell me about your wife's death?"

"I can only tell you what I heard on the news a minute ago. But then that's rehashing it, isn't it? I can't add anything."

"Humor me."

"Sure. Why not?" he stood there arrogantly openly defying Benicki to rile him.

"Where were you this morning?"

Kimball laughed loudly. 'You'd like it if I couldn't come up with a good answer, wouldn't you? If I give you a sure thing, will you fuck off?"

"Try me."

Kimball shook the papers in his hand which included some sort of catalog "Here it is, smart ass. It's all here. Look for yourself in the front pages."

He handed it to Benicki who remained seated.

The catalog title was, 'Defensive Driving Course'.

"Open it!" snapped Kimball impatiently.

Benicki turned the cover. Lying there between the pages was a certificate. He read it slowly. It stated that Edward Kimball had satisfactorily completed the 8-hour course this Saturday, August 28th. There was no way he could have killed Julia Hochstetter this morning.

For a moment the weeks of investigative work seemed to go down the drain. There was only one saving grace. The cockiness Ed Kimball was showing at the moment seemed to be something he was relishing. Something he had anticipated doing. Was he strutting the ramparts of Elsinore Castle? Dagger in hand? Defying the fates?

PART XI

Benicki paced up and down in the office. It was already Monday morning. He felt like a racehorse chaffing at the bit, but scratched from the race the last minute. The odds seemed heavy against his getting back into the race. His mind kept dwelling on Kimball standing a few steps below him. He wished he had wiped the smirk off his face, had knocked him down the flight of stairs. Not only for what he had done to Holly, but also in view of his gut feeling that he was involved in the two women's deaths.

He wished he were on the latest case instead of being the tail wagged by the dog. Not that De Morro wasn't a good bird dog, but he agonized over the feeling that Kimball might kill again.

A little before nine, De Morro phoned.

"I know how close you are to this case. The doc's got it wrapped up. Want to meet me there in half an hour?"

Charlie Blake had performed the autopsy the previous afternoon, carefully inspecting the body for marks and lacerations aside from the stab wounds. A specimen was taken from each of the vital organs for examination.

Benicki was already in the Medical Examiner's office when De Morro arrived.

"Let's take a look," said Blake making his way through the heavy stainless steel swinging door leading to the storage room. The temperature was in the high 30s. A dozen gurneys stood in rows on either side of the room. Off to one side was a door to a small separate room used for storing badly decomposed bodies, victims of the ravages of desert temperatures. At the far end was another door leading to the loading dock.

They walked past two bodies of infants, an old bearded man, a terribly obese woman in her mid fifties. Near the door to the loading dock was the body of Julia Hochstetter. The sheet covered all but her feet and her face. Blake pulled the sheet down from her neck.

"Whoever did this took hold of her by the neck. The

slight contusion you can notice is more pronounced on her left side, your right as you face her. I'd say he held her by the right hand. There was no apparent attempt to strangle her. Instead he pounded her skull against the stone wall. Small bits of the lava rock were embedded in the skin which was severely lacerated. The force he used against her, using her head as a mallet, was so concussive that she would have died within five or ten minutes. There was no need to stab her six times."

"Six times?" asked Benicki.

"Yes, Karl."

"When do you figure she died Charlie?" asked De Morro.

"It's hard to be exact when a body's lying around in the heat. I don't imagine the air conditioning was left on in the house."

"No," said De Morro.

"We checked on everything. Only the circuit breakers for the lights were thrown on."

"That's what I assumed when I tried to estimate the approximate time of her death."

"Could she have died on Friday instead of Saturday?" asked Benicki.

"Not Friday."

Benicki's heart sank. If not Friday, it was Saturday and Kimball had the perfect alibi.

"She died on Thursday," said Blake.

"Thursday!" half-shouted Benicki. "Are you telling us she died on Thursday?"

"As best as I can tell."

"How do you figure?" asked De Morro.

"The heat had already taken effect on the tissue, as you can imagine. With the degenerative process going on, I figured she had been dead about forty-eight hours. What helped me pinpoint it, however was the examination of the contents of her stomach. The digestive process of her noon meal on Thursday had continued for approximately four hours. If she had ingested the food at noon, the time of her death occurred around four. Depending on how late she ate, you have a span of a couple of hours. Six at the latest, possibly."

Benicki couldn't believe what he was hearing. It was like the bugle call echoing across the distant mesa. The flashing lights at a rail crossing warning of thousands of tons of steel that would be roaring by momentarily. The cavalry was coming to the rescue. The battle hadn't been lost. The flashing signal told him to stop, look, and listen.

"Charlie, you made my day," said Benicki. "I never realized a shot of adrenaline would feel so good."

De Morro wondered about his enthusiasm as he turned to Blake. "Charlie, send a copy to Karl as well. Would you?"

"No sooner said than done."

Benicki walked over to De Morro's car with him.

"That was a twist. All this time I thought she had died on Saturday, or maybe Friday."

"You'll let me know of anything you come up with?" asked De Morro.

"I'll help all I can."

"I appreciate that. If the lab boys come up with any thing, I'll call you."

"Good luck'"

Suddenly the doubt that had hung over him since Saturday had given way. Blake's time frame was the ray of sunshine penetrating the dense clouds. That certificate Kimball had thrown at his face wasn't worth the ink used to print it. It was a stage prop. Wrong act. Wrong scene.

He spent the rest of the morning typing up his theory on the killings and walked into his boss' office.

"Ben, how about breaking bread with me? I need to sound you out."

"Sure, Karl."

They sat off to one side in one of the smaller, but more expensive downtown restaurants. It was in an old Victorian house that had been meticulously remodelled. Tables were placed on the second floor as well and service was provided by means of an old-fashioned dumbwaiter from which the waitress brought their dishes. A large shade tree shielded them from reflected light coming through the window.

"It all fits," said Benicki. "Even what doc stated about the slight contusions. The fingers of the right hand that he had to use."

"But if he battered her brains out, why stab her?"

"Doubts. Having the use of only one hand he couldn't be sure. Both hands and he could have choked her easily. He had done it before. But this time, he had to provide another MO. Leaving telltale marks with one hand would point suspicion directly at him. Even if she were unconscious at the time, how could he be sure she might not recover and confront her assailant. What if she were so thick skulled that she survived. We've seen it in major head injury cases. Weeks in a coma and suddenly they're back."

"That's true, Karl. So it's a case of overkill."

"Exactly. He couldn't take the chance. Moreover, the different MO could remove suspicion from himself if he had a good alibi."

"What now?"

"I guess sit down with De Morro. Give him what I have and let him follow up."

"I've got a better idea. Maybe we can keep the pressure on."

"What's on your mind?"

"I'll get back to you." He reached into his pocket.

"No way. This is on me."

"What's the occasion?"

"A special kind of birthday. I've been reborn."

The Arizona Republic had devoted its editorial this morning to this latest murder of a real estate agent. It echoed the fear and indignation of the public, especially the real estate segment, and spoke of the measures being taken. The local real estate boards had circulated flyers to all member offices since the first incident took place in the Scottsdale area, where the agent's car was found parked at Sky Harbor Airport. Subsequent warnings were issued upon Anne Pearson's death and later the discovery of the first agent's body in the Pinnacle Peak area. With the latest killing, persons were tending to work in pairs rather than individually. All were cautioned not to make appointments late in the day with prospective clients whom they hadn't carefully screened. The Arizona Association of Realtors was putting pressure on the District Attorney's office of the county to put all their efforts into apprehending the person or persons responsible. The real estate industry was systematically being demoralized.

The Investigative Department of the county, under the D.A. had been conducting its own investigation from information channeled through to them, as well as using their own crime lab. To date, they too had come up empty handed as far as putting together enough evidence to request an indictment.

Ben McKenzie, after having lunched with Benicki, went straight to the D.A.'s office and at four o'clock that afternoon a press conference was quickly called. It was to be a show of strength.

Seated behind an oblong table were the D.A.; Abe Clinton, his chief investigator; John De Morro; and Karl Benicki. The cameras of the major networks were lined up. District Attorney, Perry Lanham started speaking.

"Our entire community is sickened by this latest tragedy involving the brutal murder of a real estate agent. For most of this month, Detective De Morro of the Scottsdale Police Department has been investigating the disappearance of William Binder, whose body was recently identified when discovered in the Pinnacle Peak area. Now Detective De Morro has another agent's murder to investigate. It is our consensus that these two killings are unrelated. Three weeks ago, Anne Pearson, another real estate agent was killed here in Phoenix. Detective Karl Benicki, on my right, of the Phoenix Police Department has been investigating her death. It is his belief, and shared by this office from our review of his findings, that this latest murderer is linked to that of Anne Pearson. Our joint investigations are continuing and will continue until my office hands down an indictment. My chief investigator, Abe Clinton, will coordinate the investigation with Detectives De Morro and Benicki. They will each have full authority to proceed with their investigations regardless of overlapping jurisdictions. The full cooperation of this office will be put at their disposal. Whatever warrants or subpoenas it takes to wind up these cases will be speedily issued. I spoke with the governor before this conference and have his complete backing to reach out anywhere in the state, should our investigation extend beyond Maricopa County. Again, let me emphasize that our citizenry demands that all parties responsible be brought to trial as quickly as possible."

Benicki had hoped for this kind of latitude, to be able to carry on his own investigation. He had no doubts that De Morro would fully cooperate, keeping him informed. But he functioned best landing by parachute, like in Vietnam, cutting loose, and being on his own those first threatening moments. Once again he had landed in enemy territory.

It was almost time to drive home from work. Ed Kimball had been flying high all day. His confrontation with Benicki on Saturday had been one of his most memorable performances. He complemented himself for having learned the scene and the lines so well. Nobody had to cue him. The success of it was much like the box office goodies on Broadway, where the audience is led to believe they have all the answers. They sit back in their seats complaisantly, projecting the anticipated lines the actors will voice. They know exactly what's coming next.

How unexpectedly this drama had played out, however. He laughed, recalling Benicki's expression. Benicki was determined to place him at the scene. Then the switch. The alibi.

He had already anticipated that his being in class would be found to be unimportant to the case. No medical examiner could possibly shave all those hours off the resulting rigor mortis. Kimball knew that eventually Benicki would want him to explain his whereabouts on Thursday afternoon.

The past weekend had also gone well for him.

It was three weeks ago that he had cut his hand. The pain had subsided. He had returned to the hospital to have the stitches removed. There was little feeling in the area, however. The doctor had cautioned him not to expect too much, too soon. On Saturday night he broke away from his recent pattern of celibacy. Away from the routine that had voluntarily confined him to his apartment, he was feeling the high from the ephemeral audience he imagined had witnessed him at his best. He still luxuriated in their applause. He discovered a new lounge on Van Buren and 30th Street, captivated a sparkling young thing who fussed over him because of his injured hand.

In bed with her in the early morning hours on Sunday, he realized what a handicap it was not to be able to touch, fondle and grab with both hands. Putting pressure on the bad hand was out of the question. Resting over her on his elbows, awkward, and trying to lie on one side without use of the other hand, disconcerting. By backing her against the wall and holding up her left leg, he found that he could force himself into her without use of the bad hand. She clung to his neck feeling his hairy chest rubbing her breasts as his thrusting increased in tempo.

Suddenly pain shot through his bad hand as he unconsciously reached out to catch his balance. It was enough to reverse the peaking pleasure he was experiencing and stopped his movement.

"Come on, lover, don't let me down now."

His ego was at stake. He blocked out the pain in his mind and brought her all the way with him.

On Sunday he had remained in the apartment. He read the account of the discovery of Julia's body in the paper and marked the television news schedule. Switching channels in rapid succession, he managed to view coverage of the crime where programming overlapped. Even though his name didn't appear, he knew he was the star.

He pictured Benicki sitting in front of the TV in complete frustration. For a moment he sympathized with the man. He disliked failure himself. But the sympathy quickly reverted to the hatred for the man that had built day by day. The predictable sight of him, the challenges he had thrown out, the bombast in predicting his downfall, goaded Kimbal. From time to time, Benicki's threat of confinement still sent cold shudders through him.

This morning he had been surprised not to see Benicki's familiar face lurking somewhere. What upset him now was the tan colored sheriff car that fell in behind him as he left the office. What was going on? He thought it might be coincidental, but as it remained on his tail, he became annoyed. Why this all of a sudden? It spooked him.

The elation he had felt all day turned to depression by the time he reached the apartment and found Benicki parked there. He felt like a trapped animal. He fought the feeling. They didn't have a shred of evidence on which they could build a case. But he had the jitters. He hurried to his apartment.

When the early edition of the news came on he had already finished two beers. The news conference at the D.A.'s office knifed him. His idea of dividing and conquering, to have two separate police departments running their asses off into blind alleys, collapsed like a

215

house of cards. The D.A. was calling out the fuckin' army, navy, and marines. So that's why the sheriff car had followed him from work. They were all going to climb on his back. The whole goddamned stinking bunch of them.

On Tuesday the pressure increased. No matter where Kimball drove, on the job, or to and from work, there was always a law enforcement vehicle tailing him. When one dropped out of sight, another would pick him up. When he returned to the apartment around four, he found Benicki waiting for him with a warrant to search both the truck and the apartment. It also authorized Benicki to take him in for questioning.

Kimball's eyes darted around to see if there was any backup. There was.

The search failed to turn up anything that resembled the type of weapon that had been plunged into Julia's breast.

"What the fuck were you looking for?" he asked one of the officers.

Benicki supplied the answer. "The nails to nail down the lid on your box."

"Up yours!" snarled Kimball.

"OK. Let's go downtown. Would you follow me in your truck, please."

"That'll be a change. To follow you."

Kimball followed Benicki into the parking area behind police headquarters, then through the rear entry to the elevators by the lobby. Benicki pressed the button for the second floor.

"This way!" he said as he lead Kimball into room 242.

As they walked past the control desk the girl on duty pushed one of the numbers on a lighted panel to show that Benicki was back in.

"I need an interrogation room," he announced.

"The outer ones are occupied. The first two down the hall are vacant," he was informed.

"Down here!" said Benicki leading the way past a dozen work stations lined up next to one another where detectives could fill in their reports. Separated by a four-foot wide hall were two rooms. The door to the one on the right was open. Benicki stepped off to one side of the doorway.

"In here!" he ordered.

Kimball stopped in the doorway, hesitating.

"Sit down over there!"

Kimball stepped into the room and turned around as Benicki was about to close the door. "No! Leave it open!"

Benicki knew he wouldn't get anything out of Kimball if he shut the door. "OK, but sit down."

The room was 8' x 8'6". The suspended ceiling was slightly less than eight feet and contained an air conditioning vent and recessed lighting. A desk behind which Benicki now sat and one chair for the person being interviewed were all the furniture in the room. The metal-framed chairs were padded with vinyl cushioning, hard and uncomfortable. The severity of the room bespoke its purpose.

Benicki realized that Kimball was already uncomfortable.

"Why have you brought me here?" asked Kimball, his face getting moist.

"We're conducting an investigation into two recent deaths."

"What's that got to do with me?"

"You were formerly married to one of the victims.

217

Now, if you please for the record, what is your full legal name?"

Kimball decided that the quickest way to get out of here was to cooperate. "Edward V. Kimball."

"What does the V stand for?"

"Victor."

"What is your home address?"

"710 West Turney."

"Is that here in Phoenix?"

"Yes."

"How long have you lived in Arizona?"

He took a moment to answer. "Nine years."

"Where were you living before you came here?"

"New York."

"Would that be New York City?"

"Yes."

"Do you have any known relatives?"

"I have a son."

"What is his name?"

"Jeff."

"How old is Jeff?"

"Six."

"What is his mother's name?"

"While she was alive, Julia."

"When did Julia die?"

"Saturday according to the media."

"Would you disagree with the media?"

"How should I know?"

"If I told you that the coroner pinpointed her death occurring on Thursday afternoon instead of Saturday, what would you say?"

"I'm not qualified to differ with his opinion."

Benicki sat quietly while referring to his case file. He noticed that Kimball's eyes kept straying to the doorway, making sure in his mind that the door was still open. Drops of perspiration were, by this time, forming on his brow and he was wiping them off with his palm. Kimball knew what the next question would be and was prepared for it.

"Did you drive directly home from work last Thursday?"

"No."

"Where did you drive instead?"

"Yuma."

"Why would you drive to Yuma that late in the day?"

"I had business there."

"What kind of business?"

"I went to collect a debt."

"Who did you collect the debt from?"

"Mike Perez."

"Where can we contact Mike Perez?"

"On the construction job at the air base."

"Can you be more specific?"

"He wanders all over."

"Where did you meet with Perez?"

"Ernie's Bar."

"What time did you meet Perez?"

"Let's see. I left work around 3:30. I make Yuma in 3 -1/2 hours. I'd say close to seven."

"What did you do in Yuma?"

"Drank a couple of beers."

"Is that all?"

"I told you I went to collect a debt."

"What did you do after finishing the beers."

"Drove home. Had to work the next morning."

"What time did you arrive?"

"Oh, 11:30 or so."

"Anybody see you?"

"Yeh. The manager stuck his head out."

Benicki had gotten the information he needed regarding Thursday. The next step would be to verify it.

"I guess that's all I need at the moment. Thank you for coming down."

"Big deal!" said Kimball getting up and stretching. Christ! It was good to get out of there.

The D.A. decided that it would be a good idea if the investigating officers attended the funeral of Julia Hochstetter. Not only to show by their presence a sign of support to the family members, but also to publicize their unity of purpose.

Roger Hochstetter decided on a chapel which served the Sun City area. The grief he and his wife were experiencing had sapped their strength. Actually it was Scott Harrison who had suggested this, realizing that the day of the service would add extra stress.

The chapel was filled with flowers and on the closed casket lay a single red rose. This was from Jeff. Betty Hochstetter had told him that his mother was asked to visit God. Both she and his mother had taught Jeff something about God and his son, Jesus. Jeff wasn't quite sure what to make of it all, but he had great faith in whatever his mother and grandmother told him about God. His grandfather also talked about God, or rather to God, when they bowed their heads at mealtime. It was strange to Jeff, that his father never did. Sometime he'd have to ask, why?

Benicki, De Morro and Abe Clinton drove together and were talking quietly in the larger reception room of the memorial chapel. Suddenly Benicki stopped in the middle of a sentence and stood open mouthed. The others turned to see what he was looking at. Ed Kimball was dressed in dark blue slacks, a blue short sleeved shirt with a dark blue tie.

He was the last person in the world Benicki would have expected to see here. He marveled at the man's unmitigated gall. If by appearing he was out to convince those who knew better of his innocence, he was having the contrary effect. Both De Morro and Clinton shook their heads in disapproval. They watched as he went into the chapel. Most of the others had already seated themselves. The music had been played softly in the background. A few seats remained empty. Clinton moved to a single seat and Benicki and De Morro managed to find seats together.

To one side at the front of the chapel was the private area for the family of the deceased. The elder Hochstetters had come in unnoticed. From his vantage point, Benicki noticed Jeff trying to see who all the people were in the main room. Suddenly he spotted his father. The music was now being played even softer and coming to an end since the minister from Hochstetter's church had taken his place at the podium.

"Daddy! Daddy! We're in here," this high-pitched voice called out.

All eyes turned in the direction of the child who was standing by his seat. Most of the people couldn't see him. Roger Hochstetter held onto Jeff's arm trying to quiet him and get the boy to sit down again, but Jeff resisted his effort.

"Come, daddy! Sit with me!" he cried out insistently.

Edward Victor Kimball rose from his seat, and hugging the wall, made his way up the aisle as swiftly and quietly as possible to the boy's side.

The service began.

There were few dry eyes during the service. When the minister gave his benediction and closed the service, most people left. Those closest to the family remained.

The day after the funeral Karl Benicki got off to an early start. Liz had asked about the funeral, and he had told her about Jeff calling out to his father. She couldn't help laughing picturing the scene. After all, as she told Karl, how was a six year old to know. Even though there had been a recent divorce, his father was still his father and he naturally wanted to be near him.

As he drove along I-10, the large correction facility in Litchfield Park reminded him of his promise to lock Kimball up so tight that fresh air would never reach him. He had carefully observed the man during the interview at headquarters. His hesitation in entering the room, his insisting the door remain open, and even with that the beads of perspiration that formed on his brow, the tension that had built up during that short period. The sigh of relief when the interview ended. The way Kimball stretched to relieve his tension. None of this had escaped him as he wrote down his notes after the interview.

He turned off at the Gila Bend exit which would lead to Interstate 8. In Gila Bend he stopped for breakfast. By quarter of six Benicki was on his way again. The early morning hours at this time of year appealed to him. There was a freshness to the desert air that was the harbinger of cooler days. Soon the mornings would be crisp, daytime temperatures mild and comfortable. The past weeks had been anything but that. If all went well, he planned to take Holly out for lunch tomorrow. He had stopped by the previous day to see how she was coming along. Three weeks had passed since Kimball had struck her. The discoloration was almost gone. She was in high spirits.

"I'm thinking of going back to work right after this weekend."

"Are you sure that's what you want to do?"

"Don't be silly, Karl. Of course. It's a job and I need a little more material for that book. Besides, I might want to spend Christmas in England. Wouldn't that be neat?"

"Sounds like fun. Why England? Why not Paris, or maybe the Mediterranean? Rome, perhaps."

"I've been reading Dickens. Old stone buildings hundreds of years old. Fireplaces and the smell of burning logs. Hot toddy. Reminds me of home."

"You've never said anything, Holly. Don't you have family you'd like to spend Christmas with?"

"I have, back east. Providence. My father owns a large manufacturing company making auto parts for all the majors. You know, that chrome trim around the windows?"

"That's quite a business, I'm sure."

"Mother's into all kinds of charities. She's always had time for them, but as for me, what was it? Boarding school. Miss Jane's finishing school. Then off to college. I've always been on my own."

"Didn't your father have time for you either?"

"When I was little he used to play with me. We had wonderful times together. But then later, he seemed almost afraid to come near me, to touch me."

She laughed. "I guess he had a Freudean hang-up. I blossomed out at an early age. Maybe he was afraid

223

he might become aroused if he held me close or kissed me."

"Do you ever see them?"

"I rented a car and drove up for a few days when I returned from Venice."

"How'd it go?"

"Lousy, if you'll excuse the expression. It was what we used to say in finishing school, the pits. You'd have to know my parents. Their ancestors came over on the Mayflower and all that garbage. You'd think they were still decked out in their Pilgrim hats and bonnets and starched white collars. They felt a young woman, especially their daughter, shouldn't be gallivanting around overseas by herself. Unchaperoned, as it were. They don't seem to realize that their little baby girl is now twenty-four."

"What do they think of your dancing?"

"You must be kidding, Karl."

"Would they have a fit?"

"Mother would die and daddy would go to an early grave." She started giggling.

"What's so funny?"

"I was thinking I might provide entertainment at one of mother's charities or at one of daddy's smokers."

Karl joined in on her laughter. Holly was indeed a mischievous pixie.

"What have you told them?"

"That I do public relations. Well, I do!" she added defensively.

There had been serious talk as well. Karl described the funeral service.

"Was Ed embarrassed?"

"I'm sure he must have been."

Holly kissed his cheek when he had to leave.

The drive to Yuma went quicker than he had anticipated. Even the construction detours caused no delay. When he reached the air base he explained to the guard at the main gate what his problem was. He only knew the man's name, that he was involved with the new construction that was going on.

They gave him directions to a new hanger and repair facility to the south of existing buildings. It was already 7:30 and construction crews were hard at work. Cranes and heavy equipment were moving huge precast concrete panels into place. He stopped at the construction checkpoint. Benicki showed his badge.

"I'm looking for Mike Perez."

"See that fellow there with the blueprints?" he pointed. "That's Mike."

"Thanks."

"You can't go in there without a hard hat. Regulations. Park your car over there," he pointed. "I'll get you a lid."

Benicki looked like any of the other supervisory personnel when he approached Perez.

"Mike Perez?"

"Be with you in a minute," he said. He was still going over the blueprints with the worker standing next to him. He rolled up the prints and turned them over to the man. He turned around and spotted the gun in Benicki's belt. His first thought was that the Feds had caught up with him. After all he'd been ripping off government property. He cleared his throat. There was a hint of nervousness in the man's voice now that hadn't been there while he was talking with the construction worker. The nervousness didn't escape Benicki.

"You looking for me?"

"I'd like to ask you a few questions."

"Who are you?"

Benicki pulled out his badge and noticed the man's expression of apparent relief when he said, "I'm Detective Benicki of the Phoenix Police Department."

"What do you want of me?"

"Are you a friend of Ed Kimball?"

"He's no friend, but I know him."

"Do you see him often?"

"He's been down here a few times. Why?"

"When did you last see him?"

"Christ! How should I know?"

"Was it in the last couple of days?"

"No."

"How about a week ago? Last Thursday?"

"Could have been."

"If I told you that Kimball said he saw you last Thursday, what would you say?"

"Guess it must have been."

"Did he tell you he was coming?"

"No."

"He didn't phone in advance?"

"No. He just showed up."

"How would he know you'd be here?"

"I'm here during the week."

"Where did the two of you meet?"

"He came to the bar."

"Which bar?"

"Ernie's."

"That where you usually hang out?"

"Most of the time."

"What time did Kimball meet you?"

"Seven."

"You're positive?"

"Why all these questions?"

"We're investigating a homicide."

"You mean Kimball's dead?"

There seemed to be a note of relief in his voice.

"On the contrary. He's very much alive."

Benicki paused to observe his reaction. His face had lit up with the thought that Kimball was dead. Now he frowned. He continued his interrogation.

"Are you sure of the time?"

"Yes."

"When you weren't sure of the day you met, how come you're so certain of the exact time."

"I just know."

"What did the two of you do?"

"Drank a couple of beers."

"Then Kimball left?"

"That's right."

"What time was that?"

"Eight."

"You're sure of that, too, are you?"

"You're damn right!"

"Do you want me to believe that a man drives all the way from Phoenix to have a couple of beers and then turns right around?"

"That's what he did."

"Why would he do that? Any special reason?"

"He came to see me."

"A social visit? You said you weren't friends."

"He collected a debt," said Perez angrily.

Benicki mulled over the interview as he drove back to Phoenix. There were a number of points that were particularly noteworthy.

First, there was his uncertainty of the day of the

week, yet the positiveness of the exact time of Kimball's arrival. Next, he had noticed the man's relief at the thought that Kimball was dead, which was immediately replaced by a worried look on learning that he was very much alive. It appeared that Kimball had something on him. Blackmail? Apparently that was the answer. Furthermore, if Kimball had come down to collect a debt and had been paid off, then Perez wouldn't owe him anything. But this was a remote possibility. He doubted that this debt had anything to do with money. If a debt were to be repaid, arrangements would have been made. You'd call Perez and tell him you were coming down, to have the money ready. No man in his right mind would carry a bankroll into a bar night after night waiting for someone to come in to collect.

There was a final flaw in what Perez had said. The two beers. How long does it take to drink two beers? He had done it on numerous occasions. A half hour was a reasonable time. Yet, Perez had testified that Kimball had left at eight. That was probably the truth. But taking half an hour away, that made the time they started drinking seven-thirty. Not seven. From the expression on Perez' face at the first mention of Kimball, there wasn't any love lost. They wouldn't stand at the bar if they didn't have anything to talk about. There had also been that fleeting sneer of contempt at the mention of Kimball collecting the debt. That, too, would suggest dealing with a blackmailer.

Shortly after eleven, Benicki was back in his office. He quickly typed up a record of the interview and went in to talk with Ben McKenzie.

"I wouldn't be surprised if they've been ripping off the government," summarized Benicki.

"Kimball's company is one of the suppliers. What if Kimball has looked the other way?"

"Sure! That would give him a hold over Perez."

"I'd fear a man who could send me to the pen."

"It all fits. I'd like to see a warrant issued to look into Perez' bank account. If he's smart it won't show up there, but if he finds there's pressure on him, he might come up with something. If he's been covering for Kimball, I want to know about it."

"I'll get on it right away, Karl. With the Labor Day weekend coming up, you may have to wait till Tuesday."

"Can't be helped."

After downing a fast-food lunch, Benicki drove to Kimball's apartment and knocked on the manager's door.

"Yes, Mr. Detective?" asked Marge.

"Is your husband around?"

"David's downstairs here in A-4 cleaning up after a tenant. You won't be bothering him."

"Thank you."

The door to the vacant apartment was open and he walked towards the noise of the vacuum cleaner in the bedroom. The manager saw him and shut off the motor.

"More problems with B-6?"

"I have a question."

"What is it?"

"You told me you know pretty much what goes on here. Who's in, who's out. Is that right?"

"I try."

"How good's your memory about last Thursday?"

"A week ago?"

"A whole week."

"What should I remember?"

"What time did Kimball come home that night? He claims you saw him."

He stood stiffly with one hand on top of the other leaning on the upright Hoover.

"Think!"

He lifted his head smiling. "Sure! I remember. I thought it was those kids again. I went outside to chase them."

"Was it?"

"No. It was him. He was leaning on the horn."

"Was he drunk?"

"He walked OK"

"Was it an accidental beep?"

"No. He held it long enough for me to come out. He must have woken all the tenants."

"What time was it?"

"Eleven thirty. I was on my way to bed."

Why was it so important for Kimball to establish the time of his return to Phoenix? He had to account for the hours he had been away. The travel time from Yuma to Phoenix, would make his departure from Yuma eight o'clock. Backtracking, if he arrived at 7:30, he would have left Phoenix around four.

That would have given him half an hour to go from work to the house in Scottsdale, kill his wife, and reach Yuma in time to establish an alibi. That's all Perez was. An alibi. That was the debt he had collected.

It all fit, now. The man was more clever than he had credited him to be. Benicki had thought of him as a wife beating brute of untold savagery. A sadist with an uncontrollable temper. He had never considered him as having a devious criminal mind as well. At the same time it fitted in with his personality. If he had an affinity for playing the roll of Hamlet or Macbeth, of course he would plot carefully and well.

Somehow he felt a new sense of urgency. If Kimball's mind had planned so well, he would also have taken into account contingencies. Had he considered that, if an investigation into Perez' affairs showed that he had been ripping off Uncle Sam, and the F.B.I. prosecuted, he wouldn't give a damn what Kimball held over him? Kimball would be holding an empty gun to his head. If Perez blew the fuse on the time alibi, what then? How could he be sure that evidence linking him to the killing might not be turned up by one of the crime labs? He couldn't. Then he'd have to be ready with another alibi to save his neck. But what? He went into Ben's office again.

"There's no way of getting a warrant to wrap things up tomorrow, is there?" asked Benicki.

"I'm pressing, but I doubt it. Why the sudden urgency?"

"I've got a hunch that something will go wrong. Pit of my stomach. You know the feeling."

"What did you have for lunch?"

"Grabbed something on the run."

"That's your problem, Karl. Indigestion," he laughed. Nobody's going to run away. We've got a long reach."

"You're right as usual, Ben. Guess that's why you're sitting there, as you keep reminding me."

He spent the rest of the afternoon routinely, then parked in the usual space. When Kimball arrived he could see from the man's expression that the sham cockiness and bravado while answering questions during the interrogation, was once more replaced by hatred.

Like a wild caged animal always being prodded by a sharpened stick, those eyes told it all. At the first opportunity it would claw its keeper to death. He watched the body language as Kimball walked by. The tension was showing. Benicki knew that surveillance was now constant by the combined efforts of the law enforcement agencies. How long would it be before there'd be a flaw in his scheming? What would it take to break the man?

Benicki knew it would be a question of time. A time of patient waiting. Watching. Criminals never knew when an investigation came to an end, only to be suddenly reopened as an ongoing investigation when a shred of evidence came to light. The circumstantial evidence was building. Only a few more pieces could bring it before a grand jury and a possible indictment.

PART XII

Ed Kimball didn't know what to do when Jeff called out to him. He hoped Jeff's grandfather would quiet him down and that would be the end of it. When attention was focused on him again, he had no choice but to move forward. He felt the two hundred pairs of eyes bearing down on him. It was as if he were carrying a heavy pack up a steep grade, even though he moved up the aisle swiftly and quietly.

Jeff shifted over to make room for him, gave him a big smile. He couldn't help but notice the icy stares of Jeff's grandparents. They conveyed the message - *'how dare you defile this day? We know how you abused our daughter'*. They knew nothing of fun escapades spent in bed all weekend, of smoke rings, of golden moments shared together. Fuck them! They were Hochstetters, stuffy old farts. Rigid and stiff like his cock with a hard on.

The small hand thrust into his made him forget the grandparents sitting on the other side of Jeff. The minister's voice was mellow but firm. He spoke about Julia as a warm and lovely person whose capacity for growth was unlimited. A loving daughter, a mother of a handsome, bright son who could forever be proud of her. A devoted wife who had recently experienced the trying time of a divorce. 'Bullshit!' thought Kimball. The only 'trying' was to stick it to him.

As the minister continued, sniffles could be plainly heard in the audience. Those who had been close friends wept openly. Even persons whose lives had only been casually touched be hers, couldn't remain dry-eyed.

Betty Hochstetter was quietly sobbing. The cushioned pew was quivering with her emotions. Her husband's eyes were tearful but he kept his head erect stoically. Jeff patted his grandmother's arm, leaned over and whispered,

"It's OK, grandma. Mommy's with God."

She tried a halfhearted smile and took his hand.

Jeff looked content. He had his dad on one side and grandma on the other.

The Hochstetters had spent a brief time at the chapel the day before when friends came by to pay their respects and sign the memorial keepsake. When the service ended and soft music cradled the people's voices, Jeff's grandparents prepared to leave.

"Come, Jeff," said his grandfather.

"In a minute," he answered and before his grandfather could say anything, he tugged on his dad's arm. "I want to show you."

He led him to the casket, reached up and removed the rose. "This is from me."

"It's beautiful," said his father.

"Do you know where Mommy's going?"

"To heaven."

"That's where God is. Mommy told me that."

"She's right, Jeff. She's going to be with God."

"Do you know much about God?"

"I know he watches over little boys like you."

"Did he watch over Mommy, too?"

"I'm sure he did."

"Well, how come she's going to him then, if he's been watching over her?"

"I guess...."

He didn't have a chance to finish what he was about to say. Jeff's grandmother took him by the arm and led him away. As he was being ushered out, he turned towards his father, "See you!"

Kimball walked to his truck where he had parked in the street. He hadn't paid attention to the eulogy except for the part that referred to the recent divorce. He felt sorry for his son. Remorse was foreign to his makeup, but for a few moments he had regretted what he had done. He had betrayed his son. When he drove off, that instance of compassion reverted to anger and frustration. When, for Christ's sake, would they stop? A sheriff car was following as usual. Didn't they have any respect? She had been his wife. He was coming from her funeral. Couldn't they see he was distraught?

He had arranged for the day off.

"Sure," said Mel, "you go ahead. Sorry about your wife."

All the guys at work had been sorry when they heard of her murder.

"I hope they fry the guy in hell!" is how Mel Greer had put it.

Mark had figured there was some fuckin' nut running around loose who seemed to be cutting notches in the handle of his six-shooter. "I wonder how many more he's going to knock off."

"What makes you think it's one guy doing the killings?" asked Ed.

"Some of the guys were talking."

"How come you didn't cut me in?"

"Jeese, you were married to one of them. We figured you wouldn't want to talk about it and get upset."

"What'd the guys figure out?"

"It must be the same guy who's knocked off two people in the same company. Maybe he's got it in for the owner. Maybe he got a bad rap on some real estate deal. Who knows? If it's got nothing to do with this particular outfit, well, shit, there are lots of other companies in the valley. He might as well thin out their ranks, spread his stuff around, if he's got it in for real estate agents in general. Maybe the guy has a license and got fired for some reason. You hear about guys all the time who go back with a loaded gun and start shooting up the place. It doesn't matter who they kill just as long as they're getting their beef off their chest. Or a guy will set the place on fire. They get their kicks in all kinds of goofy ways. Know what I mean? Whoever this guy is, though, he must be way out there. The way he cut into your wife. Oh, Christ! man. I didn't mean to mention that. Sorry!"

Kimball didn't feel like going home. It was early yet and he didn't relish going back to the apartment. The place was starting to close in on him. He wanted to forget the whole damn business. Maybe a flick. When he drove past Cine Capri where he had met Julia before they started running around together, he didn't like what they were showing. Sentimental garbage. Who'd want to see that? Behind him now was a Phoenix Police car.

"Fuckin' bastard! Get off my back!" he shouted as he drove. Weren't they going to let up?

He drove past all the new office construction that was inundating Camelback Road. Far ahead of him loomed the hump of the camel against the bright blue sky. The Praying Monk rock formation on the north slope, shining in the afternoon sun, caught his eye. "You'd better pray, mister. Pray for this fuckin' town. If these cocksucker cops don't get off my back, I swear it'll be a hot day in hell."

Fuckin' and cocksucking. That was it. He drove to Scottsdale, left the truck in the public parking area and walked over to one of the adult theaters. He got himself a large container of popcorn as he entered.

Benicki woke with a start during the night. He had

been hanging in between sleeping, dreaming, and thinking. The frustration of the case was getting to him. The thing that troubled him the most was the feeling that time would run out soon if he couldn't put the necessary pieces together. All at the same time, Perez, Kimball, Jeff, McKenzie, were vying for his attention in his dozing state. Each was crying out to be heard.

"To collect a debt."

"While she was alive, Julia."

"Daddy! Daddy! We're in here."

"That's your problem, Karl. Indigestion."

He looked at Liz. She was sound asleep. Thank God for Liz. She looked so beautiful even in the turquoise blue light emitted by the digital clock on the bedside table. Quietly he slid out of bed and went into the kitchen. He was now wide awake.

Overhead a police helicopter made a sweep above the sleeping city. The kitchen clock said three. Three o'clock. A crime statistic showed a high percentage of violent crime occurring around this time. Why? Bars closed? People milling around? Arguments? Violence? One thing leading to another?

Like Kimball. Stages. Anne Pearson killed by mistake. This in turn leading to Julia Hochstetter's death. Leading to what? That's what he was afraid of. That sinking feeling Ben had called indigestion. It was getting to him. No doubt about that.

He put water on and stood staring at the kettle till the water started to boil. He made tea and sat down at the kitchen table. As he bobbed the tea bag up and down, he tried to sort his cluttered thoughts. Words began to associate as he kept an eye on what he was doing. Tea. Caffeine. Stimulant. Drugs. Doctor. Charlie

Blake. Autopsy. Julia. Julia? Reflexes?

Charlie had found nothing in her system that would have slowed her reflexes. That was in the written report. Why would that have been important if she knew the person confronting her? She had no reason to believe that she was about to be killed.

He took the tea bag and dropped it onto the saucer. The hot tea tasted good.

The killer was waiting for her in the family room. There was no sign of a struggle. He hadn't chased her. The lab people had scrutinized every inch of the room, almost microscopically. He must have been hiding behind the half opened doors. De Morro had interviewed Jean Schaeffer who was showing the house to the Edlys. According to her statement, she found the family room doors swung back to make a 45° angle to the wall. Plenty of space for the killer to stand behind either door.

In his mind he pictured the photographs taken, the sketch of the floor plan showing the position of the body in relationship to the room. The room was approximately 28' x 20'. On the right hand wall, when Jean Schaeffer entered, the fireplace was centered in twelve feet of gray-black lava rocks flanked on either side by four foot wide bookcases. The doors from the living room were off center in the family room to allow for a wet bar to the left of the doorway. Directly across from the fireplace wall, windows and French doors overlooked a large patio. The entire area had adjustable shutters that blocked out light and permitted privacy. The wall opposite the entry was paneled to allow for a large built-in television, high fidelity equipment and multi-use storage. A family room in the true sense of the word for fun and hobbies. A door near the fireplace wall led to the kitchen area.

   With the layout clear in his mind, he assumed the roll of the killer. If he couldn't make use of his left hand, he'd have to position himself behind the door to the left. The one by the wet bar. The killer heard the front door being unlocked. There were two ways the intended victim could enter the family room. Through the kitchen or directly from the living room. He imagined Julia crossing the tiled entry and continuing into the kitchen. Would he hear her steps on the tiled kitchen floor? He didn't. She had set her things down for the moment. He imagined her walking down the hall and listened to her steps on the tile. Then quiet. She must now be in the living room. Why isn't she coming in here? Oh! She's adjusting the shutters in there. I can hear her. Her next move will be to come into the family room Why didn't she come in here directly? Wouldn't this be a better place to leave her papers? Place them on the wet bar? Wasn't this the room for fun and games? Why let people talk business in the kitchen? That meant nothing but work, no matter how much somebody enjoyed cooking. Preparation? Cleaning up dirty dishes and pots used in preparing the meal? Polishing silverware and crystal glasses? Making up menus and ordering from the store? Everything's quiet again. The soft carpeting must be cushioning the sound as before. She's bound to come into the family room to open up the shutters. Isn't that what Jean Schaeffer was doing when Jennifer Edly followed into the room and screamed? Benicki imagined it all.

   Jean Schaeffer was lucky. The killer wasn't waiting for her. What about the victim? She steps into the room. I step out from behind the door. She stops in her tracks and asks what I'm doing here. In that split second of her indecision I grab her neck with my good hand and push. She steps back to escape the pressure of my hand. A half dozen steps brings her in front of the fireplace wall. Her right foot strikes the front edge of the hearth throwing her off balance backwards. As her body tips I push hard. Her head makes contact with the wall. In rapid succession I continue to bang her head against the rock. Even as her body sags I use all my strength to prevent it. Then her body is limp and I let go. She slumps to the floor in a sitting position. I have to make sure she's dead. I stab her again and again.

Benicki leaned back in his chair not realizing how close to the truth he had pictured it. The lab people stated that the killer had wiped the blade off on her skirt. The bloody imprint showed the weapon to be a standard hunting knife, the type commonly sold in a leather sheath with a strap that fastened across the handle with a metal snap. A five inch blade, one inch across at the widest area, pointed towards the top of an arc. The type sportsmen wore on their belts.

The knife was Benicki's trump card. A lie detector test would determine whether or not Kimball had owned and used a knife of this type. But there was more ground to cover before that. Kimball, he knew for a certainty, wouldn't voluntarily undergo one.

The mental exercise he had put himself through stimulated him. He wasn't tired in the least. After closing the bedroom door he turned on the television to watch, of all things, a rerun of the Ironside series.

Liz ambled over to him. The alarm clock set for 7 had wakened her. Karl was snoozing in his recliner in front of the TV. The Today program was in progress. She bent over and kissed his cheek. He tilted his head and opened his eyes.

"Hello, lover," she said. "Since when have you taken to separate bedrooms?"

He smiled back. "Since you started snoring."

"I snore?" she asked in a concerned voice.

He laughed. "I woke up. Too much thinking going on. Figured I might as well stay up. Guess I didn't make it."

"Tell you what we'll do this weekend."

"What?"

"Absolutely nothing. How does that fit you?"

"Like a glove."

Benicki stuck his head into McKenzie's office. "Anything?"

"Mid afternoon's the best they could come up with. Too late to do any good today. You'll have your hot little hands on all the legal tools to do the job. Tell you what, go down Monday night. The department will pick up the motel room and expenses. You'll get an early start on Tuesday."

"I'll buy that!"

"Thought you would."

At mid morning he phoned Holly to confirm their tentative luncheon date.

"You thought you might have to go out of town."

"Postponed till Monday night. Can you join me?"

"Love to."

"I'll pick you up at eleven thirty. Try to beat the crowd."

The Town and Country Shopping Center consists of 68 assorted businesses under a rambling Spanish tile roof complex at the corner of 20th Street and Camelback Road. By the approach to the northeast parking area stands the Black Angus restaurant. Clad in old weathered planks, that designers had also utilized on the interior decor in conjunction with lofty timbers, there was a feeling of spaciousness and quiet dignity. Despite the rustic look, it was anything but a cow town stomping place. The mood was intimate. The bar and cocktail tables near the entry overlooked a stage where groups of talented musicians provided nightly entertainment and dancing. When Benicki and Holly entered, couples were already lined up. The hostess was taking down names. It was first come, first serve.

When Benicki moved to the head of the line he gave his name and showed his badge. "I've got a heavy schedule. Appreciate anything you can do."

Five minutes later his name was called out.

Holly squeezed his arm. "Rank has privileges," she said with a laugh.

"You'd better believe it."

They were seated in a horseshoe-shaped booth with comfortable upholstered cushions and backs of heather-colored striped material that extended to a height of seven feet. The corners of the booth were curved gently so that additional guests could be seated comfortably. Overhead lighting was suspended from the heavy timbers crisscrossing the vaulted ceiling. On their table a candle flame flickered in an amber glass cylinder. Across from them were smaller tables separated from others by heavy plate glass that allowed conversational privacy, yet prevented them from becoming cubicles. Intimate, but open.

The waitress came over. "Cocktails?"

"Let's celebrate," said Benicki.

"OK. Daiquiri."

"Dry Martini. Beefeaters. Onion."

"What are we celebrating?" she asked.

"Your recovery. When I first saw what he had done I thought you'd never be the same. But now, if at all possible, you're more beautiful than ever."

"Aren't you sweet. If I didn't know you so well I'd think you were making a pass at me."

"If circumstances were different, I would have long ago."

"That's flattering."

"You've decided to go back to the club?"

"I start Tuesday."

"How did you get started anyway? I don't believe I ever asked you."

"You mean you didn't see me pirouetting around in my ballet slippers in Swan Lake when I was ten?"

The waitress brought their drinks. She told them what the luncheon specials were and they ordered.

"Hold up for a little," he suggested.

"I'll bring your salads when you finish the drinks."

"Here's to my handsome prince," she pouted her lips in a kiss to him.

"How long did you stick with ballet lessons?"

"Till I was fourteen. Then I quit."

"Why?"

"I think I told you about daddy. That he must have been afraid to get too close to me. That's what happened. I developed. You've never seen a ballerina," she lowered her voice to a whisper, "with teats like mine. Have you?"

"What I've missed in life," he said in a scholarly voice.

"In all seriousness, I'm sure you never have. They're mostly skinny and tend to be small breasted.

There's nothing wrong with that. But I'm the way I am and that's all there is to it."

"I can assure you, Holly, you're one of God's more masterful creations."

"Why is it the right guys are always the married ones."

"Guess that keeps us out of trouble."

They both laughed.

Benicki was of the Catholic faith, but he never associated a certain type of food with the day of the week. He didn't care if he ate fish on Friday, or beef, or anything else. Food was food. Provided by the Creator for people to eat. In moderation, of course. He didn't believe in gluttony. Since the day he was assigned the Pearson case he hadn't been to the gym. Weight lifting for the moment was replaced by weightier problems.

Holly had ordered thin slices of steak in teriyaki sauce, with wild rice and asparagus spears. His order, a rare New York steak with asparagus. 'No potatoes' he had specified. He did, however, join her over desert. New York cheese cake with strawberries. Black coffee.

They talked about many things. She asked how he and Liz had met. He told her about Vietnam and his early days with the police force. Except for Benicki referring to what Kimball had done to her face, they didn't talk about the case at all. Benicki had wanted to show his appreciation for the Eggs Benedict and her hospitality at other meetings.

The Benickis had done absolutely nothing over the long weekend exactly as Liz had suggested. Except for church and brunch on Sunday, it was theirs to enjoy in any way they wished. Karl had surprised Liz by his rummaging around and finding a carton that contained a ship model he had started a few years before, but had never completed.

"Well, look at you."

He smiled as he unpacked the carton on the kitchen table.

"What brought all this about out of the blue?"

"Thought I should try to finish this."

"Well this weekend's a good time to start. Have fun." She kissed him on the forehead.

In no time at all he was engrossed gluing small parts. Strong hands worked delicately. What had spurred this sudden interest was the face of a small boy reaching up for a rose to show what he had given his mother. Maybe Jeff would like to have this ship model in his room someday.

Benicki drove carefully and defensively on his way to Yuma. He was in no hurry. The secretary in his office on Friday had confirmed a reservation at the Quality Inn. He had timed his departure from Phoenix to arrive sometime before ten. At the second detour for road construction a semi and a car collided. Traffic was halted in both directions. Because of the slower speed zone, the driver of the car wasn't killed. A lucky case of D.W.I. It took more than an hour to clear the road and by the time Benicki arrived in Yuma it was after eleven. He put in a call for six, showered and went to sleep.

The sky was overcast in the morning. Dense clouds hugged the mountains to the north. An occasional streak of lightning flashed through the gray backdrop. "Is it going to rain?" he asked the waitress.

"Probably. They had a bad one up north a way last night. Lots of flooding from what I heard."

By seven thirty Benicki was once again at the construction checkpoint.

The man recognized him. "You're not looking for Perez, I hope."

"In fact, I am."

"Didn't you catch the news last night?"

"I was on my way down here."

"He got killed yesterday. Their plane went down in the storm."

Benicki realized his intuition wasn't indigestion as McKenzie had suggested. Kimball's alibi couldn't be refuted.

"Where was he coming from?"

"Used to fly up to Las Vegas almost every weekend. Him and those other two. Jeese, we have to replace three superintendents. They must have been rolling the dice pretty good up there. Never seemed to need their pay checks."

Benicki found himself talking with a naive but honest man.

"Thanks!"

"Too bad you came all this way for nothing."

McKenzie found the news hard to believe. "I'm sorry, Karl. Real sorry."

Benicki touched base with De Morro. "Anything at all, John?"

"Nothing on the Hochstetter case. We may get a break on the Binder case. Some guy answering the wanted man's description, tried to use one of the stolen credit cards in Atlanta. They've got everybody from the F.B.I. down looking for him. Maybe we'll get lucky. How about you?"

Benicki told him about Perez.

"Shit! That blows another lead."

"You think you've got something," said Benicki, " and it blows up in your face."

It was raining when Benicki saw the light blue pickup drive up. Since early afternoon, the storm that had downed the plane in Blythe had moved into the valley. He had learned the details of the crash through the Transportation Department's Aeronautic Division. The plane had apparently suffered wind damage to the controls and in trying to make a forced landing had struck a power line. The plane's occupants had died in the resulting fire.

He watched Kimball head up the stairs.

"Christ! You again? I wish the hell you'd get out of my hair."

"I was down in Yuma to talk with your friend."

Kimball laughed.

"Yeh! I heard about him. How lucky can a guy get?"

"Yes. I am lucky."

"You?"

"Sure. Your alibi went up in smoke. There's nobody to say you weren't right here. In fact, I'll pinpoint where you were. In a certain house in Scottsdale."

"You're fuckin' crazy."

"You say you'd like me to back off. Frankly I'd like to close out both cases."

"What do you mean both cases?"

"Anne Pearson and Julia Hochstetter. I don't have to tell you."

"If you guys don't stop hassling me, I'll file a complaint through my attorney. That'll shut you up for good."

"I'll make a bargain with you." His voice was calm

and free from any indication of hostility. "As I said, I'd like to wrap it up. Why don't I arrange for you to take a lie detector test? If you've got nothing to hide. "

He didn't have a chance to finish.

"You can shove it up your ass! Now get out of my way!" He raised his left hand to motion Benicki to stand aside as he stormed by. The door was slammed louder than ever before.

The left hand? The bandage was gone. Even the strips of adhesive gauze that protected the skin in the final healing stages were gone. Benicki wondered how much use he had of the hand. There was nothing to do except keep the pressure on the man, ever mindful not to overstep the fine line that could justify a complaint of harassment.

He rarely took a case file home, but tonight he studied all the documentation. It was well after midnight before he set it all aside and went to bed. He was stymied for the moment but felt there'd be a break in the case. Investigative work was mostly patient digging, but sometimes there was a bit of luck involved.

Kimball spent a miserable long weekend. The depressed feeling started closing in on him by Saturday. When he had driven home from the porno film on Thursday, a Scottsdale Police car trailed him. No matter where he drove it was always the same now.

This Friday before the Labor Day weekend was more of the same. They were slowly driving him mad. He had never felt so tense, nor hated so vehemently. The good thing this day was not seeing Benicki. He knew he hadn't seen the last of the man. As certain as death itself. Alone in the apartment with a paper bag full of liquor he had picked up on the way, he got himself stinking drunk and lay around the apartment all day on Saturday. On Sunday he had to break and run. He couldn't take it anymore. The walls were closing in. He drove north on the freeway. For a time, a sheriff car followed a quarter of a mile behind him. Then the car took an exit ramp.

This was the answer. Get away as far as possible. He drove through Black Canyon City and eventually took the Bumble Bee exit towards Crown King. Away from the highway on a gravel road he could breath again. It wound down a gentle slope. Lush desert plants were everywhere. The air seemed cooler and fresher, free from the pollution that hovered over the city. Spread out before him the mountains loomed majestically, towering over Horse Thief Basin.

He found a place to park and got out. The rocks in front of him dropped down some fifty feet to Turkey Creek which was dry except for a few small pools of water. A small brown rodent drank nervously as a hawk circled overhead. Kimball stretched and let the fresh air fill his lungs. Suddenly the hawk swooped down and clutched the squeaking rodent in its talons. Kimball felt fear. It somehow reminded him of Benicki. Benicki intended to do the same. Swoop down on him. He tried to shrug off the feeling and almost succeeded. It was only a short while since he had pulled off the highway, but overhead he heard a familiar clop, clop sound. He glanced in the direction of the sound and spotted the police helicopter that was swooping closer in circular flight. He could now see their faces. He felt like the rodent, looking desperately for a place to hide, but unable to escape the dive of the hawk. In sudden panic he ran, stopping abruptly in time to prevent a fatal fall.

He turned in their direction waving his arms frantically and shouting invectives. One more swooping pass and they headed south. With a bottle in his hand he continued shouting every oath and filthy invective he had ever learned on the streets of New York. They echoed from the rocks into the hidden caves and canyons. They spilled into the dry washes and the reflecting pools ever hidden from the direct sunlight. It proved nothing, but it unleashed the tension that had been holding him tied down to the medieval rack while the inquisitor turned the ratchet one more stop.

Kimball was oblivious to the chill of the night air. Sunrise found him stretched out once more on the vinyl seat. The morning temperature was far lower than it had been near the McDowell Indian Reservation some eight weeks before. When the sun reached down the slope and he awoke, his mouth was dry. His mind was clear, but his muscles were cramped from the night-time chill here in the Bradshaw Mountains, where prospectors in the 1880s had torn gold out of these gullies with their bare hands.

His anger had left him and as the sun rose in the sky and noontime temperature heated the rocks, his mind was made up as to what he had to do. Like the lonely prospector with his burro, he too, felt alone in the world at the moment. Everybody was against him. Survival was up to him and he was determined to survive.

Kimball was in no hurry to return to Phoenix. What little remained in the last bottle he drank down, holding it to get the last drop. In the distance to the northwest heavy clouds gathered. He watched the bolts of lightning as they streaked downwards behind the mountains. The wind increased dramatically as the clouds touched down on the mountains and seemed to roll over them. Then came the first drops of rain. Large as pennies. As small catch basins filled, he cupped his hands. He couldn't bend the fingers of his left hand much, but he was able to quench his thirst. The rain became a downpour. Water ran down his face, his clothing was soaked. He didn't care. It was a cleansing rain. For him a renewal.

The storm was directly overhead. A bolt of lightning struck a pinon pine some hundred yards away. The dry creek directly below him was now surging with turbulent water. Elsewhere water was cascading down canyon walls. He knew what this meant. He climbed into the truck and headed back towards the freeway, driving through two-foot high water in the washes and dips in the road. Another half hour and the gravel road would have been impassable.

PART XIII

Benicki read the reports filed on the surveillance of Ed Kimball over the Labor Day weekend. He paid particular attention to that filed by the officers in the helicopter. Their description of him running berserk in Horse Thief Basin fitted the pattern. The pressure hadn't been let up. In fact it had increased. Only the strongest, most self-confident person, having nothing to hide or fear would be able to withstand it. He couldn't himself in all honesty say what he would do under similar circumstances. He remembered in Vietnam how some of his group had become separated by an enemy ambush. After the Vietcong had melted back into the jungle, when his group counterattacked, they had swept through the forbidding jungle looking for the bodies of their comrades. The interpreter with their force learned from villagers that the men had been captured and led through the jungle, their arms bound behind them to bamboo. He knew how torturous that would be. It was difficult enough to make one's way through the underbrush without getting impaled on spiny plants or splintered bamboo stumps. Making one's way bound, would rip the flesh, exposing it to insects and maggots. He remembered seeing some of his missing buddies years later in a North Vietnamese propaganda film. Cowed, spiritless, they had admitted their atrocities against the Vietnamese people. All the time they faced the cameras, their vacant stares complemented their puppet dialogue. Yes! He realized what pressure could do to a man.

This didn't mean that he felt any sympathy towards Kimball. On the contrary. They hadn't been able to prove he was the murderer, but proving and knowing were in this instance synonymous because he knew the truth. He wasn't interested in being judge and jury. All he wanted was evidence that could hold up in court. An indictment that would bring Ed Kimball to a speedy trial. It would then be up to them to decide whether or not he was a psychopath who required treatment in the facilities for the criminally insane. Or a hot-tempered, sadistic bully, fully aware of his acts, who should be confined for the rest of his life. There was no question in his mind that Kimball would prefer death to this sentence.

Benicki pondered on the justification of fate, the justice that is summarily meted out. How often the fate we fear most is waiting patiently at the end of the trail. His father had been a three-pack-a-day smoker, who as a boy developed a fear of water after seeing his dog get caught in an undertow at the beach. Rufus washed up on the sand an hour later. Who could blame his father for not wanting to go into the water, other than a bathtub? That heavy smoking brought him down the trail, one cigarette at a time. The coughing troubled his mother.

"Father, don't be so stubborn! I won't have this any longer."

He had lost weight, gotten hollow-cheeked. Their doctor gave them the terrifying verdict.

"Lung cancer."

When his father died, he literally drowned. The doctor gave the medical term for it. Pleurisy. Karl looked it up in the dictionary at the time. It all sounded so technical. The Romans called it pleuritis, the Greeks pleuras derived from pleura, side or rib. The doctor explained that the acute infection which occurred, resulted in excess body fluids collecting in the lungs. Like slipping under the waves ever so slowly. A tidal wave, or that undertow that had dragged faithful Rufus to his death, would have been kinder.

Benicki wondered what fate had in store for Kimball. Would he be faced with rotting away in a cell? The thing he feared most? Strangely, Benicki had a feeling that time was running out.

Throughout the remainder of the week the pressure was kept up. Kimball, for some reason, again reverted to a monastic existence after hours. The routine was clockwork in simplicity. Off to work in the morning. Back to the apartment around four. No side excursions other than shopping.

The routine triggered Benicki. It was similar to the pattern established just before Julia Hochstetter became a victim. This time, however, he was never let out of sight for long. Benicki wasn't going to give Kimball the slightest opportunity to strike again, if that's what he had in mind.

He didn't underestimate the man. Some of the world's most creative geniuses throughout history would have been judged totally insane by modern standards. His concerns went to law enforcement agencies in the form of an 'Alert Bulletin'. Surveilance would have to be flawless.

Overlooking the awesome vista of Horse Thief Basin, Ed Kimball cast the die when the helicopter had swept by the second time. He had to take one final gamble to get them off his back, to convince them to look for somebody else. He had reached the point where he didn't look forward to anything anymore. His food tasted lousy. Even liquor was losing its kick except for the fact that it dulled his senses. He slept restlessly. Sex also had lost its savor. At the moment if pussy were waved in his face, he would have looked away. At least that's what he told himself.

It was one thing to come to a decision. It was something else to implement it. His conversation with Mark a couple of days before the long weekend was fixed in his mind. Mark had said, '...*there are lots of other companies in the valley. He might as well thin out their ranks, spread his stuff around, if he's got it in for real estate agents in general'.* That was pretty good thinking on Mark's part. Sure! Why not make it look as if it were a vendetta.

Mark had the answer. Mark was the answer.

He waited around for him after work and was all smiles. For days he had passed his fellow workers by without acknowledging their existence. Mark was surprised when he was asked to join Kimball for a drink.

"You feeling all right?"

"Feeling great."

"Well, you sure as hell fooled me and the other guys. We've been figuring you've had a hornet up your ass, the way you've been growling around."

"Sorry, guy. Didn't mean to be a bastard. Things on my mind. Had to solve some problems."

"The smile, then. Got them solved?"

"Will have. By the way, old buddy, I like your beard. Look older."

Ed led the way to a bar on Van Buren not far from the freeway. Mark followed in his car. The bar was a hangout for a certain element in the valley, popular as a restaurant for it's Sicilian cuisine. Kimball had always figured it was mob owned.

"How about a plumber and helper?" he asked Ed..

"Sure."

"Let's have two. Make it Bud," he told the waitress.

They were seated in a booth overlooking Van Buren. The Friday afternoon traffic was backed up bumper to bumper for blocks. It sent a chill through Kimball when he thought of the recent tie-up on McDowell, the detour and the kid climbing into the freezer. "Christ!" he said out loud.

"What is it?"

"Happened to think of something It's nothing."

The shot glasses and bottles of Budweiser were placed in front of them. Ed picked up his whiskey glass.

"Here's to you, Mark."

"Thanks. Likewise."

They drank down the whiskey and poured beer into their frosty glasses.

"Remember?" said Mark.

"What?"

"That fuckin' weekend down Nogales. That was a ball breaker."

"Whatcha hear from that guy, Paul?"

"He's in L.A. working some kind of deal."

"What does he do?"

"Promoter of some kind."

"How'd you get to know him?"

"He used to screw around with my sister."

Their conversation lagged while they drank and refilled their glasses.

"The guys were wondering how come you've always got the law tailing you. They got something on you? I noticed it now again when we drove over here. Jeese, even the Governor doesn't get that kind of attention."

Ed had rehearsed his answers. He knew what was on all their minds.

"Hear about that small plane that burned over in Blythe on the weekend?"

"Yeh! On TV. Those three guys who got fried."

"They all worked on that job in Yuma that I've been handling. Knew one of them. Got chummy. He

256

was ripping off the government, running up to Vegas with the dough. The fuckin' cops think I know all about it. They're out of their fuckin' minds if they think I'm going to testify."

"How'd you learn about the rip-off?"

"This guy, Perez, wanted to cut me in if I'd go along."

Ed saw no point in telling Mark that Perez had been bombed at the time.

"That's heavy stuff, monkeying with the Feds."

"That's what I figured. I told him no dice. I didn't want to get fucked up by the mob, either. Once you're cut in they've got your balls in the wringer."

Ed drank down his beer and held up two fingers to the waitress who was leaning on the bar.

"Ever get your balls hurt?" he asked Mark.

"Sure. Hurts like hell."

"Can you picture some mobster grabbing one with a pair of pliers?"

"Jeese! Just the mention of that gives me shooting pains."

"That's just it. I've told these guys I won't testify, but they've got some jack-off D.A., who's trying to make a name for himself. Stinkin' politics."

"Whatcha going to do about it?"

"That's the problem I've got. I've got to see this one guy, but if the law follows me I'll lead them right to the bosses. I'm liable to wind up like little pieces of link sausage. Know what I mean?"

Mark's eyes were getting bigger with the thoughts of what mobsters would do to Ed.

"It's got me scared shitty, Mark. Couldn't sleep too well last night. The longer it takes for me to see this guy, the worse it gets. They may figure I'm going to squeal and take me out anyway."

"No wonder you've been looking the way you have," he pitched in sympathetically. He was also starting to feel mellow from the drinks.

Ed continued. "I had the idea that if I could give them the slip for a couple of hours and manage to pick up a rental car, I could do it."

He had tossed something to Mark to think about.

"What if you drove somewhere and grabbed a cab without their knowing it?"

"The trouble with that, if the cops learn of the switch, they'll trace where I went from the trip ticket."

"Shit! I didn't think of that."

Ed watched his expressions. Mark was one of those transparent people whose minds were constantly exposed. You always knew what they were thinking or were about to say. Like a seaman waggling his signal flags on the ship's deck. Like a puppy with his tail going a mile a minute.

"I wish there was a way," said Mark.

The words were sweet music. Kimball was prepared to offer him a hundred bucks for the use of his car. His blood started coursing with excitement. With dogs running up ahead catching the scent, he had the rifle cocked ready to shoot the treed animal.

"Got an idea," said Mark. "Park Central Shopping area's handy. Leave your truck over by Diamond's. I'll wait in my car on the north end of Penny's."

Ed remained silent. He wanted it all to be Mark's idea.

"Give them the slip and make your way over. When you come out the door, I'll slip out of the car and you take the wheel. How does that sound?"

"Brilliant! You're a goddamned genius. We'll do it

tomorrow."

Mark's face beamed. Yeh! he thought, it wasn't bad.

"Can you be there at noon?" Ed asked.

"Sure. Anytime you say. I've got nothing till six."

The pieces had fallen into place so smoothly Ed couldn't believe it. "You're really a good guy, Mark. I'll never forget how you saved my skin."

"And your balls," he laughed.

The sudden smile. The smug look gave Benicki the signal when Kimball pulled in later than usual. He knew where he had been for the past hour. The car that had followed him to the bar had reported in. Something was brewing and from the way Kimball walked and looked it would happen soon. He was a ticking time bomb. The door wasn't slammed, the drapes not drawn.

All the signs.

Benicki picked up his radio phone. "I want a back-up standing by tomorrow."

Chirping birds woke Ed Kimball as the first light dispelled the gossamer that remained of night. Like the hand of a master Acoma potter smoothing his clay, a mass of pale yellow gold spread across the sky accenting the stray clouds lost over the desert. He stood by the window watching the birds hopping around on tree branches, then suddenly flitting off to another tree. The lingering warm temperature necessitated keeping the air conditioning on at night. He turned it off and slid back the aluminum window to breath the morning air. There was a crispness with promises that in another month the nights would encourage open windows and walks in the park.

He thought of Jeff. He hadn't made any attempt to see him since the funeral ten days ago. He couldn't believe that only ten days had gone by. In some ways it seemed like a lifetime ago when Julia's terror-stricken eyes confronted him. He had tried to shut that moment out of his mind, but it was indelibly etched. When he least expected it, her final words spun uncontrollably in the vortex of his apprehension.

"Why?"

That was something he had asked himself. Why? The first killing was a mistake. A stupid mistake. Sure, he had frightened her by the way he looked. If she hadn't been about to scream, how different it would all be. Or would it be different? Was his Karma to go through this living hell? For in some ways it had become that. A living hell in which he could no longer call his soul his own. Rationality had reverted to irrationality. No matter how he tried to justify his actions, was there really any justification? Survival? That's what he had decided was all-important as the rain drenched his body and lightning jabbed the earth with electron stilettos. Survival? Why? What was so all important about that? Living was important, but survival, no.

When this business was over with, would he be able to live again? Live, without swimming about in a fishbowl with a hundred hungry cats' eyes watching every move? Or wouldn't they ever believe that he had nothing to do with any of it?

At six o'clock Kimball went across to the neighborhood Circle K and bought the morning paper, a couple of glazed twists and a large container of black coffee. He didn't want to fuss in the kitchen this morning. He took the same red felt pen he had used to mark the houses he screened before killing Julia. He had to find someone who was having an open house today. Now that the weather was a little cooler, interest in real estate encouraged more open houses. It also had to be a vacant house. Too often home owners were reluctant to leave and inhibited potential buyers by remaining within earshot.

Patiently he went over all the houses shown and, when he had finished, found he had checked off three. He spotted their locations on a Phoenix map and zeroed in on the property closest to Park Central where Mark's car would be made available.

First he showered, then shaved. Always in that order. Creatures of habit from birth to death. Mostly predictable. Sometimes, however, quite to the contrary. The expected becomes the unexpected. Once more he saw Julia's face. She had expected him to act civilly despite their differences. The unexpected had caused her to trip on the hearth and all her expectations for the future, for Jeff and herself, had ended in a blood bath.

The backup team Benicki had requested the previous day was parked in the side street across from Kimball's apartment. The men had strict orders not to let the suspect out of their sight for a moment.

Benicki's gut feeling or intuitiveness had proven right on the previous two occasions. Julia's danger, and the need to meet Perez again. He cursed the fact that he hadn't been able to prevent her death. Perez' death was tangential to the investigation. Now he had to make up for Julia's death by keeping someone else alive and nailing Kimball to the wall like the skin of a wild beast that no longer posed a threat. The skin, a reminder and a warning to other predators.

He was cruising the central Phoenix area. Whatever direction Kimball was going to make his move in, he wanted to be ready. The call came through to his car.

"He's heading downtown."

"Don't lose him!"

They reported that he turned east on Osborn, then south on Third Avenue.

"He's parking by Diamond's."

"Stick with him!"

Ed Kimball moved quickly. He didn't want to arouse suspicion, but being 6' 3" tall he had long legs that wove around the parked cars. Glancing back he saw the men leave their police vehicle which he had spotted tailing him. He had to elude them quickly. Hurrying into Diamond's store he glanced around. He was near the men's department where a sale was in progress from all the merchandising banners. In a second he stepped into the dressing area and into an unoccupied booth. With the confusion generated by the sale, he knew that salespeople were preoccupied and wouldn't pay attention to what he was doing, unless he came up to them with merchandise.

He visualized what the officers would do. They would suspect that he had hurried through the store to one of the other exits. They would each branch out in opposite directions to search for him. Waiting just long enough for this to happen, he left the booth, made his way past the escalator, the crowded jewelry counter and the women's shoe department. Outside the entry he glanced down the arcades. He spotted one of the men moving in the direction of Goldwaters. What about the other one? There were two routes he could take to reach Penny's. Straight through the connecting mall, past Dalton's bookstore and the other shops, or by way of the sidewalk that separated the stores from the west parking area. If he were to be spotted entering the arcade, there was no way to go except to run back in the direction he had come or duck into a store. Only the ones to the east had exits at the rear as well. Either way, he could get trapped.

With long strides he chose to go by way of the outer sidewalk until he came to the next arcade leading to Penny's. He hadn't taken more than a dozen steps when the other officer turned the corner up ahead in the direction of the two level parking garage. Ed knew he might turn and glance back at any moment. He was alongside Great Expectations Beauty Salon. Stepping sideways, he moved into the doorway, entered, picked up a magazine and sat down. One of the girls walked over to him.

"Are you here for a haircut?"

"I'm meeting someone."

She smiled and moved back by the cash register. He cast sideways glances at the door, but neither of the men appeared. Putting the magazine down he strolled to the door. He took his chances and hurried across to the entrance and quickly disappeared inside Penny's. He breathed a sigh of relief at not spotting either of the men as he made his way through the store. He pushed open the glass door and stepped across the outdoor display area to the sidewalk. Mark was waiting nearby. The white Fiat hurriedly pulled up across from the entrance and Mark slid out of the driver's seat.

"Good luck!" he said. But Ed was already moving away even though he hadn't pulled the door shut.

"We lost him."

"You what?"

"He gave us the slip."

"I'm on the way."

Moments later an angry Detective Benicki pulled up behind the diagonally parked blue pickup which he recognized.

"How?"

"Went into Diamond's."

"And?"

"He must have run through the store."

"Talk to anyone?"

"Not yet."

"Well, get going! Ask around. He's six three. He can't be missed."

His frustrations hit an all-time low. Complete surveillance was the key today. Letting Kimball slip through their hands was sheer incompetency, but then he realized that he, too, had been caught off guard two weeks earlier.

Benicki hurried to the line of cabs off Central Avenue. His first thought was that he had transferred to other transportation. Cabs would be obvious. Would Kimball do the obvious and spit in his eye? He stepped out in front of a moving car oblivious of what he was doing in his hurry, jumped back and in two strides crossed over.

"Did a cab pull out of here in the last ten minutes with a big fellow in it? He's six three."

"Not here. I've been in line longer than that. Maybe he jumped into one of those scab cabs. If so, wish him luck."

"Why?" He was curious.

"He'll be robbed blind on the fare."

Robbed blind? Blind to realize that Kimball wouldn't leave anything to chance. He couldn't rely on transportation that might not be there. He'd also have to get back from wherever he was going. No. To the contrary, it would be planned out carefully. If that were the case, someone else had to provide the transportation. Did that someone else drive, or turn the car over to him?

Which?

Knowing the way Kimball acted and reacted, he was a loner. A man who would sit by himself all night out at Horse Thief Basin, undoubtedly drinking, didn't need anyone. He'd want to be on top of the situation every moment. Furthermore, he wouldn't want to involve anyone who could be a witness to his actions.

The officers combed the area. There was no sign of the suspect. Nobody in Diamond's had noticed the man. He had obviously left. They stood in the arcade area between Diamond's and the J. J. Newberry store.

"Would he possibly be hiding somewhere?" asked one of the men.

"That wasn't his purpose in coming here," said Benicki with the patience of a saint, despite the fact that he was fuming inwardly.

To be faced with the prospect of sitting around waiting for the suspect to return, was the last thing Benicki wanted to do. Time was running out. Whatever Kimball intended doing could be a question of minutes or hours at the most, before he accomplished his mission. An area the size of Greater Phoenix was impossible to comb. If Kimball had transferred to another vehicle, what were they to look for? What make? Color? License plate?

They needed something to go on as starters and take it from there. But they had nothing.

"Is that Kimball, Detective Benicki?" asked one of

the officers pointing to a man heading towards the pickup.

The man looked as if he were in his twenties. Blonde. Bearded. Tan slacks, brown and white striped jersey with short sleeves.

"No, but let's see what he's up to."

As they approached, they observed the man trying the door handle on the passenger side, and finding it locked, also the other door. He turned to walk away as the men surrounded him.

Benicki didn't recognize Mark with the beard as he showed him his badge.

"This your truck?" he asked.

"No."

"Trying to steal it?"

"Hell no. Checking to make sure it's locked."

"Why?"

"Belongs to a friend."

"Would that be Ed Kimball?" He recognized Mark from his voice.

"Yeh! How'd you know?" Then he recognized the detective. "Oh, I remember, you're that detective."

"That's right. Benicki."

The stakes were high. He played a different card.

"Ever go hunting with Kimball?"

"Yeh! Why?"

Benicki had to tie up loose ends.

"Does Kimball own a hunting knife?"

"Yes."

"Would you know where he usually keeps it?"

"Glove compartment."

"How do you know?"

"I borrowed it a while ago without asking. Almost chopped my head off when I returned it."

They had searched the truck when they went through the apartment. Could he have returned it? Was he planning to use it again?

"You don't have a key, I gather."

"He took it with him. Thought he was going to leave it under the floor mat."

"With him? Where?"

"Hell! I don't know."

"Did somebody drive him?"

"No! He drove."

"In your car?"

"What about it?"

"I won't go into that at the moment. You had a white car, as I remember, Garrity. What make?"

"Fiat."

"Plate?"

Mark Garrity gave it to him.

"Put out an APB," directed Benicki.

"Ken, open up the truck!"

Ken went back to the squad car and came back with a special iron to slip in between the weather-stripping and the glass. In a moment he had the door open and was checking the glove compartment.

"Nothing!"

Benicki turned his attention to Mark Garrity. His face was clouded. There was an impatient and almost angry tone in his voice.

"Why'd you let Kimball use your car?"

"Why the hell not? You guys were hassling him."

"What'd he tell you?"

"You want him to testify."

"Testify? That's news to me."

"That's what he claimed."

"Testify? About what?" asked Benicki impatiently.

267

"Those guys ripping off the government. The ones who died in that plane crash on the way to Yuma."

"I don't know what he's been feeding you. He's a murder suspect. That's why we're after him."

"I don't believe you," said Garrity looking worried.

"Let me give it to you straight. Right now I believe Kimball's going to commit his third murder."

"Christ! You're putting me on."

"Do you know what the commission of a crime through the cooperation of a second party involves? If Kimball does kill again, you're as guilty as he is in the eyes of the law."

"Jeese, what are you saying"

"I'll put it in simpler terms. If I lend you my gun and you use it to shoot somebody, I'm in trouble. If I lend you my car and you drive it somewhere to commit a crime, I'm also in trouble. In your case, if Ed Kimball does murder someone and the only way he could do it was to reach that person by using your car, you're in for big trouble. You're an accessory to murder. Before you say anything you should be advised of your rights. Ken, read him his rights."

"Holy Christ! What did I let myself in for?"

Mark Garrity's deep tan lightened by several shades as he listened to his rights.

Benicki stepped aside. He prayed to the Trinity, the Holy Mother, and all the saints that Kimball could somehow be stopped. The officers had been here a good thirty minutes. In that time Kimball could have driven to Scottsdale, Glendale, or north of the Phoenix Mountains.

He wondered at the simple trust people held to. He guessed it was man's nature to have faith in others from the time primitive man was attacked by the saber-toothed tiger and his survival lay in a common defense. Kimball was equally as dangerous as that prehistoric predator. He sent another silent prayer to God asking for guidance in regard to the car.

"Please, Lord, let them spot it in time."

PART XIV

The Kreugers had moved out of their comfortable home at the end of June. They loved the location and this neighborhood of ranch style houses built in the sixties. Home owners took great pride in keeping their lawns manicured, their flowering shrubs tended to, and towering palms that lined the streets pruned of dried-out, yellowing fronds.

No back-yard mechanics were permitted to re-build junked cars in driveways. In fact, cars were rarely parked in driveways, but mostly driven out of sight in uncluttered garages. Homes put on the market in this neighborhood usually sold within 90 days. Being just west of Central Avenue, which runs north and south in the city and acts as the dividing line between east and west, their house was only three miles from the midtown financial district and six from downtown.

Being older homes, they didn't have huge walk-in

closets, now featured by local home builders, nor sunken tubs in master suites. Rooms were practical in size, not overly large and certainly not cramped when properly furnished. It was an ideal neighborhood for upcoming executives like Bill Kreuger, who if they wished to save parking fees downtown, could ride the city buses to and from work. There were also financial considerations involved. A similar house on the east side of Central Avenue usually cost much more. Snobbery had a price.

Bill and Jenny Kreuger loved their house which stood on a corner, but six months before they moved from the neighborhood, when they were spending a skiing vacation in Aspen, their home was robbed. Whoever broke in was selective. It wasn't a case of vandals taking off with portable TVs, tape decks, cameras, and fast-selling items. Treasured heirlooms that had been handed down on both sides of their families were taken. Miniatures, carved ivory figurines from the golden age of China, a treasured Ming vase, an ornate silver box from the days of Victorian England, along with a dozen other irreplaceable treasures.

Jenny Kreuger was heartbroken. Bill was furious. He had the latches replaced with dead bolts that required use of a key inside the house as well. The burglars had come through the garage somehow according to the police. Perhaps he hadn't turned the garage door handle far enough to secure the door. In any case, he had the doors leading to the laundry room, which opened to the garage, kitchen, and back yard, replaced with steel-clad ones.

For further protection against intruders, in case the outside locks were picked, the door from the kitchen to the laundry room was unlocked only from the kitchen side. The laundry room side had no keyhole. For additional security, Bill Kreuger had iron grills mounted on all the windows.

Despite these precautions, it was never again the same. An intruder had entered the sanctity of their home. The feeling that Jenny had was almost as if she had been violated, raped. She felt terribly depressed over the loss of their valuables. The burglary detail assigned to the Phoenix Police Department had managed to recover one small Japanese figurine in an antique store in Tempe, but held out little hope for recovering other items. The insurance coverage was a mockery adding insult to the injury.

In the spring she spotted a house on the east side. The yard was a bouquet of yellow blossoms that spelled out promises of hope to her. It had just come on the market according to a little girl who stopped beside her on the sidewalk. For the fun of it she telephoned the lister and made an appointment to see it. Bill was told nothing of her plans. It was love at first sight for Jenny. This home, a little later vintage than their own, had recently been completely remodeled and redecorated on the inside. The owners hated the idea of having to move after their four months of upheaval, but the husband was being transferred to their head office in Atlanta and an executive position commanding a healthy increase in salary and benefits.

"You must see it!" Jenny told Bill.

"We can't afford to make a move right now."

Jenny was convincing, however. She got her way. To manage the financing, they worked with a Realtor who gave them an advance against their equity in their house at a reasonable rate of interest. It all sounded good at the time.

Now Bill was getting worried. Their old home had been on the market more than two months. They were already into September. He voiced his concerns to Maggie Hill. She said that people in her company and other brokers were frequently showing the house. Being vacant and on lock box made it easy for them. There was no need to pick up keys or make arrangements to show it.

"I'd like to pass on one comment made by one of my colleagues, Bill."

"What's that, Maggie?"

"One of her clients, when walking through the house, commented that it looked like Ft. Knox."

"Ft. Knox?"

"With all the grills on the windows and all the dead bolts. She voiced concern that in the event of a fire you'd have to find your key to unlock the door to get out. You could die of smoke inhalation in the meantime."

"That's ridiculous. We left our keys in the locks at night. No problem."

"I've got a suggestion for what it's worth. If we don't get a good offer in the next couple of weeks, I suggest we take the grills down and store them in the garage. Then if people want to put them back, that's their option. How would you feel about that?"

"It's a thought. I'll talk to Jenny."

"There's one more thing, Bill. We're scheduling open houses for every Wednesday, Saturday, and Sunday till it sells. We're as anxious to close escrow as you are."

"That'll be great. Thanks!"

Maggie Hill was an experienced real estate broker. She had started with Clinton and Sullivan, Inc. ten years ago and had specialized in home sales in the central corridor. At one time she had been president of the Women's Council, had held numerous posts with both the State Association and the Phoenix Board. Currently she was one of the directors of the Phoenix Board of Realtors. There were few people in the business who didn't know Maggie, or whom she didn't know.

Ever since the disappearance of William Binder in Scottsdale, whose car was found parked at the airport, she had been involved with the local boards in better security measures for real estate agents. Their vulnerability due to odd hours, traveling alone to scattered locations, and exposure in vacant homes, called for a reappraisal of their industry.

When Anne Pearson was killed, it was her suggestion that the ladies pair up. The problem relating to productivity, since it was halved, proved that working in pairs was economically unsound. The major effort was directed at better communication. Letting people know where you would be, and with whom, and when you could be expected to return. Emphasis was also placed on knowing as much as possible about the people with whom you were planning to meet. If they had nothing to hide, they would gladly tell you what you needed to know, such as phone numbers and addresses. Maggie Hill recommended that any agent, when given a phone number, phone back immediately to verify the number as being that of the person talked with.

This was all fine and good, but the problems relating to open houses were completely different. There was no earthly way a customer could be screened at the front door. It hadn't come to the stage where a person wasn't allowed to enter a house being held open until they produced proper I.D.s.

It was perfect weather this Saturday and Maggie Hill was determined to give the Kreuger house her best shot. She was an attractive brunette in her early forties and efficient in the manner in which she conducted her business. The early part of the morning had been spent on a listing appointment which she completed by 10:30. From there she went into the office, made sure that her new listing was programmed into the computer, grabbed a quick sandwich and coffee, and drove to the Kreuger house. She always kept a number of open house signs in the trunk of her car and when she arrived at the corner of Central Avenue and the street leading to the Kreugers, she placed a sign at the corner.

It was her practice not to put signs outside a house until she turned lights on in the bedrooms and dark areas, opened drapes and shutters, and generally had the house in its most presentable condition. Her routine today was no different.

She pulled into the driveway, went over to the door and took the key from the lock box. Strangely she found the door unlocked. She pushed it open and thought she heard water running.

"Hello!" she called. "Anybody here?"

Ed Kimball had been in the house for only a few minutes. The newspaper ad said the house would be open between noon and five. He figured there'd be plenty of time before the agent arrived. His left hand still bothered him. Remembering how he had attacked Julia, he wanted this woman's death to be different. He planned to strike her when she came into the bathroom, then submerge her body in the tub. He was running the water when he was caught by surprise. He stepped into the hallway by the bedroom and saw her in the entry.

"Oh, hi! Checking out the plumbing."

"You surprise me. I didn't see your car."

"I'm parked around the corner in the shade."

She remembered seeing the small white car.

"I don't believe I've ever met you at any of the meetings. Who are you with?"

The only name he could think of at the moment was that of one of the Realtors he passed on the way to work each day .

"Lloyd's Properties."

"Do you have a card?"

"I didn't bring any."

Things didn't sound right. Signals were flashing. Maggie had a quick mind.

"Tony Lloyd's a wonderful man to work with and so's his wife, Ruth."

"They're both great people."

Now she knew she had trouble. Tony was a widower.

"Oh, damn!" she said. "I forgot my open house signs. I'll be back in five minutes."

With that she edged to the door, drove around the corner. As she passed the Fiat she made a mental note of the license plate. In the middle of the block she spotted Herb Taylor polishing his car. She had sold the Taylors their house.

"Herb," she said rushing past him, "I have to call the police."

Benicki got the alert. It was Garrity's car. Kimball.

275

He gave specific instructions. No sirens whatsoever on the approach. He sped up Central Avenue, red grill lights flashing, followed by Ken and the other officer. The Kreuger house was at the southwest corner of the cross streets. The living room faced north with other windows to the east. The room opened to the kitchen as well as to the bedroom wing. Benicki spotted the parked Fiat and pulled up on the wrong side of the street facing it. Ken right behind him.

"Cover the rear!" Benicki ordered. From the north other police cars converged simultaneously. Benicki held up his hand for them to position themselves behind their cars. He drew his gun while crossing the lawn.

Kimball was unaware of what was happening He had walked back into the bathroom momentarily to check the level of the water. Stepping into the hall he saw who was coming in the door. He leaped into the kitchen as Benicki pointed his gun and ordered him to 'Freeze!'

Kimball experienced the feeling of the rodent by the pool of water at Horse Thief Basin. No place to hide. He went through the first door he saw and pulled it behind him figuring this way led to the back yard. Instead he had plunged into a dark cubicle. He groped frantically at the wall for the light switches which, unknown to him, were in the garage and kitchen. He bumped into one wall and then the others. His hands told him he was in a laundry room when he felt the washer and dryer. He pushed his weight against the doors when the handles turned aimlessly. In a matter of seconds he was in a state of panic. He pounded furiously on the door he had come through.

Karl Benicki waited on the other side. He realized

what Kimball was going through, the fear that was gripping him. He glanced at his watch and decided to let him sweat it out a little longer.

Kimball was fouling the air with curses. His voice rose and fell as he kicked wildly at the door. For a brief moment he stopped and Benicki took advantage of the silence.

"Come out nice and easy. Hands behind your head."

He reached over and turned the latch in the center of the doorknob. As he stepped back the door was pushed open and Kimball hurled himself into the kitchen like a man possessed. He caromed off the refrigerator and collided with Benicki knocking the gun out of his hand. Benicki lunged for the gun on the kitchen floor, but Kimball's foot caught him in the side of the stomach knocking him against the kitchen stove. Kimball held the gun in his hand as he raced out the front door. His actions were like one who might have witnessed Dante's Inferno. Oblivious of orders to halt, he started shooting at random. Despite the return fire, he kept charging until no rounds were left in his gun. He had been hit, but the frenzy with which he charged propelled him across the lawn. Finally a bullet severed his carotid artery and he fell face down in the middle of the street.

Benicki had witnessed those last moments from a prone position in the doorway as bullets whizzed through the air. He scrambled to his feet and walked over to Kimball. Bending down he pried the fingers loose from his gun and slipped it back into his holster.

John De Morro walked into Benicki's office. He had hurried over the minute the news had been flashed through. He held out his hand.

"Congratulations!"

"For another death?"

"Oh, come on, Karl, you know that's not what I mean. You solved the case."

"I hope you're right. There's only one way to be sure. Come on!"

They crossed the street and on the way to the Medical Examiner's office, Benicki told him how Kimball trapped himself and the final moments before he was shot down.

"You're lucky he didn't kill you first. You were his Nemesis."

"I don't think he knew what was out there. You should have heard him screaming in that laundry room. The terror he was experiencing was real. Sanity had escaped him by the time he rushed out."

They entered the building and went directly to the receiving room. Benicki and De Morro walked over to the gurney on which Ed Kimball lay. A red tag was lodged between the toes of one foot. The body was still slightly warm to the touch, still retaining the tanned color in the face. His features in death were relaxed. There was no sign of the hatred, the fears that had racked his body. Benicki took the sheet and covered his face before walking away.

"You wonder what happens to people along the way, John. Kimball had it all going for him. Handsome, tall, intelligent. Maybe too intelligent for his own good. How different things might have gone if he had wound up on the stage to play lives of make believe. Who knows. Reality and make believe could have been working at cross purposes in him. Make believe became reality and reality make believe. I guess we'll never know."

Dr. Charles Blake walked in on them. "Is this the one you were after?"

"He's the one."

"We've got all his things listed for you to look over."

They followed Blake. Kimball's clothing was neatly folded into a large plastic bag In a smaller, separate bag were all the contents of his pockets. Cigarettes, wallet, keys, change, a Bic disposable lighter, handkerchief.

Benicki slipped his hand into the opening and pulled out the keys attached to the Playboy Bunny key chain. There were only three keys attached. His apartment key, the key to his pickup, and a short, stubby cylindrical key. He slipped it off the key ring and looked at the number stamped on it. 6048.

"My hunch was right," said Benicki handing it over to De Morro. If he had done his homework for the joint investigation, surely the number would be significant. De Morrow looked at it.

"Anne Pearson's key!" he exclaimed.

EPILOGUE

The cliché that time heals all wounds is to adults as a tablespoon full of castor oil is to children. It's terrible to swallow, but it does produce the desired results. A year had passed since Jeff placed the single rose on his mother's casket and called out with childish abandon, "Daddy! Daddy! We're in here."

It was a year of adjustment for his grandparents. They found it almost impossible to accept the tragedy that had so mercilessly engulfed their lives. But their responsibilities to a young life, expressed by small hands that reached out, and endless questions that sought answers, gradually made the acceptance of Julia's death possible.

Jeff had adjusted quickly to his roll in school. He liked his teachers who made special efforts to go out of their way. All knew what his family had suffered. He liked the organized athletics and his skinny arms and legs suddenly developed.

Over the summer the Hochstetters were given the use of an apartment overlooking the beach at Coronado. Old friends of the Hochstetters, with whom they had remained in contact, were off on an extended European cruise. It couldn't have come at a better time to be away from Phoenix this first August. Away from sad memories.

The year brought another change into Jeff's life. Karl Benicki had felt a certain closeness to the six year old whose mother's death he predicted, but was unable to prevent. After the case was closed he sat down with the Hochstetters to explain why things had happened as they did. It was no consolation to them at the time, but unanswered questions linger to plague one's mind. Answers, no matter how unacceptable, finally shut the door.

"I'd like to look in on Jeff sometime, if that's all-right with you. Maybe take him to the zoo. Just kind of spend the day."

They thought that was kind of him to suggest. The outings became a bi-monthly ritual on Saturdays, taking in all kinds of activities. Karl took him to Lake Pleasant and taught him how to slip a worm on a fishhook. He presented Jeff with a Boy Scout knapsack and camping gear and for the first time in his life, Jeff experienced what it was like to sleep out under the stars.

During the year the Benickis became Jeff's godparents. His father had never been a churchgoer and Julia hadn't pressed the issue. But when Julia died and explanations were given about her visiting God, the Hochstetters made sure that he participated in Sunday school while they attended church services. Soon he was baptized in a private sanctuary of the church.

The Hochstetters returned with Jeff in time for school. He was soon to start in the second grade. This Saturday morning his grandfather drove Jeff to Encanto Park. They were all going to have a picnic lunch with the Benickis who had become Uncle Karl and Aunt Liz. Jeff now considered them to be family. He ran across the green expanse of lawn when he spotted them.

"My how tan you are, Jeff," said Aunt Liz kissing him.

"And grown? You must have shot up an inch over the summer," added his Uncle Karl.

"And I put on weight. Three pounds," he exclaimed proudly.

Liz and the Hochstetters walked several paces behind Jeff and his Uncle Karl. Liz was amused to see the little swagger in Jeff's walk. The kind of body language that says *hey, make room for me. I'm growing up*. He didn't have his hand in Uncle Karl's. He wasn't a baby anymore. In fact they were having a serious man-to-man conversation at the moment.

"You should see how I can swim now, Uncle Karl. Grandpa lets me go out in the ocean up to my armpits. Doesn't have to worry about me."

"Can you crawl?"

"Sure. Backstroke, too. I can hold my breath under water. That scares grandpa," he giggled and looked around at him.

"Wonder what they're cooking up," said Betty.

"Man stuff," said Liz.

They were heading towards the lake and the boats.

"Are we going rowing?" asked Jeff.

"Would you like to?"

"Sure"

"Good! That's what we'll do."

He turned around to announce, "We're going rowing."

"Have fun," said Liz. Up ahead the men's conversation continued.

"Who's going to do the rowing? You or me?"

His uncle Karl laughed heartily.

"You must be kidding. You, of course. This is my day off."

****

About the author

ABOUT THE AUTHOR

Dick Beyer was born in Berlin, Germany. He spent his second and third years in St Moritz, Switzerland, before his mother brought him to the United States. Growing up in the New York City area, he attended college to become a chemical engineer like his father. However, he decided that this wasn't for him and majored in advertising.

After having served in the Counter Intelligence Corps of the United States Army, he returned to the advertising profession and in 1950 started his own agency. With major corporate clients, he became involved in mergers and acquisitions and subsequently began traveling frequently to Europe, the Caribbean and South America.

In 1970 he moved his family to Scottsdale, Arizona, where he tired of flying to service his clients around the country and became interested in the real estate business. Since then he has headed his family-operated company and is currently living in the Pacific Northwest.

The author has traveled to most of the locations of which he writes. Man's inhumanity to man surfaces in all of his novels, and in view of the tragedy befalling children all over the world, fifty percent of profits generated from his writing will be donated to organizations such as UNICEF, Save the Children, and others.

"The Scorpion Affair" & "Golgotha II" were the first of his novels to be published in a shrink-wrap package at the bar code price of only one novel. They can be ordered through your bookstore.

Other novels

287

Golgotha II

What is the reaction to the
long heralded return of the
Messiah? Follow the upheaval
in the Holy Land over a period
of only 16 fateful days.

The Scorpion Affair

Agents of the world's largest
armament dealer are murdered.
The trail leads from London to
Paris, Berlin and Ile-ā-Vache
as this strange web is spun.